SUCCESS STRIKES

THE 1990 IAN ST JAMES AWARDS

Judges

FRANK DELANEY

MALCOLM GIBSON

PETER GROSVENOR

DES HICKEY

NANETTE NEWMAN

KATE PARKIN

IAN ST JAMES

MARK WAIT

SUCCESS
STRIKES TWELVE

The winners of the
1990 Ian St James Awards

FONTANA/COLLINS

William Collins Sons & Co. Ltd
London · Johannesburg · Glasgow
Sydney · Auckland · Toronto

All royalties from the sale of this book will be
paid to the Ian St James Trust and used for the
furtherance and expansion of the Ian St James Awards.

First published in Fontana Paperbacks 1990

Photoset in Linotron Sabon by
Rowland Phototypesetting Ltd
Bury St Edmunds, Suffolk
Printed and bound in Great Britain by
William Collins Sons & Co. Ltd, Glasgow

Foreword

To found a Charity is to become a beggar. I must confess not to have realized the full truth of this when we launched these Awards two years ago. In those, what already seem far off days, the concept was clear cut and simple – to extend a helping hand to aspiring authors, to help twelve people each year make that first, all important breakthrough into print. Simple and clear cut, yet like so much in life, what seems easy becomes far more complex in execution. The truth is that these Awards could not function without the help and support of literally hundreds of people. I, and my fellow published authors whose work you are about to enjoy, are in their debt, and this brief introduction would seem the perfect place to say thank you.

Where to begin? So many people have helped. Collins, my publishers, have been supportive from the outset. Like me, they have been dismayed by the vast amount of work involved. Like me, they have worried about the resources consumed. Yet they have consistently helped with time and money, they have tolerated my short temper when things have gone wrong, and above all they have shown the patience of Job in waiting for my next book. Such is the stuff of true friendship, which is never taken for granted.

The Book Trade abounds with generous people. Book-sellers give up precious display space to make entry forms to the Awards available on every high street in England, Ireland, Scotland and Wales. It is they who take these

Awards to the people. Without their help we could not get our message across.

Indeed people in the world of books, or who love books, seem endowed with an unusual amount of generosity. Our judges – all extremely busy people, pre-eminent, indeed often famous in their own right – freely donate their time and expertise to reading and judging the fifty stories which our team of professional readers deem the best from the thousands of manuscripts received.

So many people to thank. David Frost, who helps make the Annual Awards Luncheon such a gala occasion. And our friends at Parker Pen who not only help alleviate the financial burden of running the Awards, but who contribute so much by way of encouragement and involvement.

These then, are my partners – a partnership in which, as I confessed at the outset, I have been the taker and they the givers. Their giving has enabled twelve new authors to make the breakthrough. Here are twelve *excellent* and very different stories. They had to be; they were judged the best of more than *eight thousand* stories submitted for this year's Awards. These authors are fine writers. They are now professional writers. Some, I feel sure, will entertain us with splendid novels in the future. They are names to watch. This, therefore, is their book. I wish them every success and I wish you, their reader, every enjoyment as you settle down to read *Success Strikes Twelve*.

IAN ST JAMES

Contents

SUCCESS
STRIKES TWELVE

BORDER INCIDENT

Valori Cowie

Valori Cowie from Suffolk is a trained occupational therapist, weaver, designer and secretary who has spent many years in Kenya. She has always enjoyed writing and has had various articles published in *The Times*, *The Field* and papers based in Africa.

BORDER INCIDENT

As the car slowed down, then stopped, the trail of dust which had been following it finally caught up, and as if by way of revenge for having been disturbed, wrapped itself round the ancient jalopy like a coffee-coloured shawl, momentarily engulfing it in the opaque folds of itself. Then, its anger spent, it subsided, settling back upon the track – and there was the car with its battered box body standing directly above its own shadow that huddled beneath, as if trying to escape from the rays of the sun. The car might have been standing in a pool of oil.

Two men got out and their shadows in no way reflected their respective sizes. One was slight, of medium height with thin grey hair and shoulders rounded from a life of prayer. He wore the long white robe of a priest in the tropics and the silver cross on his chest glinted in the African sun.

The other, younger, in his thirties, was a giant. Nearer seven feet than six, his body had grown in proportion making him a magnificent mountain of a man. His reddish hair fell in a mane around his shoulders and a huge beard covered most of his face, leaving exposed his high cheek bones, a nose as long and slender as a paperknife, opening into proud nostrils, a mouth with mobile lips and one blue eye that glowed like a gentian. The other was covered by a black patch, giving him a piratical air.

Meeting by the bonnet of the car the two men clasped

hands, the elder with head bent back, looking up with concern into the one blue eye above him.

'My son, from here you must go alone. I know there is nothing more I can say to stop you trying to cross the border. But be careful, my son, be careful. You do not know how things are these days. You have been away nine years and the people have changed. Now one man will shoot another as easily as a woman breaks an egg into a bowl. I myself have seen a guard shoot a child running after a butterfly which flew beyond the barrier. They could shoot you too, Roderick.'

'Don't worry, Father. No one is going to shoot me. But if they do', and his teeth glistened like an ivory keyboard in his beard, 'where better place to die than here, near to the place where I was born, with the sun above and the African bush all round me?'

'You make light of these things. But as I know I cannot stop you going, then, go well, my son. And may God go with you as I can't.'

The hands of the two men met and gripped each other. No more was said. Then the priest got into the car, turning it swiftly and with no backward glance he drove back along the way they had come together, raising more dust as thick as the feathers in an ostrich tail.

Roderick waited until the dust and the car had disappeared, then turned and strode off down the track in the direction of the barrier. He was dressed in shorts and a bush jacket and his feet were protected by sandals having a single thong between the great toe and the next. A modern John the Baptist heading for the wilderness. He carried nothing but a bunch of flowers.

Roderick was no stranger to Africa, and now that he was alone in the bush, with its vastness stretching all around him he felt at ease and he listened to the scrunching sound

4

his sandals made in the dust as the copper-coloured columns of his legs propelled him along the rutted track.

The priest had felt it wise to leave him at a place that was still two miles from the barrier. As Roderick walked he hummed and then he listened to the sounds of the bush – birds calling, cooing, singing, screeching in the wilds. He passed a snake asleep in the sun, an emerald ribbon coiled on a tuft of grass. Once a monkey with her young one clinging to her belly, loped across some way in front of Roderick, then sat down to watch him go by, the eyes too close together in the wizened face, as she held her baby and let it drink her monkey mother's milk. Dotted at random along the way were what might have been giant cauli-flowers. But as the walker approached each one exploded into a cloud of pale green butterflies which fluttered and flew about until he had passed, and then they settled back to feed once more on the dried mounds of elephant dung dropped perhaps a week before. Far off on the horizon the one blue eye noted the familiar frieze of giraffe browsing off the tops of flat-topped thorn trees.

His shadow had lengthened a little when Roderick came in sight of the barrier, a single pole across the road. It and one round mud hut marked the boundary at this particular spot between one central African territory and the next.

If the hut had an occupant he did not hear the approach-ing footsteps. A transistor radio stood near the ashes of last night's fire, its aerial erect and absurd as a trotting warthog's tail. Out of the small plastic box came pouring forth the rhythmic, tuneless, joyless, monotonous strains of an African pop tune. As Roderick came closer the record ended and he heard the discarnate voice of the announcer euphorically chanting in the vernacular a jingle which offered listeners a sure cure for round worms, flat worms, tape worms and every sort of intestinal infestation. The giant from Europe rolled his one blue eye to heaven, groaning inwardly. But he called out, 'Hodi – anybody there?' And an African came to the doorway of the hut, his rheumy eyes like rotten tomatoes, crinkling in the sudden sunlight. Although it was many months since a white person had passed this way, Roderick's appearance, apparently from nowhere, left him imperturbable. He belonged to a part of the world where nothing has the power to surprise. Roderick had him summed up at a glance. He walked towards him, his hand held out.

'Sabalkheri – good morning. Hujambo? – how are you? Habari gani? – what is your news?' Rather reluctantly the man with the darker skin held out a pink-palmed hand that felt cool and flabby. His natural African friendliness battled with his acquired surliness so that when he replied he was well and that his news was good the words were hollow and as empty as a calabash.

'I wish to pass the barrier.'

'You may not pass the barrier.'

'I wish to pass the barrier. Why do you say I may not?'

'You may not pass the barrier.'

'I have heard you. But I am asking why is it so?'

'Because I have been told so. And if you try to pass, I will shoot you.'

'Why will you shoot me?'

'Because those are my orders. It is forbidden to pass this way.'

Roderick was no stranger to Africa and he understood something of the psychology of the man who now barred his way. He pressed on patiently. 'I hear that it is forbidden for me to pass the barrier. I want you to tell me why this is so. The trouble between the Regions ended many months ago. So why are people still not allowed to pass this way?' The guard was beginning to tire of the conversation as a

6

person does when he feels himself getting out of his depth. However, he replied once more, with the tolerance of one who holds the trump card. 'I do not know. It is the law. If you pass, I will shoot.' And he slid his rheumy eyes to the rifle leaning against the wall of his hut.

'This is a very foolish thing.' Roderick spoke quietly. 'If I came at night, when it was dark, and passed silently by here, when you were sleeping, you would know nothing, and no one would shoot me. But because I come in daylight, and do not try to hide myself, and ask permission to enter the other Region, you refuse to give that permission, and you say you will shoot me if I try.'

Roderick glanced at the ground and saw that his shadow had lengthened. He knew he must pass soon; he also knew that the man with the gun must not be hurried. He tried again. 'I have come from the far side of the world. I come in peace. The quarrel your people have with the people over there is not my quarrel. So what harm will it do you if you let me walk past your barrier?'

'It is more than one year since anyone passed this way – and lived', and a glint of pleasure swam through his eyes as he remembered those who had died, shot in the back with the rifle provided by the government. The guard sniggered when recalling his skill. Then, suddenly self-conscious, he began to pick his nose, poking a finger up each nostril in the manner of his kind. 'Besides, you have not told me what business brings you from the part of the world that is far away, and gives you reason to pass over into the other Region.'

Recognizing the fleeting flicker of interest, Roderick's one eye fixed the guard. He knew it was now or never. He said, 'I have come', and he spoke very slowly, 'to visit my father's grave. I have brought flowers to show him he is not forgotten. That is the purpose of my visit.' And he

7

showed the fading flowers to the man in front of him.

The African, who understood respect for one's father, and also about death, did not know what to say. He kicked the dust with one toffee-coloured plastic sandal. Then he scratched himself through one of the holes in his vest, thus giving himself time to think.

'If you crossed the bridge that passes over the Great River you would have no trouble. There are no barriers there. The people are free to pass between the Regions.' He shrugged his shoulders and showed the pink palms of his hands. Happy to have found a solution, he began to turn away.

Roderick's voice arrested him. 'That bridge is more than one hundred miles away from where we stand. If I were to cross over it there would be another hundred miles for me to walk to reach my father's grave. From this place, where we both are standing, it is less than one mile to where my father lies. Do you think I am a *fool* that I should travel for many days to reach a place that you could reach with your voice if you were to hurl it from your throat with sufficient force!'

The guard who understood distance and what it meant to walk for many, many days, looked at the eye that blazed at him from deep within its socket like some blue torch. He said nothing because he could think of nothing to say. Then, feeling the situation to be slipping from his control, fearing the other might yet make a fool of him, and remembering his official position of border guard, he sought refuge in the formula that proved the solution to similar problems. The needle of his mind was stuck deep in the one groove. 'I will shoot you if you pass this barrier.'

Now Roderick knew that the avenue of reasoning had been fully explored, and that any further efforts in that direction would only end in the promise of a bullet.

Movement on the ground attracted his attention and he saw a mother hen and six chicks scratching in the dust. Their beaks made little tapping sounds as they pecked at dried scraps of maize meal left clinging to the side of a metal sufuria. They were unperturbed by the sounds from the transistor radio which still fouled the air with its plaintive music and confounded commercials. 'When the box goes silent what do you do? Batteries do not grow on trees.'

'It is not easy. They are hard to get, and expensive too. Sometimes when my brother comes to visit me he brings batteries.' A faint glimmer in the guard's dark eyes communicated itself to Roderick. He said, 'I am going to visit my father's grave. I am going to pay my respects to my dead father who was an honourable man. I am going to take these flowers to the place where he lies and you will not stop me. When I return I will bring batteries for the radio. I will come back before the shadow of the hut has reached the barrier.'

This made good sense. The European only wanted to visit his father's grave; it was as well to respect the dead. He himself needed new batteries. His brother might not come for many months. Where was the harm? No one need know; after all it was five months since anyone from the government had visited here, and on that occasion his superior had been drunk and had broken the barrier. Failure to apply the brakes had resulted in a mess of splintered wood and a crumpled Land Rover that had rolled twice. Besides, if the stranger with the red beard came back as he said he would, he could, after all, shoot him then, if he felt like it.

Now that the situation was resolving itself the guard relaxed, leaning back against the wall of the hut, clasping his hands behind his woollen head and the pungent smell of his armpits wafted across into Roderick's nostrils. He

9

grinned broadly and a sudden charm banished his former surliness. 'See to it that you are not late back.' He reached for his rifle, then ducked back into the darkness of his hut. Roderick turned and vaulted over the single bar that formed the barrier, and the drooping heads of the flowers he carried bounded and shook, then drooped again as he walked away.

The walk to the customs post in the next Region took only a few minutes; as the track he was following led him round a corner, it came into sight. Here also the barrier was marked by a single pole across the road. Once it had been painted white and red, but now the paint was peeling and patches of rust showed along its entire length. A small square building of rough stone supported a corrugated-iron roof which shimmered in the midday heat.

As Roderick approached he heard the sound of voices coming from inside, rising, falling, laughing. He bent his head and peered in through the open door, and his huge bulk blotting out the light of day attracted the attention of the two men squatting on the concrete floor. They stopped the game they were playing with pebbles and the tops of Coke bottles and gazed up at the intruder. What they saw seemed of little interest to either of them and they resumed their game. Accepting that the ball was in his court Roderick made his verbal gambit with a greeting that came most naturally in that area. 'Sabalkheri – good morning. Hamjambo? – how are you? U hali garni? – what is your condition?' The squatting men continued their game but one replied, 'Njema – we are well. Sijambo – we have no troubles.'

'I wish to pass the barrier.'

'It is not permitted for any man to pass the barrier. The connection between the Regions has been broken.'

'This I have heard. But why is it so?'

'It is so.' The now familiar reply seemed loaded with the logic of foolishness. Roderick pressed on. 'The troubles between the Regions ended many months ago. Why should the borders still be closed?'

'What you say is true – the troubles are over. But no one is permitted to pass this way.' Having scored a direct hit with reasoning that defies questioning, the guard smiled broadly up at Roderick, and the smile held no malice. 'The government order is that if a person tries to pass this way he must be shot.' And the two men squatting on the floor exchanged the looks of dogs that remember where they have buried their bones.

'It is a foolish situation.' And Roderick shook his great head. There was something in the gesture of this huge red giant that appealed to the Africans, and the one who had already spoken felt that he wished to explain further. 'Even if you passed this barrier, you would not be permitted to enter the other Region. You would be killed if you tried to do so.'

'But I have just come from the other Region! It is *your* Region I wish to enter.'

'That is not possible. No one has passed here from that side for over eighteen months.' And he rolled the stones in the manner of the game being played.

'Nevertheless, what I have said is true. And now you will let me pass here too.' The note of authenticity communicated itself to the black men who finally showed themselves capable of being roused when the impossible occurs. Now, more interested in the bearded stranger than their game, they both stood up and the one who spoke said, 'What did you give the other guard that he allowed you through?' Roderick perceived the changing wind and trimmed his sails accordingly.

'Nothing, you rogues! Except my word that I would

return before the sun has fallen from the sky this evening.' The one blue eye beamed good humour and amusement. The white teeth flashed within the fiery beard.

'Who are you? What is your business?'

'My name is Gomez – Roderick Gomez. I have come from a country far away. I have come to visit the place where my father lies.'

'Gomez? You say your name is Gomez? Are you the son of Old Gomez, the Hairy One?'

'I am his son.' And Gomez began to laugh, and the laughter began in his belly, ran round inside his ribs like thunder in a cave and cascaded over his lips. Then the guards began laughing. And suddenly there they were, three strangers united in the memory of a man who was dead.

The older of the Africans then spoke for the first time. 'I remember Old Gomez. He was a tall one, like you. He too had a beard that was red and hair that was as thick and as long as the mane of a lion. Yes, I see now. You are your father's son. There can be no doubt of that.' And he shook his head and his face wore a smile as he remembered a man who was good. 'He was killed when the troubles started.'

'Yes, he was shot when the country became free.' Roderick's eye regarded the man who had known his father. 'When the people gained their freedom they burned the school my father built, they murdered the teacher my father paid to teach their children – and that man was one of their own people. They plundered the dispensary and stole the drugs and sold them in the forest, and many died from this, and now they have no medicine, no dispensary and no one to care for them when they are sick. My father's death was part of this madness. It is nine years since he died. Now I have come back to visit his grave, to pay my respects to a good man and one I loved, and to put these flowers on the place where he lies buried so he may know he is not forgotten.'

'You may pass – but it will cost you money.'

'How much?'

A moment's pause – a summing-up – the hesitation before trying one's luck. 'Two hundred pesquidors.' The tarry eyes gave away nothing, toes kicking the dust, fingers scratching hair.

'Do you take me for a fool who carries money in these parts? I have not got two hundred pesquidors. I will give you what I have.' And Roderick felt in his pocket and pulled out a note for half the sum demanded. 'Do I get a receipt?'

The guards grinned, enjoying the implication. 'The receipt book is finished. We are waiting for a new one but it may take many months.' The note was accepted and inspected briefly.

'You may pass the barrier.'

Roderick vaulted rapidly over the rusting pole, giving the guards no time to change their minds. Then he began walking fast along the winding track that took him in the direction of the place that had been his home for the greater part of his life.

As the red-haired son of the red-haired father, still clutching the flowers with the drooping heads that bobbed in rhythm with his strides, neared the place that had been the hub of so much happy activity, his thoughts raced back over the years of his early boyhood.

He remembered the house, cool and bright, white and green, standing peacefully surrounded by flowers and lawns, the garden that his mother had created and loved. He thought of his father, mounted on his stallion, Arab tail held high, riding out at dawn to direct the labour force on the plantation, and he saw him in the evenings, visiting the

13

place where the farm workers lived and raised their families – the neat settlements of round huts, their mud walls white-washed and capped with thatch shaped like witches hats that kept them marvellously cool. He remembered the packets of seeds with their bright pictures of poppies, zinnias, marigolds and daisies which at Christmas time he and his brother took to the wives, for Old Gomez used to say, 'By sowing the seeds of flowers in their gardens, they will one day find beauty blooming in their eyes.'

But when he came to the place where all this had happened, it was no longer the same. Weeds and ruin now met his gaze. Roofs caved in and walls stripped of mud by succeeding rainy seasons lolled like drunkards on a Saturday night. Grass and weeds sprang from the shells of empty homes.

Roderick walked past fast, his single eye taking it all in. Up over the brow of a mound below which lay the dam which had been his father's special pride. Instead of the clear sheet of water on which he used to fish from his own small boat, Roderick saw the tangled mass of weed and water-cabbage that had transformed it into a stagnant morass, a paradise breeding ground for mosquitoes.

Then he was crossing the lawns and nearing the house. Only the lawns had reverted to forest grass two feet high. Where once his mother's flower beds had splashed colour around the homestead, there were now ragged patches of maize and sunflowers ten feet tall, their vacant faces following the sun. He saw odd flashes of scarlet and pink, proof of the dogged determination of geraniums not to die. In some cases these bright heads owed their survival to stalks twelve or more feet long that had pushed their way through undergrowth before emerging into the light. Roderick thought, 'Africa is a whore. She gives her body freely to the highest bidder. But when she finds herself bearing the fruits of the intruder she grows resentful, throws him out and falls again into the sleep she has slept for a thousand years.'

The house had died. Quietly, without resistance, the lights had gone out, the doors been ripped off, the windows broken, and the house had died when its heart had stopped beating.

The entrance was a gaping hole, like a crone with a front tooth missing. The great curved door had gone, chopped up for firewood, and only the broken hinges still hung there, bent and useless with nothing to support.

Roderick stood in the hall and he smelt the smell of cobwebs, dust and decay, and anger and disgust rose in his throat. The walls and ceiling were criss-crossed with the tell-tale tubes of mud, made by termites to protect them from the ravishes of daylight as they wreak their silent works of destruction. Given time, they would destroy the whole house.

Roderick's eye followed the curve of the banisters, curling away to the floor above. He put his sandaled foot on the lowest stair. It crashed through the rotten woodwork as if it had been made of biscuits and the jagged splinters ripped into his flesh. In fury and frustration he kicked at the rise of the second stair and it too crumbled, spilling out a mess of white ants which ran hither and thither, seeking to hide themselves from the sudden light. He ground his foot with precision where the mass was greatest, felt it slither slightly and heard the faint sound of squashing as his weight obliterated the pale jelly bodies. He turned and left the house.

The lonely pilgrim strode down the track that had once been the driveway to his parents' home. His temples throbbed as he jumped the pot-holes and straddled the deep ruts gouged out by seasons of tropical rainstorms, and he had the feeling that he was not alone. Unseen eyes were watching him. But he felt no curiosity – only anger. Anger mixed with sorrow, which together make a man despair.

He must find his father's grave. Then he would leave this place that once he had loved, but that now, along with his father, was dead. This place that had known love and laughter and fruitful activity now belonged to the white ants.

Roderick found the place where the graveyard had been. He was able to locate it by the ruins of the church. He glanced in at the doorway, saw the empty spaces where the benches and altar used to be, saw the sky above and the streaky droppings of the birds that swooped and nested among the rafters, and the grass growing in the aisle. Only the font in which he had been christened seemed unharmed. It still held water – rain water, green, slimy water in which floated an upturned frog.

Around the ruins the rows of graves were nowhere to be seen. Now the whole area was covered with a crop of sweet potatoes, their dark green, closely packed leaves creeping and crawling, covered over the whole churchyard. Roderick walked among the leaves until his foot felt the hard plinth of his father's grave. Then he stopped and parted the leaves and saw faintly the inscription he and his brother had inscribed in the concrete before it had set. Here he set down the flowers that he had carried since dawn that day.

He knelt and tried to pray. But anger still rolled through his soul, and the thoughts he wanted would not come. So he stayed there quietly for a while, waiting till the anger drained away; and then his father's father face came back to him – and he thought of his life and all it had meant, of the things he had worked for and believed in. Behind the black patch the empty socket filled and overflowed so that both his cheeks were wet as he wept in the afternoon sun, and then peace came to him.

16

As he knelt an awareness came to him that he was not alone. The eyes that earlier he had sensed were watching him, he now knew were nearer still. He was not afraid, only interested.

When he judged the time was ripe, he opened his eye and saw two Africans standing a little way off, watching him. The younger was wearing a cloth round his loins, but his bird-cage ribs were bare. The other, old enough to be his father, was dressed in tattered shorts and the remains of an old dinner jacket, the silk lapels still recognizable, though both sleeves were gone, leaving the shoulder padding hanging down like thatch on a dilapidated roof. Roderick recognized the older one. Does a man ever forget another he has known all his life, from whom he has learnt to track and hunt and fish, who has taught him how to fashion a bow and arrows?

For a moment Roderick stayed silent, feeling humbled by a dignity that could shine through such a sartorial travesty. The round head was quite white now, and the skin stretched tightly across the cheeks and jawbone so the old man looked like an ebony carving.

'You have come back. It has been a long time. Bwana Gomez, why did you leave us?'

'You would have killed me as you killed my father.'

'It was not us who killed the Hairy One. It was the government forces. They came and killed and burnt and destroyed and then they went away. And what was left for us? Nothing! Nothing!' and he threw out his pale-palmed hands in a gesture of despair.

'You wanted your independence and you got it. You did not want the white man in your country, so you drove him out. Now you have your freedom. Why are you not satisfied?'

'No Lodlick, you are wrong', and the familiar mispronouncing of his name was for Roderick like opening a wound that had healed. 'We did not want things to happen the way they did. When your father was alive, life here was good. There was work for all, and food and houses and medicines and we were happy. At the end of each week we brewed beer, and there was singing and dancing. Now it is different. There is no work. We have no school, no church, no priest to pray for us, no one to look after us when we are sick. Life is not easy. It was different when Old Gomez was alive.'

'My father was a good man, as you have said. Why then did they kill him?' And the white man's voice rose as grief returned.

With the anguish of Africa in his old black eyes, the other answered, 'I do not know. Those people were mad.' And with great dignity and sadness the two black men knelt down and each in his own way prayed for the soul of the man who had been murdered.

The simple gesture moved Roderick unbearably, so that he shut his one eye tightly as he listened to the words being mumbled in the local dialect.

When they stood up, suddenly the three clasped hands across the concrete plinth. Then Roderick said, 'This is no way to treat the dead. Why do you plant your crops above the place where they are sleeping?'

For the first time the younger man spoke. 'You do not understand. My father has told you the people here have no work. There is no money and nothing in the shops. We have little to eat, so we must plant wherever the soil is good. And here the soil is good', he added.

Time was passing. The sun was sliding down the sky and shadows growing longer. Gomez knew he must go, but his heart held him where he was.

'Perhaps one day I will come back and we can be happy together again. I do not know. Perhaps . . . '

'Come back, son of the Hairy One. Come back and we will work again. We will have food in our bellies and our children will go to school again. There will be things in the shops and we will have money to buy them. Life will be good and we will laugh as we used to before the bad times happened.'

Roderick stepped over his father's grave and stood close to the man who had once been his servant and was still his friend. He put his arms round the bony shoulders and his red silken beard rested on the white woollen head of the older man. For a moment in time they were one, united in the tragedy of being dwellers in a world where the hallmark of progress need not bear the stamp of human happiness. Then he took from his pocket the only two things he had with him. To the younger man he gave a red cotton handkerchief which was quickly tied round his neck. And to the older he gave a slender silver pencil. 'Find a Greek merchant whom you can trust and sell this to him.' If they could find some food to buy, at least they would not starve before the next rains came. He shook hands with the younger African and said, 'The shadows are growing long. If I am late passing the barrier I may get shot.'

'Yes, they will shoot you', they both agreed.

'Goodbye, my old friend. It is good that we have met again.'

'Kwaheri Lodlick. Mungu has been good to us today. Go well, and do not forget us.'

Then Roderick trod among the leaves of the sweet potatoes and the lush, dark leaves that covered the ground sprang back as his footsteps passed, carrying him away from the graveyard. He looked back once and saw the two still standing, their eyes slitted against the sinking sun, and the two ends of the handkerchief fluttered bravely in the evening breeze, like the wings of a scarlet bird. He raised his arm and they raised theirs. He did not look back again.

His mind felt full and thoughts kept leap-frogging over one another as he strode along, so that it came as a shock when suddenly he found himself back at the barrier. The guard was relieving himself into a bush when he arrived.

'Did you find your father's grave?'

'Yes, I found it. And I prayed for his soul and I put the flowers on his grave. The purpose of my journey has been accomplished. Now I am returning to the other Region and then I will go back to the other side of the world. What I have seen today has made me unhappy.'

'First you must pay.' A flash of fury ignited the blue eye.

'You know I have no money. I gave you all I had this morning. And when you let me pass you knew I had no more. Do you think I could have picked some from a tree, or found some in the ground?'

'If you do not pay, I will shoot you.'

'You speak the words of a fool and a coward. If you want to shoot me, do it now, as I face you. But do not wait until I have turned my back on you for that would not be the action of a brave man.'

The guard smirked and shrugged, and the shrug disturbed the flies clustered on his torso, and they flew up and buzzed around his head, soon to settle again.

Time was running out and so was Roderick's patience. He had had his fill of the threat of a bullet for one day. He addressed the keeper of the barrier rather as a teacher might caution a wayward pupil.

'If you intend to shoot me, you must do it now! You may *not* shoot me in the back. You have until I have counted to seven to pick up your rifle and shoot. After I have counted seven I shall pass the barrier and return to the other Region. I will begin counting now! One . . . Two . . . Three . . . '

The words were unhurried. At 'Four' the guard reached out his hand and took hold of his rifle. Roderick's single eye never left his two. 'Five . . . Six . . . Seven.' He turned, ducked under the pole and began walking away.

He had gone a dozen paces when he heard the click of the safety catch being tripped behind him. The temptation to look back was strong. and stronger still was the temptation to increase his speed, to kick up his heels and run as he had never run before, to run, in fact, for his very life. Yet he knew to do so would be fatal. So with every ounce of control he could muster, he forced himself to keep the same steady pace. His heart hammered in his throat, perspiration ran down his forehead, trickled down his cheeks, through his beard and down his neck. And he just kept on walking, walking and waiting . . .

But the shot never came. And then he was round the corner and out of sight of the first barrier and within sight of the one ahead. As he neared the familiar pole across the track he heard a voice close to him. It startled him – his nerves felt raw and exposed. 'You're a brave man, Bwana. I do not know why he did not fire. Other times he has.' It was the guard from the second barrier. Noting the shadows growing longer he had wandered down the track to see if he could see the traveller returning. Hearing voices and being inquisitive he had crept closer, hidden in the bushes, and overheard Roderick's conversation with his opposite number.

With a jolt Roderick remembered that he had not brought the batteries he had promised he would bring. It had, of course, been impossible. Firstly he had had to give all his money to the other guard. Secondly there had been no shops, let alone batteries, where he had been. Wearily he wondered how he was going to talk his way out of this one.

Together they reached the pole and leaning on it Roderick faced the African. 'I have not got the batteries I said I would bring you. There were none where I have been – and no shops either. In any case, your friend at the other barrier took all the money I had before he would let me pass this morning.'

The guard laughed. It was a good joke. 'He is not my friend. He belongs to the other Region. But how do you think you will pass this way if you have not brought the batteries? That was the bargain we made.'

Aware that his patience had been badly eroded, Roderick Gomez now brought the full force of his will to bear on this fellow human being. He felt the force building up inside him, like a spring being compressed. He towered above the other man. When he began to speak it was slowly and with deliberation so that each word was charged with meaning.

'My friend, it was not my fault that I have come without the batteries which I said I would bring for you. But I am an honest man. I gave you my word I would return here before the shadow of the hut reached the barrier. See!' Roderick's arm shot out like an arrow from its bow, one finger pointing downward where the shadow still had a hand's breadth to travel before it would be beneath the pole. 'You trusted me this morning. Now you must trust me again to get the batteries for your radio and I will send them to my friends at the Mission and they will bring them to you. If you kill me you will never get the batteries – and that would be your loss.' They both poked at the plastic box on the ground with the chicks still pecking round it, and canned commercials still polluting the air with the same monotony but diminishing volume.

Just then Roderick noticed a strange African seated against the wall of the hut, staring at the dust between his feet. 'Who is this man?'

'He is one like you; he wishes to pass the barrier.'

'But you will not permit him to do so. And if he tries you will shoot him', mimicked Roderick, and the guard laughed with enjoyment at finding another who had learnt the rules of the game.

Then the guard said a surprising thing. 'You know, Bwana, this country needs people like you. Men who have courage; courage like you showed back here. Courage makes a man strong.'

'Yet when we come, you threaten to shoot us. How do I know you will not decide to kill me as I walk away?'

The guard grinned broadly. 'You do not know. Now it is you who must trust me!' And he chuckled like a schoolboy who knows where the booby trap has been placed.

There was no more to be said. The moment had come to act. Roderick raised his hand in a gesture of farewell, and as he did so the strange African stood up and came and leant on the barrier, and stared down the track towards the other Region. Roderick thought, 'I hope he doesn't try it, poor devil.' Then for the last time he ducked under the pole and walked away.

Alone again in the Africa he loved, the bush on either side, his mind was like a cauldron bubbling with troubled thoughts. He thought of the farce at the barrier, of his ruined home and the choked dam, the fallen labour lines and the empty church, and he saw the two hungry figures by his father's grave. They were hungry because their own people had lost their heads, drunk on the wine of freedom, and a man who was loved was murdered merely because he was their master. He looked across the familiar, arid scene and it was lit with a golden light. The sun's fingers clung to the edge of the horizon, waiting to say goodnight. The dome of the sky blushed crimson. Far off on the plains a wind out for an evening blow developed a dust devil and whipped it up and sent it swirling madly, hither and thither, in the frenzied dance of a whirling dervish. Then, the dance done, the dust devil climaxed, lifting off the earth, rising higher and higher, still swirling, twirling, whirling until its shape was spent, and suddenly there was nothing but a faint beige gauze wafting in the air.

Through the quietness of the dusk came the crack of a rifle followed by a scream, followed by another crack and a wail. A third shot was followed by silence. A man who is first shot in the legs does not die immediately.

Roderick stopped striding. He stood stock still. He stared. He felt his strength draining from his feet like water from a bath. He threw back his head. 'Bastard!' he bellowed. 'Dirty, stupid bastard!' Then he began running. And as he ran he shouted and he shouted very loudly as he wanted God to hear. 'Bloody, wanton, futile *waste*!' His temples almost split and he felt he must vomit. And he kept on running.

Only when the lights of the Mission came into sight did Roderick's pace slacken. He sensed the bitter irony of the bell beginning to toll, calling the company to vespers. He wondered about the soul of the unknown African now separated from the body left lying somewhere beyond the barrier behind him.

A great weariness came over him. He wanted to stop thinking – and feeling too. Yet he was comforted by the figure of Father Kang'ethe, whom he had last seen at breakfast before so much had happened; now he was silhouetted against the dying day, his arms rising and falling in time to the bell he tolled.

Roderick crossed the compound and pushed open the

great door of the Mission. Inside he was engulfed by waves of exhaustion and relief – but mostly the relief was remembering the gift of Napoleon brandy which with foresight he had brought for his hosts, the holy fathers. It had been a long day. And tonight – yes, tonight – he would imbibe, in order to forget.

A WHORE'S VENGEANCE

Louise Doughty

Louise Doughty lives in London and has worked as a secretary, teacher and freelance book reviewer. Having taken an MA course in creative writing and travelled in Latin America and Africa, Louise is currently working on a novel based on her experiences in Mexico and Guatemala.

A WHORE'S VENGEANCE

'There is a promise made in any bed.
Spoke or silent, a promise is surely made.'
The Crucible ARTHUR MILLER.

My mother and father used to fight and he would end up
beating her. Then he would sob his heart out as she lay on
the floor. 'Why do you make me do it?' he would cry at
her. Then, looking up at the ceiling, he would give a great
shout, '*Why?*'

They died in 1680, when I was five. The Indians came in
the night. Later, I used to tell the other kids I had seen the
braves smash their heads against the farmhouse wall. It
wasn't true. I was nowhere near at the time. I only made
it up to scare them. My mother had been due to give birth
again and was ill with it so I had been sent to stay with my
aunt and uncle in Salem, until her time came. When I first
heard the phrase 'big with child', I thought it meant that
grown-ups looked tall when they stood next to children. I
used to think all adults were big with child.

I hated living with my aunt and uncle. They had to keep
me, of course, after my parents were killed. They stuck a
mop in my hands the minute I was big enough to hold it.
They treated me like a skivvy. Wash this, scrub that, clean
over there and don't speak 'til you're spoken to – oh, and
while you're at it, take that sullen look off your face. Sullen?

I was furious. How dare my parents dump me here? For every sweeping movement of that brush, I imagined I was prodding a pin into my aunt's face or my uncle's pious arse. He was a reverend, my uncle. *The* reverend, to be precise. Reverend Paris of Salem, and I, his niece, valued about as much as his black slave, Tituba. They made me sick.

As soon as I grew old enough, I was farmed out, to be a slave in other people's houses and earn my keep. That was how I ended up there, at the Proctors'. They had a small farm, some way out of Salem. I begged my uncle to send me to a family who lived in town. I couldn't stand the thought of being stuck out there with some fat old wife and husband and screaming, red-faced farmhouse brats. I sulked from the moment they told me I was going till the moment I arrived. My uncle drove me over in the cart. He said he was doing it to curb my wild nature. Ha. As I climbed down, clutching my small bag, Goody Proctor came forward to meet me. She smiled, the way those good women can when they know they are being nicer to you than you probably deserve. 'Welcome to our home, Abigail', she said, magnanimously. I smiled back with my mouth. My uncle came inside with us but didn't stay. More important things to do. He kissed the top of my head, bidding me farewell, but I said nothing. I wasn't going to let him off the hook. Goody Proctor walked back outside with him and I heard their voices murmuring. He was telling her to beat me, no doubt, if I gave her any trouble. When she came back in, she looked a little nervous, as if I was a stray she had been landed with unexpectedly. This one's a pushover, I thought.

She took me upstairs to my room, the usual poky little cupboard, clean and unforgiving, designed to make you look forward to leaping out of bed in the mornings and scrubbing the floors before sunrise. 'I'll leave you alone for

a while. Come down when you're ready,' she said. After
the door shut behind her, I burst into tears. To be stuck
here, out here, miles from anywhere, until my hands were
raw with housework and my face cracked by peering into
dusty corners. I couldn't stand it. Damn my uncle, damn
my aunt, damn the Proctors, damn them all. I'd run away.
I'd run away to Boston. After I had finished, I straightened
my apron and my bonnet and went downstairs. I knew as
soon as I looked at Goody Proctor that she had heard
me crying. She came forward and put her hands on my
shoulders, giving me a look of such agonizing pity it made
me want to stick something up her nose. 'It must be very
difficult for you, a young girl like you,' she said. I decided
to play on her sympathies and sniffed. 'Leaving your family.
You must miss them very much.' Miss my uncle? It was the
only good thing about being sent out to this hole. I nodded.
'Well I'm sure you'll do fine here,' she continued. 'I'll not
lie to you, the work is hard, but we have a fair farm, my
husband and I. The land is good'. She took her hands from
my shoulders and wandered over to the window, gazing
out across the fields. 'It is a good land,' she repeated, 'good,
and beautiful, a great gift.' That's all I need, I thought,
some half-wit sentimental rubbish about how great this
mother earth is. It's farming that does it, and the loneliness.
Turns their wits. The men are just as bad. She showed me
round the building and the outhouses and then we went
inside and started on a small supper. 'It'll be just the two
of us tonight,' she said, stirring a pot with some brown
muck in it. 'My husband has taken our boys out round the
farm. They'll not be back 'til late.'

Perhaps it was just hindsight. I don't know. But I'll swear
I had some sort of premonition when she said it. My
husband. She spoke of him delicately, as if she was discussing a mole on her face or some ailment it wasn't quite polite

to mention. They don't get on these two, I thought. They don't get on at all.

Later she bundled me upstairs, muttering something about how tired I must be. Not too tired, all the same, to be given a list of duties to be started in the morning. There was a basin and a jug of water by my bed, cold of course. I couldn't bear to wash. At least at my uncle's we had Tituba to heat some water for us. The blankets were coarse and the straw in the mattress packed so tight it might as well have been a slab of stone. I lay awake for a long time. After a while, there was the sound of doors opening and shutting downstairs and the murmur of voices.

In the morning, I splashed my face and dressed myself quickly. The room was so cold. It had just grown light. I went and looked out of the small square window. Goody Proctor was standing in the yard, filling a bucket at the pump. I saw her look towards the house and speak to someone I couldn't see. Then she came forward and disappeared from view. I went to my bedroom door and opened it a crack. From downstairs, I could hear voices.

'I am sorry, John, but we need wood.'

'I have a day's farming ahead of me, Elizabeth.'

'I didn't notice how low we were until after dark.'

A door slammed.

I went back to the window and looked out into the yard. From the house emerged John Proctor, striding, axe in hand. He marched over to a log pile by the fence and took a large log from it. He stood it on one end and then lifted the axe, high, high up above his head. For a moment, he was poised there, his arms uplifted and his face taut. His shirt had ridden up above his belt and a flat, brown stomach was revealed. His legs were wide apart, his feet planted solidly on the solid brown earth. The axe glinted, and fell.

There was a light tap at my door. I turned quickly and began smoothing the blanket on my bed.

'Good morning, Abigail. Did you sleep well?'

'Yes, very well, Goody Proctor.'

Downstairs, we laid the table together and I was introduced to the boys, one thin and sensitive looking and the other, the younger, tearing round from wall to wall and jumping and talking about farming. Goody Proctor smiled indulgently. 'Matthew takes after his father.' She laid out five bowls on the table. 'We all eat together as a family here, Abigail.' Well that's something, I thought. She told me to sit down while she ladled porridge into the bowls. I was starving. It was all I could do not to seize my spoon and wolf it down there and then. I noticed she put very little in her own bowl, even less than in the children's. She saw me watching her and smiled nervously. 'I do not eat well in the mornings.' Then she went to the door and called her husband.

John Proctor was not as tall as I had expected. He came in standing straight, his shoulders square. Brownish hair curled against his forehead and thick eyebrows hung over a lowering gaze. He was wearing a tough cotton shirt and dark breeches. He was glaring. Sweat from his exertions stood out on his forehead despite the morning chill. He had the axe in one hand, holding it half way down the shaft, and a bundle of wood cuttings cradled in the other arm. His hands were rough and heavy. Our eyes met.

'Thank you, John.' His wife came forward and took the axe from his hand and hung it up on the wall behind him. He walked over to a large wicker basket to the left of the fire and let the wood cuttings drop into it. Then he came and took his seat at the table. Goody Proctor chivvied the boys to sit down before sitting herself and saying a short grace. We all muttered amen, and began to eat. For a

33

minute or so, the only sounds were the spoons scraping against the wooden bowls.

The first thing John ever said to me was, 'Well now, Abigail, do you miss the great goings-on in the town?'

I looked down at my bowl, then back up at him. 'Well, Mr Proctor, I don't know really.'

'Abigail is bound to be a little homesick to begin with,' said Goody Proctor.

'Well then,' replied her husband, 'we must do all we can to make sure she feels at home.'

We were lovers within a month.

I wasn't the first housemaid to be dismissed by Goody Proctor. They had had quite a turnover, that household. Rumour in the town said she was a slave-driver and dismissed so many because none satisfied her in their work. I remember Mercy Lewis telling me about Sarah Hall, the clerk's daughter, who got sent back after two weeks. A month later, she left Salem altogether to go and live with an aunt in Andover, for her health, her family said.

My uncle beat me senseless for getting the sack. I'll never forget it, as long as I live. Afterwards, I lay face down on my bed sobbing, digging my nails into the pillow. All the same, every one of them, all the same. Always. From my room, I had overheard John confess his wickedness. I knew what was coming. Goody Proctor's feet pounded up the stairs. She dragged me down by my hair and pushed me out of the door. She was strong, for such a virtuous woman. She flung my things out after me calling, 'Harlot! whore!' All the usual stuff. I landed on my knees in the yard, grazing my hands. My bonnet was hanging from my neck and my hair was loose. John was standing in the doorway watching, completely helpless. His cheeks were damp with tears. Just like my father. Exactly like my father. These men. What good would it have done if I had begged for her forgiveness? None. Somebody has to be the bad one. Besides which, I wasn't sorry and I wasn't going to pretend I was. She pushed him back inside and slammed the door. I picked myself up, and my things, and brushed the dirt off my apron. Then I began the walk back to Salem, five miles in the dark. I knew what would happen when I got back. I knew I would be beaten. All the same, trudging along the road, all I could think about was John. John. I couldn't believe that he had confessed to her out of shame and guilt. I couldn't believe that he was just like all the others, my uncle, my father. He couldn't be. Not my John. He had held my face when we made love, in the shed, on the ground. He held my face so tightly, gazing at me with eyes that burnt holes in mine, looking, looking. As if he would die if he didn't look. Elizabeth and he hadn't made love since their youngest was born and he said even before that, when they did, she would never look at him. She would look at the ceiling, at the walls, never at him. He bruised me sometimes. I couldn't believe he had gone back to her, not after all the things he'd said and done to me. It must be part of a plan, I thought, as I trudged along. He must have told her deliberately, so that he can be with me. He's worked it all out somehow. He'll come after me on his horse. After a while I had to stop. She had thrown me out in my slippers. My boots were still in their kitchen corner. I kept stumbling in the dark and catching my toes. It was freezing cold but I was completely numb. I sat down and rubbed my feet and listened for the sound of horse's hoofs tumbling along the dirt track. It was impossible that he would not come after me. Quite impossible. There was a strong wind blowing. I strained my ears to listen. So many sounds. It's amazing how many noises can sound like the far-off clatter of hoofs. I knew he would come after me. He had to come. It was all part of his plan. We would go to Boston. Nobody would be able to find us there. We would have our own house and make love in a bed and fall asleep and wake up together. Putting my slippers back on, I began to cry, but I didn't stop believing he would come after me. I didn't stop believing it until I was on my uncle's doorstep, banging on the door to wake up Tituba. It was a stupid thing to do, in retrospect. I should have hidden in the barn or in the church 'til daybreak and then tidied myself up first. I had lost my senses by then. I was dirty and tired and freezing cold. The grazes on my hands and knees were stinging and my feet were bleeding. My head ached where she had pulled my hair. I wanted to be bathed by Tituba and put to bed, the way she would when I was little, scrubbing my back until it tingled and glowed, humming a negro song.

It wasn't her who answered the door. It was my uncle, in his nightshirt, peering out into the darkness and calling fearfully, 'Who's there?'

'It's me, uncle,' my voice was quite steady. I had stopped crying and was steeling myself for what was about to come. I stepped into the light. 'Abigail.'

'Abigail?'

Well of course the whole house had to be raised to hear of my wickedness. I didn't tell him why she'd thrown me out but I had to tell him I'd been dismissed. He only would have found out later and then I would have been beaten for lying as well. He must have known it was something bad, to be hurled out in the middle of the night. He started raging about how he had brought me up, put clothes on my back, educated me, and so on and so on. I stood in front of him, swaying from exhaustion, while my aunt clucked around like a hen and Tituba stood shaking in the corner. I think she half expected to be beaten as well. She often was when my uncle was in one of his tempers. Get on with it I thought, looking up at him while he shouted and quoted scriptures about ingratitude. We all know what you're going to do. Get on with it.

Later, Tituba came to me in my room with a mug of hot milk, mumbling soothing noises. I was in pain and could only be cross with her for not getting to the door before my uncle did, not that it would have made much difference in the end. Whilst she dabbed at my back with a damp cloth, she told me about what had been going on while I had been away. Apparently, there was some move to oust my uncle from his position. There had even been a meeting when he had been called to explain some irregularities in the parish accounts. She had listened outside the door and heard a lot of shouting. Good, I thought, not really considering that if my uncle was replaced we would all have to leave this house. Things were bad all round, she said. One of the farmers was bringing another suit against a neighbour in the county court and there was talk that if he succeeded he would be bringing them against others, including my uncle. 'These bad times, Miss Abigail,' she said, curling her bottom lip and rocking back and forth, 'bad times, bad times.'

Funny how right she turned out to be, stupid old Tituba. Everyone in that town hated each other. They had done for years. Everyone thought they were being persecuted. They all had axes to grind. They were just waiting, waiting, waiting for it all to explode. My uncle once said in church, 'Remember, when you point a finger at someone . . .' (raising a hand, making the gesture) 'there are always three of your own fingers pointing back at you.' It was one of the few intelligent things I ever heard him say. Shame no one listened really.

I didn't start, it you know, all that witchcraft stuff. They started it, my uncle and the others. I just joined in at the appropriate moment. Even then I only did it because they were pointing their fingers at me. It didn't occur to me to get my own back on John until well after it had all begun. 'A whore's vengeance,' he said in court – which is one way of looking at it I suppose.

We had to run away when things got out of hand. I took Mercy Lewis with me. She had been as much involved as me and, anyway, I needed her help to get to Boston. I wasn't sure we would make it. They probably set up blockades on the roads behind us but we had a day's advantage over them and managed to slip through. I knew we would be all right once we made it to the city. Anyone can disappear in Boston. Especially a whore. I didn't have any illusions about how we would have to earn a living. We had to go somewhere where there would be no questions asked. It was either that or thieving, and I preferred to earn an honest living.

At first, we were turned away. We were filthy. Skinny, seventeen and desperate. We hadn't eaten for over two days. Mercy was coming out in red blotches all over her face and I had a sore growing on my neck. Then, at the fourth place we tried, just as we were moving on, the madam called us back.

'Come here a minute,' she said, 'you.' She was looking at me. Mercy was near collapse, clinging to my arm. I tried to make her stand up straight. The madam took my chin in her hands. A wave of violet scent hit me and I nearly fell over. I had never smelt it before. She looked at me closely. I couldn't tell whether she was being hostile or just curious.

'You . . .' she said. 'Two girls. I've heard about two girls on the run from up-country, all that hullabaloo up there.' Mercy panicked. 'It isn't us, it isn't us,' she babbled, and began to cry. The madam dropped my chin and sighed

38

theatrically, 'Oh for God's sake get her in here, off the street.' I pushed Mercy forward and followed.

Madam led us through into the kitchen where she made a sullen-looking girl in petticoats serve us soup from a huge dark stove. Back in Salem, they were still cooking soup over fires. I stared at the stove while we ate. A real stove. The girl in petticoats flounced out, pulling a face. I suppose we smell, I thought. 'Don't mind Mary,' Madam said, 'she's always a bit uppity when it's her turn to cook.' I stared at her. She laughed. 'Oh yes, missie, you cook as well in here. We take it in turns. We have a woman in for the evening meal but we all muck in together for the rest of it. Fairs's fair.' Mercy had fallen asleep with her head on the table. Madam came and sat next to me on the bench and covered my hand with hers. 'Now look here, missie, whatever you want to call yourself. You're all right underneath that mud, you'll clean up OK and I can tell you know what goes on and you'll be good. But I'm not sure about your friend here.' I looked at Mercy and then back up at her. She had very round blue eyes and huge powdered cheeks. She reminded me of a poppet doll I sewed once back in Salem. I gave it dimples with a cross-stitch either side of its mouth. 'Abigail,' I said, 'my name's Abigail. And you take me and Mercy or neither of us.' A broad grin spread across her face. 'I knew it. I knew it.' She gave out a laugh and slapped her thigh. 'I knew it was you I'd heard about. I could tell by your eyes. You showed that Salem lot, my girl, by God you showed them. Pious fools. You showed them.' I couldn't help smiling as well. She made it seem like an enormous joke. For the first time, it all seemed like one enormous, breathtaking joke. 'OK, you're in.'

'And Mercy?' Madam looked at her, then back at me, sighing, 'Well, well, Mercy too, then. See she pulls her weight, mind. And if you go, she goes with you.' Then she went over to a cupboard and pulled out a pewter jug and two large mugs. 'Cider!' she declared with relish. 'Cider to celebrate! I hope you don't mind only cider but I never drink anything too strong at this hour.' Only the men were allowed to drink in Salem. We clunked our mugs together and drained them. Madam turned and went to the door and shouted out, 'Mary, go and see if that back room at the top is fit.'

She told me later that she turned back to see that my head was on the table next to Mercy's.

That was three years since. I've stayed with Madam. I could have moved on, even set up a place of my own, but I like it here. It wasn't easy at first. I hadn't really thought about what it would be like, lying back for some grunting animal, knowing he would pray for forgiveness on Sunday, turning and smiling at his wife and worshipping her for her ignorance. My first customer turned out to be called John. That helped in a way. As he lay there, panting and groaning like a stuck pig, all I could think was, my God, if only you could see how stupid you look. If only you could see. 'Oh my darling,' I whispered in his ear, 'Oh my love.' Madam gets good reports of me from the regulars. 'It's the way you lie to them, Abby,' she said to me the other day, 'nobody lies to them like you. It's those eyes, the way you look at them.' It was John that taught me that. He was the first man who ever touched me. He taught me how to look and look and *see* – how to lie with glances and finger-tips.

I'm Madam's favourite now. She's grooming me to take over the business when she gets too old, although that won't be for years yet. It caused some jealousy when I first got here but everything is fine now. At dawn, we all get together in the parlour to swap stories and relax. The customers are thrown out into a Massachusetts sunrise, massaging their eyes and consciences. Madam locks the door and breaks open a bottle. We have a bit of a party. I like entertaining the others with my stories of the bad old days. They're always asking me. 'Then of course there was that day in the courtroom, when John finally decides to discredit me as a witness by telling the judge him and me had done the business. I deny it, of course, so the judge summons his wife to give evidence. She doesn't know that John has come clean already and says her covenanted husband is as pure as a new born baby. I am vindicated – and he is branded a liar as well as a devil-worshipper.' Madam loves that bit of my story. She slaps her thigh and roars with laughter, that deep rich belly laugh she has. 'The best thing about Christians,' she says, spluttering cider, 'is you can always rely on them to pretend they're better than the rest of us. Leaves them wide open. Never fails.' Before I came, apparently, some of the good townspeople tried to close Madam down. She went to see a few judges with whom she was *very* well acquainted and begged for their assistance in continuing a service to wayward men with less self-control than their good selves. She promised to make a donation to the church and put a Bible in each room. We stayed open.

'Tell us about how your uncle used to watch you in the bath,' says Ann. 'Well, when I was little . . . ' I begin. They've all heard it before but they listen eagerly, waiting for the punchline. When it comes they throw themselves backwards and scream with mirth. Even Mary and Elizabeth smile, lying on the sofa, wrapped in one another's arms. Mercy crouches next to me, rubbing her latest bruise. She always gets them. I never do. It's odd really. I don't know why she should attract those types but she does. For the first six months or so, she kept having nightmares. She used to cry out in her sleep. Once she even said we should

41

go back. We would only be whipped she said. 'Don't be stupid, Mercy,' I told her, 'people died because of what we said. They'd hang us soon as see us.' She knew I was right. Virtuous people have long memories. Most of the girls here are on the run from something. Occasionally we get visits from a constable but no one tells him anything. We all stick together here. If he gets too nosy, Madam gets on to one of his superiors. Apparently, I have achieved some degree of infamy. Rumours of my whereabouts are rife.

After a couple of hours of chat, it's someone's turn to go out and buy fresh bread and cheeses, or make soup. We eat until we're stuffed, then slope off to sleep until early evening. Only Madam stays up. She must catch a few hours somewhere but she never seems to rest. She's never tired either. She is always there, beaming through her powder. Not that she's soft. Last month, she threw out a girl called Beth who made herself ugly and stupid with drink. She'd get rid of Mercy if it wasn't for me. If I ever do get my own place, I'll take Mercy off the game and let her do all the cooking and cleaning. You need a full-time housekeeper in a place like this. I don't know how Madam does it sometimes, running somewhere this size on her own. I couldn't do it. She can't delegate, that's her problem. She'll have a job handing over to me when the time comes. I ought to get my own house really, but it's difficult when you start up. You have to build up the customers' trust. You have to nurture them. It would be much easier to take over Madam's clients.

I think about it upstairs, lying awake in the room I share with Mercy. It always takes me a while to get off. White beams slip through the wooden slats of the shutters, into the darkened space around me. Traders are shouting in the street outside. Mercy whimpers in her sleep. Downstairs, Madam will be sitting at the table going through the books.

What I'd really like is the biggest place in the country, open twenty-four hours a day, with the girls working in shifts. Mind you it would mean employing a lot of other people apart from the girls, to keep it running. I might have to employ some men. My mind is churning it over as I grow drowsy. Keep it small to start off with. Several small houses. I don't dream of Salem, well, not like Mercy anyway. I dream of John sometimes, out in the yard, when I first saw him. He is standing there, the axe raised up in his two fists, his face taut and haunted. A bolt of sunlight hits him as the axe falls down and down and down and I, underneath, watch it hurtling slowly towards me. I wept no tears when they hanged him. He could have saved himself. If he had confessed, it would have bought him enough time. They released the people still in prison after I ran away. By then they had realized the whole thing was a dreadful mistake. Still they never prosecuted the other accusers. Everybody had accused everybody else by then and it would have meant prosecuting the whole town. When they looked around for someone to blame, I was handy. They conveniently forgot it wasn't me who started it. Ah, well. Enough of that. It brought down a few learned men, reverends and judges. John would move back and forth inside me, so slowly, looking at me, gazing, holding my face so steady. My eyes would stare back, wide open. Boston is growing every day. New immigrants flood in. 'Look at me,' he would say, moving back and forth and holding my face, 'look at me.' There's no shortage of customers, and the new silks are coming in from Europe. His eyes promised such volumes. Vengeance means nothing next to survival, but it's helpful when the two coincide.

SECOND CHANCE

Phil Feighan

Phil Feighan took a degree in European studies and is now a teacher in Navan, Co. Meath, Eire. Phil took up writing in 1983 and is currently working on her first novel.

SECOND CHANCE

It's rather enjoyable really, being a fugitive. Never knowing when a hand will be placed on my shoulder sends a tremble of excitement through me. One has to live constantly in the present, always on the look-out. I've lost my job, my money is running out and the guards are searching the country for me, yet I have never felt as alive in my life.

Perhaps I'm tempting fate, but we live quite openly here in Galway. At this time of year the city is thronged with holidaymakers, so we could be anybody. We stroll on the promenade in Salthill with people taking their dogs for a walk, and sit in the park at Eyre Square talking to old men. Sometimes we go to Lydon's for tea and cakes and listen to the University students moan about their exams. When the cashier smilingly bags our groceries for us, I look at her and think 'If only you knew who we were'.

I have rented a place out in Barna. They told me it was a chalet; in fact it's an old railway carriage with a door that opens outwards and gas lights inside. It nestles against a gigantic gorse bush and looks out to the Aran Islands. When the day is clear one can almost see the whitewashed houses on Aran Mor.

The mornings are the best. I like to lie on in bed, listening to the seagulls' lament echo far out across the Bay. Then I go back over all the events that brought me here.

I was Father Ennis's housekeeper, First Lady of Saint Justin's parish in one of the affluent suburbs of south

Dublin. I looked after Father Ennis for twenty-four years, ever since the time I had the baby at the age of sixteen.

We're very close, Father Ennis and I, far more than one would expect for a priest and his house-keeper. He was never the type to stick to formalities, like eating all his meals upstairs or summoning me with the bell. Much of the time he came down to the kitchen for a chat, while I ironed and starched the altar cloths. I would give him all the gossip that would never reach his ears, and though I never heard him say a bad word about anyone else, we spent many a wicked hour deliberating on the parentage of the new bishop. In the evenings we would drink cocoa by the Aga and listen to the news on the radio. Innocent times, they seem as far back as one's own childhood.

To celebrate my fortieth birthday, Father Ennis, bless him, had arranged a trip to Florida. I was to go over there and spend a fortnight with my sister whom I hadn't seen in fifteen years. Sensitive as always, he didn't spring it on me a week before I was to depart. He knows that I like plenty of time to prepare for something and often teased me that I enjoyed the anticipation far more than the event. He sprang the surprise on Shrove Tuesday – the holiday was to be in early July.

I hugged myself with delight all day, but by that evening the anxiety had set in. Esther, my sister, is younger than me by ten years, but when I saw her last she was so slim and tanned, I could have been her mother: lumpy, with glasses and permed, frizzed hair. I had a great fondness for fatty bacon and Queen of Puddings. Over there, I would have to wear shorts and sundresses, and bathing togs on the beach. I would be the laughing stock of Miami.

There and then I embarked on a regime: no more perms, a new wardrobe of summer clothes; no white bread, no more skin of the chicken; plenty of fruit to clear the skin;

two pints of water to unblock the cellulite. I had twelve weeks to lose three stone; I was sure I could do it.

But you know how it is with resolutions. All went well for a week. The cats got plump from bacon fat, and Father Ennis grew irritable with salads and yogurt. Then the Redemptorists came to give the Lenten Novena and stayed in the parochial house for the duration. Their zeal couldn't be fed on coleslaw; it had to be four course dinners every night. I couldn't resist tasting the clam chowder and the Devil's Food cake, and told myself I was just checking that everything was all right in order to make Father Ennis proud of me. Then the evening Father Ennis brought me out to dinner to celebrate my birthday, I surrendered to the crêpes suzettes. There didn't seem to be much point in continuing the diet after that.

The weeks slipped by and I was as big as ever. My hair began to hang limply around my face, and I kept it back with hairclips. I looked like a simpleton. Depression set in. Then one Sunday afternoon, when I was reading the *Sunday Press* in the conservatory, I spotted an advertisement for a toning machine . Tone up those sagging muscles, it challenged, reduce that unsightly flab. Miraculous results were assured, and though I'm always sceptical about such claims, I was desperate enough to give it a try.

I located a beauty salon in the Northside, far enough away from our parish that nobody could possibly recognize me. It was situated upstairs over a bicycle shop in Sutton. It was a single large room, covered with a navy and pink striped carpet. Several cubicles were curtained off, and I could see the purple aura of a sun-bed from behind one. Two other people chatted behind another about the shade of a lipstick to match a bridesmaid's dress.

A beautician emerged from a third cubicle. She was very young and a little too chatty for my liking, so I gave a false

49

name. When I was undressed, I sat up on a couch. To my bottom, stomach, waist and thighs the beautician attached black pads which were wired to a machine. Then she turned the current on, gradually at first, then more and more until my muscles were contracting hard from the electric impulses. Looking down at the blanket which modestly covered all the flesh and wires, I could see myself being kneaded and squeezed like a large lump of dough.

The beautician excused herself and returned to the cubicle next to mine. She had forgotten to leave me some magazines, so I listened to find out what the client next door was having done. It seemed to be electrolysis. The client, a young woman by the sound of it, was complaining about the hairs on her chin, while the beautician assured her that such growth was natural during pregnancy.

Ever since my own pregnancy, I have been interested in the case histories of other women. I sat up to listen.

'How long more have you to go?' the beautician was asking.

'Another f-four weeks or so.' There was no excitement, no anticipation in her voice.

'You'll be glad to have it over.' The beautician was drawing her out.

'I'm n-not so sure,' sighed the woman. 'I'm not m-married, you see.'

I felt sorry for her. Her voice sounded far too tired for somebody of her age. Young and silly, I concluded; fussing about a few hairs on her chin and she probably as big as a bus. If only it had been like that in my day. I felt an old twisting in my stomach, but increased the current from the machine to take my mind of what was irreversibly in the past.

I booked in for a course of ten sessions, twice a week until I went to the States. Father Ennis never missed me,

50

because recently he was scarcely in the house, except for meals. The poor man was very busy. There were the Easter services to organize, and a cash-flow problem with the new community centre that was being built. He and the bishop had long meetings from which Father Ennis emerged with tightly-lidded anger. In the evenings he was away on visitation to the homes in the parish. He would return exhausted, but smiling, and sit by the Aga, with his mug of drinking chocolate. He was less talkative than usual, so I filled him in on all the latest news, excluding my visits to the beautician. I felt a little guilty about deceiving him, but, I reasoned, once I performed my duties as housekeeper, what I did with my spare time was my own business.

I began to look forward to the sessions. There was a feeling of adventure as I embarked on the bus and changed at O'Connell Street for Sutton. From the top of the bus I could see the curve of Dublin Bay all the way out to Howth and the yachts rocking on the water at the marina. Ireland's Eye was just recognizable in the distance. There was a different way of life out here, and a smell of sea air that filled me with a childish excitement.

At the salon there were cups of coffee, magazines that I would never buy but like to read anyway, and eavesdropping on conversations in the cubicles either side of me. It amazed me how these women could open up to a beautician: stories about children causing trouble at school; trial separations; family factions at an oncoming wedding. But I suppose, if the women were willing to have someone remove hair from their breasts, or reveal buttocks mottled with cellulite, a stormy marriage wouldn't be such a humiliation.

Best of all, I got slimmer. The deep line my knickers made under my trousers began to fade. I re-discovered my waist. The beautician suggested that my problem might be due more to fluid retention than fat, and that if I cut down on my salt intake, I would lose weight as well. Already, I was looking forward to meeting Esther in Florida. I bought some new clothes for the holiday and folded them into my suitcase, even though I was tempted to wear them in front of Father Ennis to see if he would notice my figure.

Mrs Grogan from Kilmacud Road was to look after Father Ennis during my absence, and I spring-cleaned the house from top to bottom, so that she would have nothing to comment on. While I tidied out cupboards and washed curtains, I thought of all the unattached middle-aged men over in Florida with money to spend on an attractive, youthful middle-aged woman. I bristled with energy and sparkled with good humour.

One could not have said the same for Father Ennis, however. His smile faded, he lost his appetite. At first I thought that it must the pressures of the parish weighing him down, or that the bishop had upset him again, until he stopped talking to me. He did not come down to the kitchen for his supper any more. It occurred to me that he had found out about my trips to the Northside, and was filled with disgust. When he read from Ecclesiastes the following Sunday: 'Vanity of vanities, and all things are vanity'; I couldn't even stay in the same room as he for a full week.

One day, in the middle of the afternoon, he appeared at the kitchen door. He didn't come in, but hesitated on the threshold, inspecting the light-switch. It was nine days to my departure, and I was kneading dough on a floury table.

'I was thinking of going away for a while, Tessa,' he said. 'I'm not feeling well and could do with a break.'

'I'm very sorry to hear that, Father,' I said, taken aback. Surely, he couldn't be that upset with me? 'Where will you go?'

'Down to Wexford to stay with a friend of mine; Father Stevens, you remember him? We were in Maynooth together. I'll leave in the morning; Father Johnston will stand in for me here.'

'How long will you be away, Father?' I was thinking of my own holiday in Florida.

'A fortnight.' From his expression, I could see that he wished he were there already.

'I'll be gone by then, Father.' I stood there facing him, my apron covered with flour, my hands anchored with the sticky dough. I felt helpless. All I could think of were the suitcases I would have to haul to the bus-stop to take me to town for another bus to get out to the airport. There was also the prospect of embarking on the plane with nobody to see me off. I wanted to cry. Whatever Father Ennis had against me, I didn't deserve this.

'I'm sorry, Tessa. This is causing you great inconvenience, I know. But I need to get away for some peace and quiet.'

Now he was adding insult to injury. 'I'm not disturbing you with all the work I'm doing around the house, Father?' I said, hoping there was just the right measure of sarcasm to make my point.

He smiled tiredly. 'No, no, it's nothing like that, believe me. Tell you what, I'll take the train down and leave you the car – you'll be busy over the next few days. I'll collect the car at the airport when I return.'

'Thank you, Father,' I answered coldly and slammed the dough into a baking-tin.

As the days passed, I became glad of the car, and not merely for getting about. I was nervous on my own in the house. I loaded the bucket with anthracite each evening so that I wouldn't have to go out back after dark. I kept the radio on in the kitchen and the television in the sitting room upstairs. But having the car outside gave the impression

53

that Father Ennis was still about, so I was able to sleep at night.

Moreover, I needed the car for all the final arrangements. There was new underwear to be bought, a decent suitcase, and my visa to be arranged. The American Embassy could not process my application until they had my passport. When I located it in Father Ennis's filing cabinet, I discovered that it was out of date. Timewise, I was leaving it very tight, and I blessed Father Ennis's foresight in leaving me the car.

The day my passport was to be collected, I drove into town. My hair had grown long enough to be re-styled and I had an appointment in David Marshall's for that afternoon. There was one final session on the toning machine that day also, and even though I could ill afford the time, I did not want to miss that last opportunity to lose another few centimetres. I headed straight for Sutton.

I was nearing the end of my session when through the curtains I heard the door open and the beautician greet someone. Then she led the person past my cubicle into the one beside me.

'More electrolysis?' the beautician asked.

'N-no. You did a very good job the last time. L-look.' I recognized the voice and cocked my ear.

'What can we do for you today, then?'

'I'd like you to w-wax my legs,' the woman replied. 'The baby is due any day, and I'd like to have them done before I go into hospital.' She sounded close to tears.

Of course, the young unmarried girl. I pulled myself over to the curtains as far as the wires could stretch.

'How have you been keeping lately?' asked the beautician. A fragrance of warm wax rose in the air.

'All r-right, I suppose,' sighed the woman.

'Look, don't worry,' said the beautician, unexpectedly

caring. 'I know it's very hard right now, but it will be over in a week or two. My sister went through the same, and you should see the gorgeous little baby she's got now. She's never been happier.'

The young woman, moved by the solicitude of another human being, began to cry. 'I can't k-keep it. I just can't. It would cause d-dreadful problems.'

'But you could have it adopted. There are childless couples crying out for a baby.'

'I know, I know. The child's father was to look into all those matters, but he still hasn't come up with any suggestions. All we've done these past few months is to fight and b-blame one another. It's my fault for not making my own decisions, but he's terrified of somebody finding out. It would cause a huge scandal.'

'Rich, married and famous,' the beautician commented. There were ripping sounds as cloth, wax and hair were torn from the leg.

The woman made no reply. 'I'll bet he was a politician,' the beautician continued. 'They're all at it, even though the publicity would ruin them.'

'I haven't seen him in weeks,' the woman said. 'I think he's pulled out on me. What will I do? I can't go through this alone.' And she sobbed.

Suddenly, I was a teenager again, as if a thick veil had been swept back. I remembered the mornings when I rose an hour early to be sick before the family got up. At school, my mates crowded about me as we walked down the corridor, so that the teachers wouldn't notice. And every evening for two weeks after I told John Miller I was pregnant, I waited outside the Palace Cinema in case he showed up. Times haven't changed a bit. The poor, poor girl.

'Now, turn to your side, and I'll do the backs of your legs,' the beautician instructed. 'You know, I was reading

55

an article in a magazine yesterday about "The Other Woman" and the lengths they must go to in order to make the man stick to his responsibilities.'

Something jabbed my consciousness. I looked at my watch. It was past the hour. I did a mental calculation of the time it would take me to cross the city. I was going to be late. To attract attention, I shifted about on the couch. One of the wired pads slipped and began to send jabs of current into my hip bone.

Still the beautician went on. 'One woman went and stood outside his house until he came running out to her in a blind panic. He promised her everything, and what's more, she got it.'

'Excuse me,' I called at last. I didn't care any more if they thought I had been listening to them; I was frantic to get away.

Outside, the rain dashed against the pavement. Black clouds glowered in the sky and the traffic splashed water on the legs of the running pedestrians. I, too, ran for cover. I had scarcely driven fifty yards when I noticed the steering pull to the left. I stopped and got out to see what was the matter; it was a burst tyre. Breathless with panic, I wrenched open the boot and stared at the collection of tools with which one changed a wheel. I did not know what to do. I took the only course open to me and flagged down a passing motorist. He was quick and adept. Within minutes he had the spare wheel on, but when he jacked the car back down, what had seemed in the boot to be a fully-pressurized wheel flattened to the ground. I burst into tears.

'I'm so sorry,' the man said, 'would you like a lift to the nearest garage?'

By the time I was mobile again, it was past noon. I knew that there was no chance the Passport Office would be open when I reached it, yet I doggedly tore across the city, praying to Saint Jude of Hopeless Cases for a miracle. It was no good. The doors were firmly shut, and a notice hung inside informed me that I should return at two-fifteen. That meant I'd be too late for the American Embassy and my visa.

Damn! Damn! All my plans for the day had been ruined, even the appointment at David Marshall's hair salon. The rain streamed down my head and into my shoes. What should I do? I longed for the warmth of a restaurant, where I could have some coffee and wash the muck and oil from my hands. But every place was thronged with people on their lunch-break, and from where I stood the queues looked endless. I returned to my car and went home.

As I drove out the dual carriageway towards Stillorgan, I wondered how Father Ennis could rush from one appointment to another, say Mass, counsel the parishioners and keep the bishop at bay without ever losing his composure. Furthermore, he had been running the parish for the past fifteen years with a minimum of holidays; no wonder he needed a break now.

I turned off into Bedford Road. The beeches and horse-chestnuts drooped miserably in front of the houses. The rain spat against the windscreen, and through the moving blades of the wipers I saw a figure standing at the gateway of the parochial house. Mrs Grogan, I thought, come to finalize arrangements about the house-keeping while I was in Florida. That was all I needed. I looked into the mirror at somebody that resembled Medusa and cursed the day I agreed to go to America.

I nodded through the rain-spattered side window at Mrs Grogan and revved the car nastily up the drive. When I got out, there was no sign of her coming up after me. What did the woman want: to be carried up to the house? I stamped back down to the gate and startled a young woman who looked as though she were about to faint. There was no Mrs Grogan.

'Is there something you want?' I snapped, pulling a strand of wet hair from my eyes in an attempt to focus on her.

'No, thank you,' she whispered, 'I was just leaving.' Her hair hung, like mine, in rats' tails about her shoulders. Her eyes were dilated. 'I was waiting for F-Father . . .' and her voice trailed off.

The beautician's voice came clanging into my memory: the other woman; responsibilities, besieging the man's house. Oh dear, sweet God.

The woman was frightened. She had a stammer. She was pregnant.

I still don't know who helped whom into the house. We busied ourselves in getting warm and dry. I fussed about setting a tray, making the coffee, buttering the scones; servile actions to give me time until the bell stopped thundering in my head. Then we talked. We talked well into the evening. She blamed Father Ennis; I blamed her. We cried in turns and together, holding each other for comfort. My Father Ennis, my own Father Jim who had been consecrated to God, and to whom I had devoted my life, had feet of clay after all.

The woman's name was Stephanie Mitchell and she worked as a civil engineer with the Corporation. Her father had died two years previously, and she missed him terribly the first Christmas. About a week before Christmas Eve she was drifting down Grafton Street in a half-hearted attempt to buy presents when she found herself gazing at the moving puppet displays in Switzer's shop windows. All about her children jumped and giggled at the reindeer and the elves and tugged at their parents' coats to move on to the next window. She noticed a priest standing next to her, and both had laughed with embarrassment at the fact that they were the only unaccompanied adults there. He had seemed so gentle, so taken with the wonder of the children, that she didn't want him to go. She told him about a Christmas in her childhood when her father had dressed up as Santa Claus and had visited her on Christmas Eve. When she mentioned that she had noticed with pride that Santa's hands were just like her father's, she burst into tears. Father Ennis took her up to Bewley's for coffee and stayed with her until she had cheered up enough to continue her shopping. Realizing how depressed she'd be, he visited her apartment on New Year's Eve to keep her company, and somewhere between Auld Lang Syne and the final party popper on the television show, they fell in love.

That had been almost eighteen months ago.

I thought of that New Year's Night when Father Ennis had left me on my own, weeping with loneliness in the kitchen, while he attended to, as he put it, an attempted suicide. I remembered how he had grown gaunt and grim the past few weeks, how he had been away every evening. When I had imagined him to be bringing comfort to the people of his parish, he had been receiving it in the arms of this woman. And now, terrified of the consequences, he had absconded, leaving her alone and frantic.

While she told me her story, I examined her carefully. She was small in size, possibly petite, judging from the size of her hands; in her condition, it was difficult to assess. Her hair was very black and riotous with curls, and when she spoke they danced crazily about her head. She had a sudden smile that disappeared like a shadow, and lambent, hazel eyes that could melt granite. She was twenty-six years of age. I could see why Father Ennis would fall in love with her. In spite of her predicament, her movements belied an energy to contrast with his composure.

59

At times, during the endless pots of tea, I heard myself talking animatedly about adoption agencies, labour pains, post-natal depression, and I wondered if I were going mad. The house-keeper arranging a holiday in Florida and worrying about leaving a clean house behind her seemed to be in a time warp. Later, after I had put Stephanie to bed in the guest-room, I found myself unable to sleep. I tried to bring the house-keeper back and deposit her firmly in my skin so that I could pre-occupy myself with the usual daily anxieties. But my mind had returned to my own pregnancy. Terrified of my mother to whom the most grievous sin was to get pregnant out of wedlock, I had given birth to a baby boy in the phone box at the bottom of our road. It was late at night and I had been trying to ring my best friend to come and help me. We had tied the umbilical cord with her shoe lace, and wrapped the shuddering infant in my school blazer. At daybreak, I walked over to Saint Justin's parish and left the baby in the confession box just before people arrived for half-seven mass. Father Ennis was the celebrant that morning. He was the new curate, gawky with a residue of acne. When I finally came forward after his repeated pleas from the pulpit, he got me to sign some adoption papers and offered me a job helping out at the parochial house. I took it up as soon as I finished my exams.

Nobody ever found out, and Father Ennis never mentioned the baby again. Whether he was just trying to help me to forget, I do not know. But something inside refused to let it go, and the more I tried to ignore the pain, the more persistent it became. For years afterwards, I cried bitterly on the baby's birthday. I fingered matinée coats and bootees long after he would have outgrown them. Sometimes in the supermarket, when no one was looking, I would squeeze some baby lotion on to my hand and smell it. And I hated every smiling mother I met.

In the middle of the night, there was a rapid knocking on my door. Stephanie appeared, clutching the handle.

'The pains have started,' she groaned. 'I don't think I'm going to make it to the hospital.'

I led her over to my bed and made her as comfortable as possible. Then I phoned for an ambulance. I was on the landing when her shrieks brought me into the bedroom like a shot. There, in my own bed which no-one else had occupied in twenty-five years, she gripped my arms and began to push.

Her baby was born within minutes, in the quiet of the night when not a car nor a rustle of leaves was to be heard outside. Having read every book on childbirth for years after giving up my own baby, I knew exactly what to do. I placed Stephanie's child, slippery and smelling of warm blood, on her stomach.

'It's a beautiful baby boy,' I whispered through a blur of tears. She would not look at him.

'He's the image of his father,' I persisted. 'Let me put him in your arms.'

'Take it away,' she moaned.

I took the baby downstairs, and in the heat of the Aga which still burned loyally I baptized him, in case he would die. Then I washed him in the sink. His cries sounded like an old, creaking door. I looked for something warm to wrap him in and found an un-starched altar-cloth in my linen-basket. When he was warm and dry, I sat in my armchair and rocked him. I sniffed him, indulging in that baby smell which is such a delight to the senses. I kissed his head, watched his hand grip my forefinger in an attempt to fathom these strange, solid surroundings. Then he nuzzled into my neck, and something in me shifted, like an ancient fracture finally settling into place.

As the ambulance siren wailed up the road to the house,

I knew that I wouldn't be able to let this baby go as easily as I had my own.

Stephanie and the baby were brought to Holles Street, where both were examined and found to be in perfect health. Stephanie was put into a ward with five other women who talked to one another from their beds, or lingered over their meals at the table in the middle of the ward. Beside their beds, an infant slept in a clear perspex crib.

Nobody else knew about Stephanie's baby, so I was her only visitor. I came to see them every day. Invariably, I found her in bed, staring dully into space, and a lone crib in the far corner of the nursery. The nurse on duty would wheel it out for me and around it I would place blankets, baby clothes and toys with the reverence of the Magi. I would sit by the bed holding the baby and talking about the weather while about us milled the other visitors to the ward.

The woman opposite us was always cut off from view by the crowd of people standing around her. Bouquets of flowers staggered against the wall; gifts wrapped with pink ribbon were heaped up beside the bedside locker. Instamatic cameras clicked and flashed. Once, I heard the pop of a champagne cork. It reminded me of a book launch, though I had never been to one.

'Did Jim call?' Stephanie asked one day.

Every time I heard her refer to Father Ennis as Jim, the jealousy clawed at my heart. She possessed a part of him that was beyond my reach. In addition, she had a baby, his baby.

'He hasn't been in touch yet,' I replied. At that, she turned against the wall.

'Don't be too hard on him,' I said. 'He's not expecting you to have the baby for another week. He'll be back then, I'm sure of it.'

Stephanie turned on me. 'Don't be so naive,' she cried. 'You know as well as I do that he has no intention of seeing me again.' She sat back against the pillows and narrowed her lips. 'Well, I have a surprise for him.'

I didn't like the spite in her voice. 'I shall tell his bishop,' she announced. 'That will put the wind in Jim Ennis's sails.'

'I think the bishop knows already,' I said, remembering and now understanding the long sessions in Father Ennis's study.

Stephanie, however, was hell-bent on revenge. 'Then I'll contact the newspapers. The entire country will know within a week.'

I left her to her plans and wheeled the baby back to the nursery. Her attitude disturbed me, not because of what it might do to Father Ennis's reputation, but because she was using the baby to strike back at him. She didn't want the baby, that was clear; she certainly didn't deserve him. Odd how we should have crossed paths. I should have been in town all day. She would have given up by the time I got home, and I never would have known. All because of a burst tyre. I looked down at the fuzzy head yawning in the crib. Florida could wait; I was being given a second chance.

Visiting time was past by the time I got to the hospital the following afternoon, having spent the morning making new arrangements. There was no problem about my being there, however, since I was treated the same way as a husband. As soon as I entered, my throat dried up. I carried a holdall with me, into which I had stuck a bunch of flowers to make it fill out. To me, it looked so conspicuous, I was sure I would be asked to leave it at the porter's desk. I joined a queue for the public telephone as a pretext for looking about me without attracting attention. My eyes darted about, taking in everything: the watchfulness of the porter; the frequency of doctors and nurses; how the visitors seemed as they left the hospital. I could feel a pulse throbbing behind my eyes.

Satisfied, I went over to the lift. As I was about to get in, a couple emerged, accompanied by a nurse holding a baby. I stepped back and watched them walk to the entrance. There, the nurse produced a pair of scissors and cut off the identity straps from the baby's ankle and wrist. Only as the parents stepped outside did the nurse hand the baby over. I lost my courage. I mounted the stairs numbly, as though I were walking in my sleep. I couldn't do it.

Stephanie was asleep in the ward; the baby, for once, was beside her bed. He smiled when I stroked his temple and curled his fingers with pleasure. It was wind, I know; he was too young to smile, but it reminded me who I was doing this for, and strengthened my resolve. I began to arrange the flowers in a vase.

Opposite me, the woman and her husband were sorting out gifts and bouquets after another rush of well-wishers had died off. The waste-paper basket was crammed with envelopes and wrapping paper. The woman moved slowly, her face set with secret pain, and every now and again, she sat on the bed to rest. Her husband said something about getting some refuse sacks to carry everything out to the car and left the ward.

I fed the baby and changed him. As long as I was doing the usual things, I could keep my panic under control. When I placed the baby back in his crib and began to wheel him out the door, I thought my legs would betray me and bring me crumpling to the floor.

I was crossing the threshold when Stephanie woke up and turned around. Desperation made me bold.

'Go back to sleep, love,' I said. 'I'll look after the baby.' The words broke the spell. I believed the authority in my own voice. A calmness fortified me like an invisible coat of armour.

The corridor was deserted. I passed the mop room and heard the nurse and the man from the ward searching for refuse sacks. Some yards further down, I picked up the baby, blankets, sheets and all, and placed him in the holdall. There was a vacant private room beside me, and I wheeled the crib in and shut the door. Downstairs, the porter was joking with two student nurses. A doctor was in consultation with two anxious-looking parents. I walked out the door and into a light breeze whipped up by the trees in Stephen's Green.

That was a month ago. I cashed in the airline ticket and took my savings out of the bank. That enabled me to buy everything the baby needed and to pay a month's rent in advance for this house in Galway. The police reports on the radio asked listeners to keep a lookout for a stout, middle-aged woman with brown, curly hair. As for the television, when I saw the photograph on the nine o'clock news, I laughed so hard, I woke the baby. There I was in a suit that had always been too tight, growling through a pair of thick spectacles. Poor Father Ennis, being so caught up in his troubles, hadn't noticed the changes while I was getting ready for Florida. I'm only half the size I was and the clothes I had been keeping for Miami Beach are ideal for Salthill. My hair is now cropped and dyed blonde. As for being middle-aged, the baby has brought a joy to my life that has knocked ten years off me. I have called him James, after his father. When I see that gummy grin of his, I could do a somersault. To be on the safe side, I have dressed him in girl's clothes. They haven't a hope of finding me.

Father Ennis won't betray me. He knows that I'm the only chance he has of ever being able to see his son. It will be wonderful. He'll be able to come here on holidays. We'll walk on the beach like any normal family and go on picnics to Connemara. Then in the evenings, when James has gone to bed, Father Ennis and I will sit in the kitchen, drinking cocoa and making plans for our son's education. A Holy Family; a perfect Trinity.

I'll have run out of money by the end of the week. I'll phone him then. But it would be better not to take any risks yet and tell him where I am. Just in case. For the time being, he can transfer the money I need into my bank account in Donnybrook. Then I'll sit it out until the heat is off. I'm not taking any chances when so much is at stake. Nobody shall touch this child of mine.

I'd kill us both first.

THE GREEN
MOUSTACHE

William Harley

William Harley from Oxford is married with three daughters. Starting his career in a Copyright Library, he then became an Official Handicapper for the Jockey Club. William now spends his time in front of his typewriter and playing golf.

THE GREEN MOUSTACHE

He started school as a little monkey, and left as a big ape. He lumbered along. He swung his arms long and loose, in simian fashion. He held his head at right angles, as if searching the ground for edible insects. The girls never looked at him and, if they had, Gilbert Green would not have known, because he could only see people's feet.

'He's in that yobbo stage,' said his father, in excuse for their shambling son. 'He'll soon grow out of it.'

'If he does, it will be more than you ever did,' said Gilbert's mother.

This was almost an affable remark for Gilbert's mother, at any rate when addressing her husband. She had never forgiven him for continually demanding sex, even after the birth of Gilbert, when, in her opinion, they had both of them done their bit, and could conveniently shelve the sticky, degrading exercise, and forget about it. In point of fact, it was a long time since Gilbert's father had made any such plaintive request, though, sleeping in the spare bedroom, he frequently found his thoughts occupied with visions of his wife undressing on the other side of the wall.

They were sitting opposite each other now, in the two leather armchairs given to them by Mrs Green's mother when they were married. It was a situation Gilbert's father tried to avoid, because whatever Gilbert's mother happened to be wearing it outlined her thighs, hips, and breasts in such a thought-provoking manner that he often rose hastily

with the strong conviction that his Y-fronts were full of
itching powder. She was approaching forty, but looked in
her twenties, even in broad daylight. Look what giving up
sex had done for her, she said to her feminist friends, most
of whom had to do without it anyway. She never invited
anyone to look at what it had done for her husband.

'We can't send him to the university, because his granny
with the money ain't dead yet,' said Gilbert's father, whose
venture into the armchair had only been out of a feeble
sense of the duty to discuss their son's future.

'My mother isn't seventy yet,' snapped his wife, and
glared at him as if he had implied that it was her fault that
her mother was still alive. The eyes she glared with were
like a houri's, smoky beneath their drooping lids; the mouth
she snapped with was red, full-lipped and sensual; the angry
jerk of her head moved her heavy dark hair like a banner
in a small breeze. She was the biggest living falsehood ever
perpetrated upon this earth.

'There are plenty of people dead by seventy,' pointed out
Mr Green. He did not mean to suggest that they were if
they had done the decent thing, but his wife's expression
seemed to indicate that she thought he did. He went on
hurriedly. 'Anyway, seeing how things are, and what the
marmalade factory pays me, we'll have to find out what he
wants to do with himself. See what sort of job he wants.
We can't have him hanging around here till kingdom come.'

'I won't have him doing rough work. He takes after my
side, not yours,' said Gilbert's mother. She was taking the
opportunity to remind him whence he got his uncouthness
and his brutal carnality. Her own mother was good at
genteel pursuits, such as watercolours and tapestry, as well
as at staying obstinately alive. Mr Green's lot had all been
in the army, as privates.

Gilbert's father got up. Exposure to the sight of an

exquisite body moving carelessly under a thin dress could only be endured for so long when a man was not allowed to grab it. Apart from which, he thought he had displayed sufficient sense of responsibility in bringing up the subject of Gilbert's future at all. 'Perhaps he can answer a few adverts, or see what they've got along at the job centre,' he said. 'I'm going up to my study. I've got a couple of letters to see to.'

His wife wrinkled her delicate nose and made a noise with it that was like a *pizzicato* note on a viola. In a plain woman, it would have been called a sniff. 'I looked into that so-called study of yours this morning. You keep it like a pigsty,' she said.

Gilbert's father was glad he had had the foresight to hide Ruby May under the sofa up there. Not that it had required much foresight. When a man is supposed to have a private room, it is just the place that a woman will always find an excuse to poke into.

He had no letters to write, of course. It was an escape, a retreat into the shade after too much dazzling sunshine. It so happened that he had answered an advert himself. It had appeared in his *Purty Gal Magazine*, with an attractive illustration of the commodity and a form on which you listed your preferences. The package had arrived very early that morning, and, in order to avoid enquiries concerning the parcel's peculiar shape, Gilbert's father had gone out in his dressing-gown and ambushed the postman up the road. It was a good job he had a sofa, or there would have been a problem where to keep it. After it had been inflated with the small foot-pump provided – a longish job that was fairly hard on the calf muscles – it was as tall as Gilbert's mother and went in and out in the same places as Gilbert's mother. It had cost him forty pounds including VAT, and he had been given a choice out of four shades of head hair, two of pubic hair, and any one of a dozen faces. This particular model was called Ruby May – or *the* Ruby May, as the advertisement put it – and he had chosen black head hair like Gilbert's mother's and black pubic hair like Gilbert's mother presumably still had; and this was in spite of it being Gilbert's mother's fault that Gilbert's father had found himself so titivated by an illustration that he had lashed out forty quid for the article. Ruby May had a pretty face, if somewhat immobile, and she was inclined to stare at him. He imagined himself waking in the night to find her sharing his pillow and thought it very much on the cards that he would be frightened.

Gilbert himself had no notion, past or present, of this situation, and, anyway, was too taken up with being a yobbo.

Gilbert Green, the hulking school-leaver, was no good at selling electrical components. Demonstrating a time-switch, he had paralysed his own arm and the customer's. He was no good at selling carpets. Re-rolling a length of Wilton, he always finished with a roll three times the diameter of the original roll. He was no good as a milkman. He got up all right on the first morning, but on the second morning he was still in bed when the milk floats were returning to the dairy. Finally, he spent a protracted time out of work, and spent three days of it growing a moustache.

He was amazed that it had taken only three days. He had thought it would be a long and patient job, involving much peering into the mirror, moistening with the fore-finger, and subtle clipping with scissors. It was almost as if the fully-fledged article had arrived on his lip when he wasn't looking; as if there had always been a moustache out there that was Gilbert's moustache and had flown in at the window at the first opportunity. It was thick, bristly, and of a blackness that often seemed blue, when it was not of a blueness that often seemed black. It gave off little sparks of light like a hypnotist's swinging watch. It was a Casanova moustache and a Marquis de Sade moustache; so that, when they saw it, Tracy Hart said she betted it could unhook a bra from the other side of a bedroom, and Coral Meadows declared she felt that at any moment it would bend her over a chair and give her a good hiding; only Veronica Draper said nothing; she silently fainted, and had to be brought round with a rum and coke.

The first affected by the magical growth was Gilbert himself. Under such an influence, he ceased to shamble, and walked erect. Now that his head was no longer parallel to the ground, everybody could see not only his moustache, but how handsome he was. With a mother like his, what else could he be but beautiful? Soon he had a list of girls longer than the applicants for the Royal Enclosure. And, what's more, his moustache got him another job; though his new employer did not at first realize that that was why she had given him the job. But his mother was wrong in claiming that Gilbert took only after her side of the family. There were, and never had been, any such moustaches on her side. Gilbert's moustache was a Green moustache.

Miss Amy Murchison was always telling herself not to be so receptive to other people's enthusiasms, not to make promises in the evening that she would regret in the morning, in fact to avoid all positive moves until she had had time to think things over. At a party, she had been talked into joining the local branch of Freedom For Women. In no time at all, she had been talked into becoming the Treasurer. Almost immediately, she had been talked into writing about Mrs Pankhurst for the *Oxborough Chronicle*. Researching Mrs Pankhurst for this purpose, she did not even like the sound of her. Nevertheless, the article established Miss Murchison as a prominent local feminist. It was a reputation somewhat removed from the truth. She preferred men's company and men's talk when she could get it; though that was not very often; in fact, hardly ever.

In optimistic moods, she thought of herself as slim; in ordinary moods as thin; and in pessimistic ones as downright scraggy. Once she had considered becoming a model, because, being thin, she looked well in clothes. But then she heard that models were frequently photographed without any clothes, and she looked awful undressed, being thin. One morning, when the sun was shining on to the breakfast table, her father commenced to spread himself some marmalade on toast, and then, with a soft exclamation of mild surprise, dropped the knife and slid gently and peacefully off his chair. Ever since this event, less melancholy for her father than for her, Miss Murchison had run Murchison's Music Shop in the High Street with at least as much efficiency as was demanded. She had the assistance of old Mr Tyler with the musical instruments, and she had one counter-hand upstairs and one downstairs. Old Mr Tyler would be a fixture as long as he was spared, but the counter-hands just came and went.

Miss Murchison thought it odd that she never got more than half a dozen applicants when she advertised for a counter-hand. In these days of unemployment, she would have expected a deluge. However, that was the way it was, and, as it happened, there were precisely six of them waiting in the shop at this moment, while she sat in her office. It was dusk, and the shop was shut, but she hadn't switched the lights on, and neither did she intend to emerge until she had thought of all the proper questions to ask.

The six would-be counter-hands were five girls, who, between them, knew all about music from Monteverdi to

Mahler, and the one male contestant, Gilbert Green, who thought Schubert was a lolly on a stick. With the shop facing the wrong way to catch the fading light, it was quite dusky standing there among all the electric guitars and keyboards, and Gilbert found it difficult to allot the girls their marks under the recently formulated and developed Gilbert Green Female Points System, which was so many for face, so many for breasts, so many for legs, and additional bonuses for any other noteworthy feature, such as bum. One girl in a tight cream polo-neck clocked up such fantastic figures that Gilbert was doubtful about giving them the final stamp of his authority. They could have been merely the trickery of moving shadows, and Gilbert would have liked to have taken her across the road and stood her in Beryl's Boutique, which was lit up like Las Vagas. Fat chance that she would have obliged, though. She was too absorbed in discussing sonatas for solo cello with the others; listening to which incomprehensible chatter eventually forced him to the conclusion that whatever Points System Miss Murchison might employ, he, Gilbert Green, stood a nil chance of even finishing in the first five!

He was astounded when he got the job. Miss Murchison finally came out of her office with all her questions neatly tabulated in her head, and switched on the lights. Her gaze went immediately to the one towering boy, and stayed there. Her impression of the five girls was a vague one, as of worshipping acolytes, clustered round his base. She stared at his moustache and felt a strange but warming sensation as if suddenly she were twenty years younger. Her list of careful questions vanished from her mind, leaving it in such a turmoil that she could not think straight. As a notorious feminist, she could be under surveillance. There was probably a Sex Discrimination Act, and, if she gave the post to a female, there was every likelihood that, as a notorious feminist, she would be prosecuted under it. Any lawyer would certainly advise her to . . .

When she had announced her decision and was shepherding the five resentful girls out of the shop, she wondered if she had done wrong. When she ushered the last one out of the door, she was certain she had.

Gilbert hurried home to break the glad news to his parents. Miss Murchison had taken him into her office and given him a glass of lemonade. She had seemed to want to talk – and not about the job, either. She had told him quite a lot about herself, and the listening Gilbert, whose first woman employer this was, concluded that this must be the way women employers went about putting new employees at ease. He found his father at home, but not his mother. 'She's gone,' said Gilbert's father, in a voice that contained an interesting mixture of glee and gloom.

'*Gone?*'

'Just now. Some woman about seven feet tall called and took her off in an old Volkswagen. She's gone to some protest camp outside a missile base somewhere. It was her duty, she said. She said she'd see me when the victory was won.'

'*Gosh*, dad!'

'I don't know whether I mind or not,' said Gilbert's father.

Gilbert saw that his father was holding a photograph, at which he had apparently been looking. It showed a girl with her skirt blown up so high that it covered her face. Gilbert had an idea he had seen the picture before.

'Who's that, dad? Marilyn Monroe?'

'It's your mother,' said Gilbert's father.

'Garn!'

'We were at this fun fair,' said Gilbert's father. 'They kept sending up these blasts of wind through holes you didn't know were there. Your mother didn't go much on it.' He was still staring at the photograph, and Gilbert couldn't tell whether he was smiling or pulling a face. Gilbert took the picture for a closer look. 'Well, I'm blowed,' he commented. Fancy his mother having fabulous legs like that. It had never crossed his mind that she had any at all. He handed it back.

'She told me to tear it up, but I kept it. If a man can't look at his own wife's gorgeous underpinnings, whose gorgeous underpinnings *can* he look at?' Gilbert's father said. He took the photograph between his thumbs and forefingers as if he were about to tear it up. He looked wistful, then put it in his pocket.

Gilbert told his father about the new job at Murchison's Music Shop. Gilbert's father said he knew Miss Murchison by sight and referred to her as that thin woman. Miss Murchison had, however, shown acumen in preferring Gilbert to five girls. Men were always best, even when they knew damn-all and the women knew everything. Gilbert got the impression that his father was currently against females. When Gilbert told him about the circumstances of Miss Murchison's father's death, as narrated to Gilbert by his strangely communicative new employer, Gilbert's father had a suitably sombre comment to make. 'I might have helped manufacture that marmalade,' he said.

Thinking of Miss Murchison, Gilbert wondered why she had stared at his moustache all the time. Her gaze had been the same melting gaze as he was accustomed to seeing on the faces of Tracy Hart, Coral Meadows, and Veronica Draper. He knew all about the combustible effect of his moustache on Tracy Hart, Coral Meadows, and Veronica Draper, but it was hardly likely that an old lady like Miss Murchison . . . His thoughts broke off. There was something on the sofa, something that was lying on its

77

back, with what appeared to be a face staring upwards. It also had what appeared to be legs, and they were what appeared to be apart.

'What the devil's that, dad?' he cried, and pointed, so that his father would know what he was talking about.

'I'll put the other light on,' said Gilbert's father.

Ruby May had not been not readily identifiable because of the light but because she was more and more resembling an Egyptian mummy with every passing second. A steady hissing noise was issuing from somewhere about her person.

'You'd think they'd supply a puncture outfit with these things, but do they hell,' Gilbert's father muttered.

'Yes, but what is it, dad?'

'What does it look like?'

Gilbert's father lifted up Ruby May and upended her for Gilbert's inspection. Rendered somewhat difficult to handle through loss of air, the sixty-seven inch simulacrum displayed as much resentment at this procedure as if she had been flesh and blood, and, for a space, it was as if she and her proprietor were engaged in a bout of all-in wrestling.

'Crikey, it's got a whats-it!' Gilbert cried.

'That's the whole idea, ain't it?' said Gilbert's father.

'Where did you get it?'

'There was an advert in my *Purty Gal Magazine*.'

'What's that, dad? One of those pin-up papers?'

'Well, it wouldn't be the *Times Literary Supplement*, would it?'

'And you have to blow her – it – up?'

'That's right,' said Gilbert's father, with a suggestion of a snarl in his voice. 'You have to blow her up. And, what's more, you have to do it just right. Because too hard, you roll off, and too soft, you wallow like a waterlogged canoe.'

78

'Dad!'

'It's all very well you being disapproving, son, but it's years since your mother ran down the fire curtain. She tipped me out of the bed one night yelling that I seemed to have only one thing on my mind, and that was an exercise that could only be described as ludicrous at best. Haven't you ever wondered why I sleep in the spare room?'

'Gosh, dad!' Gilbert had vaguely assumed that his parents slept apart because, at forty, they had long been past it. A surge of masculine resentment followed swiftly on the revison of his ideas. 'Gosh, dad! Wasn't that grounds for divorce, or something?'

'I didn't want you coming from no broken home, my boy. Apart from which, I didn't seem to want to never see her again,' said Gilbert's father.

Gilbert looked at his father and he looked at Ruby May, who obviously needed urgent medical attention involving a rubber patch, some glue, and a foot-pump. Poor old dad, he thought. He thought of Tracy Hart, Coral Meadows, and Veronica Draper. Compared with lucky old Gilbert, he thought.

'When you get married, son, marry someone who'll love you back, and never mind gorgeous underpinnings,' said Gilbert's father.

Gilbert's mind filed away this advice in case its proprietor ever needed it, but was more concerned with a more urgent question. 'What about our dinner?' demanded Gilbert's mind.

'I say, dad, what are we going to do about dinner?' Gilbert asked.

'Dinner?'

'Yes, who's going to cook it?'

'Oh, I'll see to that. Eight o'clock all right?'

'You mean, you can?'

79

'Of course I can. If you can cook marmalade, you can cook anything,' said Gilbert's father.

Miss Murchison was thirty-five, and a virgin all bar a tenth. George Pettigrew had sprung from the bed in a panic, because his mother's key was clicking in the front door a full hour earlier than she had said it would. Miss Murchison was left nine tenths unexplored, and, after this, never spoke to George Pettigrew again; nor his mother, either.

At the moment, Miss Murchison was asking herself if she were quite right in the head. This was because she could not stop herself peeping through the glass partition of her office at the boy, only half her age, who was her new assistant, Gilbert Green. Undoubtedly it was the moustache that fascinated her. Watching it, she found herself thinking the most fantastic thoughts, as if she were watching the whole of life, from its primeval beginnings to its final end on the last frozen star. It promised burgeoning and swelling, and her continual peeping held the same avid desire as a withering plant eyeing a water-can. It was too ridiculous for words, and one thing was certain. She would have to do something about it, and pretty soon she would have to start thinking what.

Gilbert, unaware that the gesture was making Miss Murchison feel worse – or perhaps it was better – was stroking his moustache as he leaned on his counter while he immersed himself in the *Oxford Companion*. He was doing this because he had come to the conclusion that an assistant in a music shop should have at least heard of Chopin and Wagner. While he idly wondered why Wagner wore such funny hats, and what Beethoven always looked so mad about, he softly hummed a contented tune that was certainly not the work of either. At the back of his mind, there was also his growing satisfaction with his sex life. Within weeks of its unpromising beginning with a six-second explosion in the arms of Tracy Hart, he could now endure whatever selections from their repertoire the accomplished Tracy, Coral, and Veronica chose to hurl at him, and this was without having to fight for any breather, either.

When he looked up from his substantial volume, he was slightly startled to see Miss Murchison standing there in front of him. She must have approached on tiptoe, and holding her breath into the bargain . . .

'Studying, Gilbert?'

'I try to, when there are no customers, Miss Murchison', replied Gilbert earnestly.

'Thursday is always a slack day. That's why we have it for our early closing,' Miss Murchison said.

'I can recite the Top Twenty,' Gilbert said.

'Can you? That's more than I can,' Miss Murchison said.

'I've just been reading up about Bach's Suit,' Gilbert said.

'Sweet.'

'Pardon?'

'Bach's Suit is pronounced sweet.'

'Oh,' said Gilbert. 'Thank you. I'll remember that. It says here that Bach's Air on a G string is one of the loveliest melodies ever written.'

'That's right, so it is.'

'It's amazing what you can learn. I've seen girls wearing them on the stage. G strings, I mean. I would have had absolutely no idea that you could get a tune out of a little thing like that,' Gilbert said.

Miss Murchison opened her mouth, then shut it again. Gilbert wondered what she had been about to say. He knew Miss Murchison had something on her mind. He was growing more percipient every day. Miss Murchison had not approached his counter in order to indulge in some idle musical chit-chat. So, come on, then. Out with it!

Miss Murchison was asking herself what Gilbert would think of tea on the lawn. She had cut the grass last evening and had put out the white-painted garden furniture, because they were obviously in for a warm spell. She wondered if she could bring herself to suggest it. Good heavens, why not? Surely she could invite her young assistant to tea on the lawn, without people thinking that she was trying to rob the cradle, or whatever they called it?

'What do you plan to do with yourself this afternoon, Gilbert?'

It so happened that Gilbert was taking Tracy Hart on the river. They knew a spot where interlaced branches hung over a grassy pillow like a green canopy over a four-poster bed. However, one of the several useful instincts that had been blossoming within him lately informed him that Miss Murchison might not enjoy being told about this. 'I might do a spot of gardening,' he responded carefully. Gardening! That'd be the day!

'It will be hot work, gardening in this weather,' Miss Murchison said faintly.

'I expect it will, Miss Murchison,' agreed Gilbert, nodding. He did not look at her directly in case she dried up. An instinct was telling him that here was a lady engaged in an inner struggle. There would be a punch-line to all this, and he'd better hang on until it was delivered.

Miss Murchison had a vision of Gilbert digging, shirtless, in the heat. With a moustache like that, he would have a chest like the Black Forest.

'You'll have to st . . . st . . . strip off.'

'Yes, Miss Murchison,' said the fascinated Gilbert, waiting.

'Get some sun on your ch . . . ch . . . chest.' George Pettigrew had had no more than eight hairs, if that.

'Yes,' said Gilbert.

'Well, have a good early closing, Gilbert,' said Miss Murchison, turning and fleeing, pink-faced, back to her office.

In her office, Miss Murchison sat down firmly with her back to the glass partition and had a word with herself. The situation was ludicrous. And it would get worse. If Gilbert stayed, she would end up doing something that would wake her, yelping with embarrassment, in the middle of the night for the rest of her life. She could not imagine what had possessed her to engage Gilbert. He would have to go, of course. But she could not simply throw him out on the street, jobless, when it was all her fault in the first place. It took her some little while to think of her uncle, Colonel Chetwynde, but when that scarlet-faced, military figure floated into her mind, she gave a chuckle of relief and reached for the telephone, Her aunt, after some twittering enquiries after her niece's health, told her that Colonel Chetwynde was not at home. Miss Murchison knew he wouldn't be. She wanted to know where he was. Her aunt said he was at Kempton Park. Of course, he would be. Her uncle had often boasted to her that, in his capacity as Senior Starter to the Jockey Club, he had officiated on every racecourse in the country, and Kempton was where today's racing was. She rang the racecourse. Her uncle was in the bar. Of course, he would be. She asked if someone could fetch him to the telephone. When she had finished talking to her uncle, she felt a little better, but not much. She got out the bottle of gin she kept for the Boosey and Hawkes salesmen and drank two glasses in spite of hating the stuff. She did not like what she was about to do. She did not like it at all.

*

Gilbert, who had started to pack away some miniature scores, saw Miss Murchison approaching again, and observed that she was wearing a peculiar expression. He took it for the same peculiar expression as before, but, if anything, intensified. Hullo, he thought.

Miss Murchison was wishing she hadn't drunk two glasses of gin, or even one glass.

'Gilbert, if I dismissed you, would you go to the thing?'

It was not what Gilbert's instinct had prepared him for.

'What thing, Miss Murchison?' What was all this, then? A hypothetical case? Or was he out of a job again? Why was Miss Murchison hanging on to his counter as if it were a life-raft?

'You know, the ... er ... Race Relations thing, or whatever thing, the thing is.'

'I think, if it's about unfair dismissal, you go to some other thng,' said Gilbert, looking hurt. He could see that Miss Murchison was upset. Well, that made two of them. He watched Miss Murchison's blouse going up and down. Veronica Draper's blouse did that when she was upset, only vastly more so.

'Anyway, would you go to it?'

'I don't know, Miss Murchison.'

'We can't go on like this, Gilbert.'

'Like what, Miss Murchison?'

'You and I. No, I don't mean that. What I mean is, I've been thinking. I've been thinking it over.'

Gilbert remembered Mr Dobson in the electrical shop. Mr Dobson had said he'd been thinking it over, and the next thing was, Gilbert had been out on his ear.

'Perhaps I should have chosen a girl,' Miss Murchison said.

'You had five chances,' pointed out Gilbert, somewhat stiffly.

84

'I know. I'm sorry.'

'Am I sacked, then?'

Miss Murchison hiccupped. 'Pardon,' she said.

'Am I sacked, then?' repeated Gilbert.

'Yes, you are. Well, sort of.'

'Sort of?'

Miss Murchison brushed a lock of hair out of her eyes, and it fell back again. 'What I mean is, you'll still have a job. You'll still be in the family. Well, sort of.'

'I don't understand, Miss Murchison.'

'I mean, I've found you another . . . hic . . . appointment. No wonder people oughtn't to drive cars on top of two gins,' said Miss Murchison.

'What?'

'Never mind. The thing is, I've got you another job. You'll like it, Gilbert. It's a well-paid appointment. At least, I think so. You'll be earning more than you do here. At least, I think you will.'

'An appointment as what, Miss Murchison?' asked Gilbert, who was astonished to learn that there was a well-paid job that he was fitted to do.

'As a starter,' said Miss Murchison.

Gilbert waited. Miss Murchison had begun a sentence, but, for some reason, was pausing before going on. There was more to come; such as, as a starter he would become town clerk, but, after that, he would become lord lieutenant. Something of that sort. Then he saw that Miss Murchison was regarding him with questioning eyebrows and an expectant smile. Apparently that was it. He was to be a starter. He had baffling visions of prawn cocktails and egg mayonnaise.

'I don't understand,' he said. 'What sort of a starter?'

'A starter of racehorses, of course! What else?'

Gilbert gaped. Racehorses? *Racehorses?* His ignorance

of racehorses was total. He had never even had 5p on the Grand National!

'My uncle, Colonel Chetwynde,' explained Miss Murchison, holding the counter firmly, 'is the stenior sarter – I mean, senior starter – for the Jockey's Club. He's been needing an assistant for some time. I've just told him about you, and he was so pleased I thought the telephone would light up. He said he'd come back to me as soon as he'd rung Leicester Square or somewhere. Anyway, the upshot was – is – that the Jockey's Club is – are – sending you some sort of badge, and you are to start starting at the earliest possible moment, which I understand is at Pondvale Park.'

'Good God,' Gilbert said.

'Exciting, isn't it?' said Miss Murchison.

Gilbert thought that the likes of Miss Murchison, with their colonel uncles and their jockey's clubs, probably imagined that everybody got on a horse and chased after a fox every morning before breakfast. Well, he had news for her. Half the population had never set foot in a bridle; and he was one of them.

'But, Miss Murchison!' he cried. 'I can't ride! I can't even ride a pony, let alone a racehorse! In fact, I've only ever even *seen* a racehorse once – and that was on the telly, when I happened to be waiting for Laurel and Hardy!'

Miss Murchison fought a dizzy spell. 'You don't have to *ride* the horshes, Gilbert! The *jockeys* ride the horshes! Haven't you ever been to one? A horshe race, I mean?'

'No,' said Gilbert.

'Neither have I, but I know all about starting, because my uncle talks about it all the time . . . He says the trouble with this generation is they're too yellow-bellied to answer advertisements for assistant startering. They ought to have a spell in Burma, he says. Anyway, what happens is, they all go into little boxes – the horses do, I mean – and they wait there until my uncle presses this lever. Then they all come shooting out like pips squirted from an orange.'

'Is that all?' asked Gilbert.

'That's absolutely all. After he's pressed the lever, my uncle goes to the bar and puts his feet up. He doesn't even walk. A car comes and fetches him.'

'Yes but . . .'

'There's no more to explain. What could be simpler? Selling the latest single of the Filthy Five must be a comparatively involved and complicated operation!'

'Yes, but there's still something I don't understand, Miss Murchison. If all your uncle does is press a lever, what does his assistant do?'

'I can't imagine, but it must be an extremely easy way of making money,' Miss Murchison said.

After a short spell of life in the protest camp, Gilbert's mother's hair was sticking out in all directions. Nevertheless, it looked in no way neglected or bedraggled. It looked as if Sebastano of Chelsea, plus a small army of his assistants, had spent the entire morning fixing it to look exactly like that. Furthermore, if the fashion houses of London could have seen her in her torn dress, they would have immediately ordered similar holes to be incorporated in all the top-price garments in their autumn range. This elegant wear and tear in the apparel of Gilbert's mother was largely caused by the periodic confrontations with the fuzz, when the Union Jill had to be raised, the barricades personed, and a united front presented.

Gilbert's mother, who shared a tent that had collapsed three times already with a certain Miss Loomis, was hanging up six pairs of tights on the wire fence that surrounded the base. The American soldiers were grinning at her from the other side. She was joined presently by Miss Loomis, who brought an armful of brassières with monstrous cups that could have held a sack of corn meal. The American soldiers whistled at Gilbert's mother, but not at Miss Loomis, which came as no surprise to Miss Loomis. Miss Loomis did not envy Mrs Green; she simply admired her. Miss Loomis thought beautiful women like Monica Green were the decorations of the world. They should get all their cosmetics for free and all their clothes tax-deductible. She only wished to God that she could have been one. In Miss Loomis's opinion, a woman who did not prefer beauty to brains, had no brains.

Gilbert's mother pretended the American soldiers were not there. 'I'm enjoying this life,' she said, with a peg in her mouth. 'It's so restful with no men around.'

Miss Loomis looked at the soldiers. She wouldn't have said there were no men around. 'Oh, I don't know,' she said.

'What I mean is, having men underfoot, having men making demands,' said Gilbert's mother, pinning up the last pair of tights.

One of the soldiers looked like Ernest Borgnine. Miss Loomis wondered how *he* would set about making demands. 'Oh, I don't know,' she said.

As they walked back to their grass-floored abode, which had every creature comfort, if what you meant was comfort for creatures, Gilbert's mother had a pleasant recollection. 'Have you seen what someone's written on the side of the loo, Angela?' she laughed.

'No, what?'

'A woman without a man is like a fish without a bicycle,' chuckled Gilbert's mother. 'I think that's clever, and so true, too.'

Miss Loomis thought it depended on who was the

woman. The next time she went to the loo, she climbed on the seat and wrote another message under the first one.

Well, here's one fish who wouldn't mind a bicycle for Christmas, she scrawled.

Gilbert walked into the Course Manager's office at Pondvale Park. He was wearing his best suit, which had a metal badge in one pocket and a letter confirming his appointment in another.

'I wish to see the Course Manager,' said Gilbert to the Course Manager's clerk behind the counter.

The Course Manager's clerk was extremely plump. He was eating a banana, and there were crumbs down his waistcoat. It was a banana he was eating, but there were crumbs down his waistcoat. 'Mr Pillinger is at lunch, sir,' said the clerk. He wrapped the skin round the uneaten portion of the banana and put it on the counter. 'Can I be of assistance?'

'Colonel Chetwynde, then. I'd like to see Colonel Chetwynde,' Gilbert said.

'He's having his lunch, too. They're all having their lunch except me,' said the Course Manager's clerk.

'I was told to see the Course Manager first, and then Colonel Chetwynde,' Gilbert said.

'They won't be long. It's a short lunch. At least, I always think it is,' said the Course Manager's clerk.

A superbly dressed young woman with the most inflammatory figure Gilbert had ever seen walked long-leggedly into the office, reached across Gilbert, donating him a whiff of terribly expensive perfume, and took a racecard from a pile on the counter. 'Excuse me, mister,' she said.

'Who was that?' asked Gilbert, with his nose twitching, after the vision had departed on tapping heels.

89

'Lady Chaundy,' replied the Course Manager's clerk, picking up the segment of banana and putting it down again.

'Oh,' said Gilbert.

'She modelled underwear until last May. Now she owns Dotheboys Hall, for god's sake,' said the Course Manager's clerk.

'Dotheboys Hall? I thought that was only in a book,' Gilbert said. 'I didn't know it was a real place.'

The Course Manager's clerk looked at Gilbert through his bifocals. 'Dotheboys Hall is a horse,' he said.

'Is it?'

'It only won the Two Thousand, the Sussex, the Eclipse, and the Champion, that's all. It's only worth a cool ten million. It's only fully booked at stud until the turn of the century,' said the Course Manager's clerk.

'Is that good?' asked Gilbert.

The Course Manager's clerk pulled down his spectacles and scrutinized Gilbert over the top of them. 'May I ask what your business is – that is to say your business first with Mr Pillinger, then with Colonel Chetwynde?' There was a note of genuine curiosity in his voice.

'I'm the new Assistant Starter,' Gilbert said. He wondered if he shouldn't have announced this in the first place, and saved all that dialogue about Dotheboys Hall.

'What?' said the Course Manager's clerk.

Gilbert waited. Repeating yourself to someone who heard you the first time put you at a disadvantage. He had learned that already.

The Course Manager's clerk was fingering his spotted bow-tie and looking puzzled. 'Jack Dolby is the Assistant Starter, and he arrived half an hour ago,' he said at length. 'He's having his lunch,' he added.

Gilbert thought it time he produced some documentation.

He laid on the counter a small tin badge with the single word OFFICIAL on it, and beside it he laid a brief communication on costly stationery. 'There you are. There's my gold badge, and there's my letter of authority,' he said.

The Course Manager's clerk held the letter to his bifocals, then looked at Gilbert. 'This doesn't say Assistant Starter, it says Starter's Assistant,' he said.

'So what's the difference?'

'Plenty, there are six Starter's Assistants, but only one Assistant Starter.'

Gilbert did a small sum. 'But that's eight of us!' he exclaimed. 'Do you mean to say it takes eight of us, just to press one measly little lever?'

The Course Manager's clerk ran his hand through his thinning hair. With a mechanical movement, he picked up the remnant of banana, unwrapped it, and popped it into his mouth. 'I knew they were hard up for Starter's Assistants, but I didn't know they were this hard up,' he said, with his mouth full. 'What were you doing before you had this feeling that you would like to be a Starter's Assistant?' he enquired.

'Selling hit singles in a music shop,' Gilbert said.

'I can think of more suitable preparatory exercises,' the Course Manager's clerk said. 'Like fighting a few bulls in Madrid, for instance. Have you any notion of the duties of Starter's Assistants?'

'They don't help Colonel Chetwynde press the lever?'

The Course Manager's clerk had planned not to smile until he was sitting in front of his lunch, but he smiled now. 'Have you got a pencil?' he asked.

Gilbert handed him a pencil.

'Look, here's the stall,' said the Course Manager's clerk. He drew a line across the counter top.

'The little boxes,' nodded Gilbert. 'Yes, I've heard of them.'

'And here's the horses,' said the clerk. He jabbed the pencil at random all over the counter and snapped the point. He handed Gilbert his pencil. 'It's your job to handle those horses in to the stalls,' he said.

'*Handle* them?'

'Yes, and sod your luck – especially in that suit,' said the Course Manager's clerk.

Gilbert didn't understand. He had seen horses from riding schools, walking in sedate Indian file, each one with a sedate little girl on its back. 'Why don't they just walk in? They walk everywhere else, don't they?'

'Because they don't want to. And neither would you if you knew damned well it was a preliminary to having to hare round Pondvale Park, with a little man clouting your arse all the way in from Comstock Coppice,' said the Course Manager's clerk.

'How do we get them into the stalls, then – dangle some carrots?' demanded Gilbert.

The Course Manager's clerk touched his lip with his tongue. 'Two of you take a buttock each and shove,' he replied sweetly.

Gilbert thought about this and didn't like the sound of it at all. He said so, and the Course Manager's clerk nodded. 'You can collect anything from a fart in the face to a kick into the next county. How are you for insurance, my friend?' Looking at Gilbert through his bifocals, the Course Manager's clerk had the air of one who had known duller mornings than this in the pursuit of his occupation.

Gilbert reached a swift decision. There had been only one item in the whole encounter that could be placed on the credit side. And that was Lady Chaundy. He asked the Course Manager's clerk for a sheet of notepaper. 'Have

92

you got something to write with as well? My pencil seems to be broken.'

The clerk searched under the counter and eventually came up with a bottle of ink and a quill pen.

'My God, that's a quill pen!' cried Gilbert in amazement.

'Mr Pillinger's got the other pen. They found this one when they were digging out the foundations,' said the Course Manager's clerk.

Gilbert wrote out his resignation with the quill pen while the Course Manager's clerk dodged the flying ink with his hands up.

'You might as well have your lunch,' the clerk said, when Gilbert had spread the missive on the counter, because it obviously could not be folded into an envelope for twenty minutes. He gave Gilbert a yellow voucher out of a drawer. 'You can ask for seconds if you like. I always do.'

Outside, the first person Gilbert saw was Lady Chaundy. This was because she was leaning against a rail only a few yards from the door. She was doing something to her nails. She gave Gilbert a little red smile as he passed by, and Gilbert felt flattered to be recognized as the one who had been leaned over in order to pick up a race-card. She was still there when he came down from the lunch-room, and this time she gave him a much warmer smile, with a mouth that moved like a beating heart. 'Wotcher,' she said.

Lady Chaundy told Gilbert that she doubted that a moustache like that was legal. She said she could feel it tickling from three feet away. She told him she was twenty-two. She said that Sir Bruno Chaundy, who owned half London south of the Thames and half London north of the Thames, and next year would probably own the Thames, was currently in the Far East putting in an offer for Kuala Lumpur. She said Sir Bruno was not due back until October 15th, so was Gilbert doing anything until, say, October 14th?

Gabriella Chaundy was not a girl to let the grass grow under her feet. She had not netted Sir Bruno Chaundy, not to mention Dotheboys Hall, by being a girl to let the grass grow under her feet.

Gilbert found his father watching television all by himself. 'If this is Top of the Pops, what the hell does Bottom of the Pops sound like?' he grunted, when Gilbert came in.

'Want me to switch it off, Dad?'

'Ta, son.'

His father seemed glum. Gilbert judged that he was missing Gilbert's mother. There was nothing to miss, but he evidently missed it, Gilbert thought.

'Want me to put the light on, Dad?'

'Might as well, I suppose.'

As soon as the dusk was dispelled, Gilbert spotted at once that there was something different about his father.

'Dad! You've grown a moustache!'

'Want to make something of it?' growled Gilbert's father.

'But, dad, it's fantastic! It's exactly like mine!' Gilbert made his father get up, then pulled him in front of a mirror. 'Look! Peas in a pod!' he cried in delight.

Gilbert's father pushed his face against the mirror and inspected his moustache right up close. He brushed his finger along it, and a faint crackle came, as of static electricity. Had the room been in darkness, it would have been full of dancing fireflies, for, at his shoulder, the grinning Gilbert was doing exactly the same thing.

'You know, son,' said Gilbert's father, when they had ceased their light-hearted duet, 'this is the family moustache. I've seen it in old photo albums many a time. My grandfather, Silas Green, had the best of the lot. A real champion, it was. Girls swooned all over him. My grandmother had to sweep them from underfoot like a plague of ladybirds, and that was in spite of him coming out of World War 1 with a tin leg.' He gave the moustache a final caress. 'I'm going to have a photo of this and send it to your mother,' he said.

This was not among the plans Gilbert had already begun to form for his father's moustache. In spite of the example of great-grandfather Silas, his father clearly had no idea of the potential of what he had brought into being on his upper lip. It was a good job he had Gilbert to make plans for him.

'Dad, there's a Conservative cheese-and-wine party at the Old Rectory on Friday night. Shall we go? You and I, I mean? You and I together?' It was hardly the most glittering function of the week he was offering, but he had a reason. He had thought of someone whose sex life could do with a little touching up, even more so than his father's did; and it was a person for whom he still retained a high regard, even if she *had* sent him on a job where he could have got his face kicked in. And there was another reason. He was going away on Saturday and might not see his father again until October 14th.

His father had turned away from the mirror in astonishment. 'Go *where*?' he exclaimed.

'The Conservative cheese-and-wine party. I thought perhaps we ought to sort of – er – show the flag,' Gilbert said.

'Flag? What flag? With me Labour, and you Haven't A Clue, why the hell should we go to a Conservative plonk-and-cheddar shindig?'

'I'd like you to meet Miss Murchison,' Gilbert said.

'What, that beanpole? Is she going to be there?'

Gilbert thought his father might be in for a surprise. It had certainly been a surprise to Gilbert. He fingered his moustache as he wondered what mysterious fertilizer could have set the sap rising in Miss Murchison at last. Quite a few pounds avoirdupois had homed in on Miss Murchison of late, and every one had found a perfect site for itself. Even with the high standards set for him by Tracy Hart, Coral Meadows, and Veronica Draper, Gilbert wouldn't have minded still working for Miss Murchison. 'She isn't a beanpole any more, Dad,' he told his father. 'I don't know what she's been up to, but she's sort of – what's the word? – blossomed?'

'Sprouted, more like it,' said Gilbert's father.

'Anyway, what do you think? Coming?'

'Might as well, I suppose. Might be a giggle,' Gilbert's father said.

'Dad, I want you to meet Miss Murchison.'

'That's what you said the other day. Where is she, then?'

His father sounded snappish, and Gilbert knew why. There had been a picture in the evening paper of someone waving a placard at Mrs Thatcher in Downing Street, and Gilbert's father had been positive it was Gilbert's mother, though Gilbert thought it could have been anybody with a good figure. He was not surprised that his father had not recognized Miss Murchison, because the new Miss Murchison, standing there holding a glass of indifferent white wine, not only looked like one of Hollywood's hotter properties, but had the upholstery to go with it.

'This is her, Dad,' said Gilbert, with a smile at Miss Murchison.

Gilbert's father looked at Miss Murchison with his eyebrows pulled down to the horizontal. It was almost as if he disapproved of her low-cut front which Gilbert knew was unlikely in the extreme. 'How do you do,' said Gilbert's father, in a tone as cool as the white wine should have been.

'Oh, my God,' muttered Miss Murchison under her breath. She saw before her two identical, heart-stopping moustaches. But what a difference in the countenances they adorned! In one the smooth vacuity of youth; in the other the lightly etched lines of fascinating maturity! A black misery crept over her as she realized that this terrific turn-on of a man, just a few ideal years her senior, was looking around for someone else to talk to. 'He doesn't like me,' she silently keened.

This women, Gilbert's father was thinking, may have managed to cover herself with erogenous zones, but she is on the committee of Freedom for Women. She is a protester and a feminist. I could fall for her like a ton of coal being delivered down a coal-hole, but to what purpose, when next minute she's off to Downing Street to wave placards at Mrs Thatcher? Oh no, once bitten, twice in the casualty ward, Gilbert's father was thinking.

'Let me get you another drink, Miss Murchison,' Gilbert said.

'I don't think I can drink any more of this stuff,' said the new Miss Murchison. The new Miss Murchison still kept a gin bottle for the Boosey and Hawkes salesmen, but it had been joined by brandy, whisky, vodka, and rum, in readiness for any other occasion that might crop up, such as herself feeling like a noggin.

'Gin, whisky, vodka?' suggested Gilbert. 'The wine is with the ticket, but I'm pretty sure there's a bar somewhere.'

'Yes, please,' said Miss Murchison, who wanted Gilbert to go away.

'And I'll have a Scotch and soda,' grunted Gilbert's father, who would have preferred Gilbert to stay.

After Gilbert, the disappointed matchmaker, had gone off in search of the bar, muttering to himself that he would have to have a word with his father, the new Miss

Murchison decided to lead with her left. She was using the direct approach these days, and getting results.

'Why don't you like me, Mr Green?' she asked, and, as she spoke, arranged her mouth into the scarlet pout she had practised as part of her new image.

Gilbert's father, though slightly rocked by the left lead, decided to be equally blunt. Averting his eyes from Miss Murchison's new poundage, which revealed its whereabouts with every movement, he briefly ran through the reasons for his antipathy. A mental image of Gilbert's mother added an extra sourness to his tone. He had had Freedom For Women up to here. Why did they object to being sex objects? What was wrong with being a sex object? Call a man a sex object, you wouldn't find him complaining. And so on. Miss Murchison listened to him and could hardly believe her good fortune as the flimsy catalogue of his objections finally ceased.

'But, Mr Green! That's all in the past! As far as I am concerned Freedom For Women can take a running jump! I'm finished with it!'

Gilbert's father stared at her suspiciously. She was in the paper every week. Even the *Oxborough Chronicle* couldn't get it wrong all the time.

'Oh, yes? Since when?' he growled.

Miss Murchison lifted her slim wrist. An even slimmer watch glittered upon it. She moved closer to Gilbert's father. 'Since precisely four minutes ago,' she dimpled.

It was only in the last two weeks that she had had anything to dimple with.

They went outside and sat in the mild late evening. They were still there when the sickle moon had climbed to overhead. They discussed an impending divorce and planned a partnership in Murchison and Green's Music

Shop. They kissed a great many times, using the modern engulfing technique, and Gilbert, peeping out of a doorway, witnessed several. Neither wanted to waste time because both thought enough had been wasted already. They tossed up whose bed it should be, but went to Miss Murchison's anyway, because Gilbert's father remembered he hadn't made his, and Ruby May might easily still be in it. The night was an enormous success, since one partner was endowed with natural skills, and the other was glad she had bought a sex manual.

Mrs Bannister, the camp postperson for the week, had chucked in a letter through the tent-flap.

'Sweet Christopher, who's that?' exclaimed Miss Loomis, who had come to sit on the palliasse beside Gilbert's mother, in order to lean over and share the highlight of the day.

'My husband,' replied Gilbert's mother, throwing down the barely glanced at photograph and shaking the empty envelope. 'He's forgotten to put the letter in. Typical!'

Miss Loomis picked up the picture for a closer look at Monica Green's husband. Her gaze went immediately to the moustache and stayed, transfixed. 'My God,' she whispered. A tingling sensation ran over her body, as if she were sitting with bare feet on a wet floor through which an electric current was coursing. The moustache – or so it seemed to Miss Loomis – inspected her all over, thoroughly and lingeringly. The moustache – or so it seemed to Miss Loomis – spoke to her, in the first appreciative tones she had ever listened to. 'Plenty of men prefer women in large dollops. All *you* have to do, my dear, is go out there and find one.'

Miss Loomis flushed. 'And you left *this*, to come and sit for weeks on end in the middle of a squishy field?' she cried.

Gilbert's mother took back the photograph. 'No field is squishier than your average man,' she grunted. She looked at Gilbert's father. So that was why he had sent the photo. He'd grown a moustache. Big deal! She sat with the picture in her lap. Absently she screwed up the envelope and threw it vaguely in the direction of the rubbish bucket. After an appreciable time she got up and went out of the tent in silence. She toured the camp until she found someone who had a drawing-pin. When she came back, she pinned Gilbert's father at eye level to the tent-pole. She came to look at Gilbert's father so often that poor Miss Loomis only got three turns in the entire day.

During the night, Gilbert's mother got up four times and looked at Gilbert's father with a torch.

MOTHERING SUNDAY

Annie Hedley

Annie Hedley from Torpoint, Cornwall has travelled the world and visited some 21 countries.
Now settled once again in Cornwall, Annie's
current preoccupations include writing a novel,
Mozart and trying to cure her wanderlust.

MOTHERING SUNDAY

The tiny village school at Five Lanes Ends has only one teacher but she does a good job. Year by year the school fights off closure. It's in bad condition. The children, even the infants, have to go across the playground in the wind and rain to reach the leaking toilets.

'It's a disgrace,' the governors say, quietly, every time they meet. They say it very quietly so that the county council don't use the toilets as an excuse to close the school.

Every dinner-time the teacher opens the partition which separates the infants from the juniors so that they can all have a sing song . . .

When I first came to this land I was not a wealthy
  man,
So I got myself a hoe I did what I could
And I called my hoe 'Scratch and Sow'.
Oh the land was sweet and good, I did what I could.

Down the dale at Anion life was calling Janet out. It wasn't a whim. It wasn't a rebellion. She had no choice. She was being driven by the force which compels an exhausted gosling to peck, with all its dying strength, at the iron hard shell of its dried out egg.

She would go to the YWCA. She had some money saved. She could pay a month's rent in advance and have plenty left to tide her over till her first pay-day. Perhaps there would be enough for a small second-hand car. Janet had it all worked out. Everything would be fine ... once she'd left home.

Daniel wouldn't ever leave home. He couldn't. One day he would have it all, the land, the moor, the farmhouse they'd always lived in. No farmer's son could walk away from eight hundred unmortgaged acres. So Daniel would wait as his father and grandfather had waited.

'Farm as though you would live for ever and live as though you would die tomorrow,' Grandad used to say when he was alive and he lived to be nearly a hundred.

None of them had a choice. Perhaps, like Father, Daniel would have to wait until he was over sixty before it would all be his. By then he would have earned every building, every acre, every blade of grass.

When it's too wet to go out to play the children in the school sit cross-legged in the hall and sing their favourite songs.

When I first came to this land I was not a wealthy
   man,
So I got myself a son. I did what I could.
And I called my son 'My Work's Done'.
Oh the land was sweet and good. I did what I could.

The tiny school is well known for the sweet singing of its children.

Long before Daniel had been old enough to leave school he had grown into all the heaviest and dirtiest jobs. As a toddler he'd been well schooled in patience. He'd attended cold moorland markets perched on his father's shoulders. He'd waited all day with nothing to play with in freezing Land Rovers while flocks of sheep were gathered and drenched. He'd been put to stand for hours at rainswept roadsides to watch for the knacker's man and guide his lorry across the fell to the body of a dead beast.

When he was only five he'd been given the job, with only the scurrying rats for diversion, of waiting for the afterbirth whenever a cow calved. He was charged with retrieving the steaming, slithering placenta before the cow could eat it.

Daniel became very good at waiting. The collar would rub, but he would stay in the traces, accepting drudgery, abuse, and frustration, trapped by the promise of land.

Daniel held a high trump card. As an only son the farm had to come to him or be lost to cousins. No matter how much his father might bellow, only the worst of public disgraces would cause him to leave the land to cousins. Because of this Daniel had been able to negotiate sufficient small freedoms.

In the awful ringing silence, after the shouts and blows had stopped, Daniel strode from the yard with his head high. The old bull limped into the kitchen for his crib of yeast cake and tea. His glare forbade the woman to speak.

Soon after this Daniel had been given his own car. Even when it became known that he went to the pub in it nothing was said. He came and went as he pleased.

When Daniel got his car Janet spoke up for a pony. She had always wanted a pony. Many times Father seemed to waver on the brink of permission. It had been discussed over long winter midday dinners in the dim, stuffy kitchen. The kitchen huddled under the low end of the long slate slay roof at the back where the farmhouse dug itself into the grey hillside. The warm kitchen always smelled of milk, wet working jackets and the red label cow cake which was kept in the back porch.

'You'll hurt yourself for sure,' said Father.

'Why can't I have one? Daniel's got his car. Why can't I have a pony if he's got a car?'

'Nay, lass, you don't need a car. What would you do with a car? You're too young to drive,' said Father.

'She don't need no horse, neither. Waste of grass. Riding horses don't make money . . . they eat their heads off and spoil the grass doing it . . . don't even sell well for meat. The only place for a pony is out on t' tops.'

Daniel righteously played the adult.

'You could use her as a brood mare. She'd pay for her keep,' begged Janet.

'We'll see,' said Father, 'we'll see. If there's a useful quiet mare at the next pony sale we'll think about it.'

It was strange the way things had of working out for the best. As Father said, 'The Almighty has it all arranged. Take lambing, every year God makes sure just enough ewe lambs survive to replace the ewes lost in lambing.'

By the time Janet should have had need of a car everyone accepted that it wasn't called for.

There wasn't any work for girls up in the hills, and all the family agreed that it wasn't worth the expense of running another vehicle just so that Janet could get to a low-paid shop job down in the town. Janet was glad that she didn't have to go among strangers.

There was plenty for her to do at home. Mother had always been 'nervy' and by the time Janet reached her teens Mother was a lot worse. She'd started to get 'worried up' and she screamed whenever Father went to touch her. Then she took to refusing to get out of bed during the day and not going to bed at night. At his wit's end Father had had to call in the doctor.

On prize giving day it had become a tradition for the governors to listen to the 'Farmer's Song' before the chairman announced an extra day's holiday.

When I first came to this land I was not a wealthy
   man,
So I got myself a wife. I did what I could.
And I called my wife 'The Bane of My Life'.
Oh the land was sweet and good. I did what I could.

'It's just "that time of life" come a bit early for her,' the
doctor had said sympathetically to Father. 'I know it's a
nuisance for you but try to be patient. It takes a lot of
women this way. I'll give you some tablets for her and you
get her out of the house more. Give her a few months and
she'll be looking for it again.'

'There you are,' said Father. ''Tis a good thing Janet
hasn't got a job. You're always saying you've too much to
do, Mother. You've never been strong. Leave more of the
work to Janet and get out and about . . . like Doctor said.'

So it was, that long before she'd left school, Janet became
very good at washing clothes, by hand. Mother wouldn't
have a washing machine in the house. She always main-
tained that they cost too much, didn't wash clothes properly
and wore the sheets out. There was lots more washing to
do when Aunty came to live with them because Aunty,
years ago, had had a stroke and couldn't always get to the
commode in time.

She'd come to live with them when Uncle died. He'd
farmed a nice little fifty acre 'inland' holding over on the
eastern side of the Trough of Bowland. They'd never had
any children so Aunty had to go somewhere. Brother-in-law
had wanted to put her in a home but Mother had put her
foot down.

'She shall live with us. 'Tes a poor family that can't look
after its own,' she'd said firmly, 'and now that Daniel's left
school we can look after her little farm along with ours.
That extra grass'll come in very handy, our bullocks can

go off the fell for a spell to be finished, and we'll see the advantage in the better prices we get for them. Besides, that land should come to our Daniel, there's no reason for it to go to Them over at Black Moss, they've never done nowt to deserve it.'

But Aunty was bad for Mother's nerves so Father took care to make her follow Doctor's advice.

As well as all her other jobs before and after school, Janet took on the baking. She became very good at it. Her Sunday roasts, rice puddings, parkin, Yorkshire puddings, cakes and Victoria sponges were 'nearly as good as Mother's,' Father said.

'You'm a proper little wife,' he'd say as he rose from the kitchen table and went into the parlour for his after-dinner sit down. And Janet would glow.

Janet had to do a lot of scrubbing, on her hands and knees. Mother held that these squeezy mops were all very well on lino, but lino's expensive, and when there were perfectly good slate slabs on the floor why waste money covering them?

'The proper way to keep slate flagstones clean is to scrub them. Besides, it never hurt anyone to bend their back,' said Mother.

Fortunately Janet was a strong, well-built girl. She humped buckets of coal to the kitchen Rayburn and she chopped and carried forests of wood for Aunty's fire in the poky front dining-room which had been made into a bedroom for her.

'Just because we live in the country we've no call to go about looking like clodhoppers,' was one of Mother's favourite little sayings. So Janet polished Father's, Mother's, Aunty's and Daniel's shoes as well as her own.

She washed and polished Mother's and Daniel's cars too.

Father drove a Land Rover but he had it washed only if he was going down to market.

Janet loved lambing time. For as long as she could remember she had helped Mother look after the bottle lambs. By the time she was twelve she was proud to be looking after them all by herself.

'My little shepherdess,' Father would say proudly. 'I'm thinking of putting her on the pay-roll ... I couldn't manage without her.'

When the orphan lambs were frail Janet took to getting up every four hours right through the night to feed them. Staying up made her sleepy at school but nobody noticed.

Many new people had come to live in the Pennines. Most of them were commuters who bought the houses on the newly built estates which were being grafted on to the villages surrounding the market town. Their quick children ... shot their arms up and hissed 'Misssss ... Misssss!' whenever a teacher asked a question. These parents had expectations of academic achievement and were demanding at the parents' meetings.

A younger headmaster from away was appointed. He reorganized the school and encouraged the older teachers to move on or retire. For the first time in its long history the grammar, turned unwilling comprehensive school, began to send pupils off to colleges and universities. The local children, even when adolescent, were usually biddable and easily overlooked so no one questioned twelve-year-old Janet's lack of progress.

At bedtime during lambing Janet would carefully set her alarm clock and put it under her pillow (so that its ring wouldn't disturb Mother or Aunty). At its bidding she'd put on her dressing-gown and creep down the steep cupboard stair. She'd mix and warm up the milk and carefully pour it into the big Corona bottles and struggle to get the thick teats over their necks. She'd wrap the bottles in a towel, push her feet into her wellies, and with the torch clutched like an extra bottle in her arms scurry in a pool of light across the dark yard to the barn. No matter how cold and wet the night was . . . lambs had to be fed.

One frosty night Janet shone the torch round the shed. Nothing unusual was happening. One of the ewes was heaving and pointing her muzzle up into the dark rafters, a sure sign that she was in labour. Janet got on with her bottle feeding. She settled herself on a bale and enjoyed the rush of greeting and the impatient nuzzling of her pet lambs. She laughed as they jostled for the teats and she had a hard job to keep her seat against the strong chugging pull of their sucking. Six tails waggled in milky ecstasy.

When Janet had put the lambs back behind a hurdle she lifted another, a 'wish' little thing, out of its hay nest under a heat lamp. Its skin hung in slack folds as though it was wearing a hand-me-down babygro. Its head flopped sideways as though its neck was broken. Janet knew that it needed colostrum. She went into a pen where a ewe was happily suckling the lamb she'd given birth to that afternoon and milked out half a jam jar from the ewe's engorged tits. Janet settled the weak lamb on her lap and with painstaking persistence placed drop after drop of the thick liquid on to the back of its tongue and stroked its throat to get it to swallow.

'My little maid'll keep anything alive and make it thrive.' Janet had been so proud when Father'd said this to Mr Robson the auctioneer that she'd gone red in the face and felt that she'd burst.

By the time she'd finished tending the premature lamb Janet knew that there was something wrong with the ewe in labour. She'd pushed her small hand into the ewe's hot birth passage to feel what was happening. A contraction imprisoned her arm and she had to wait until it relaxed. She'd felt around but hadn't found the expected nose, foot or tail. Not knowing what to do she'd crept back upstairs to wake Father.

'What? What? No. Do you hear me. Leave me alone.' Mother was ever vigilant.

'Don't you stir, Mother. Nay, I'll not be bothering you. I'm just seeing to a ewe,' Father'd said. He'd pulled on a jersey, put on his boots, lighted a Tilley lantern and gone out to see what the lass was making such a fuss about.

Father diagnosed 'ringwomb' — the neck of the ewe's womb instead of opening up as it should have done had gone into spasm — and there was nothing to do but wait.

'Come back to bed, lass,' he'd said.

'But she might need us. Listen to her. They don't usually make a noise like that. Please, please can we sit with her. Just for a while?' she'd begged.

'Little Miss Softheart,' Father'd said fondly.

'Please. Please.'

'She may not be ready for hours . . . '

'But by then she'll be tired and weak and need help . . . '

Fondly amused, he'd given in. Janet's lambs had settled, replete and sleepy, under the red warmth of the pig-lamp and Father had sat down on the straw with Janet on his lap. The wool of Father's old jersey, which smelled of stale milk and diesel, felt rough against her face. The only sounds were of cudding ewes snickering to their new lambs and the distressed cries of the labouring ewe when her fruitless pains came.

As safe and content as her pet lambs Janet had drifted towards sleep.

Drowsily she felt herself being lowered gently on to the straw. Then a warmth covered her, and gradually the warm blanket became heavier, became a stifling weight upon her, compressing her chest. The weight of the huge bull crushed her into the yielding straw. She screamed a long, silenced scream against the violation, the pain and the suffocation into the palm of Father's red, rough hand.

Afterwards he'd held her tenderly on his lap and rocked her like a baby and crooned, 'My little lass, my little bird, my little love,' and she'd sobbed bitterly and couldn't stop shaking.

'Sh, sh, chuck. You've had a nightmare. You're all right. Father's got you. He's got you safe. He won't ever let any man harm you. He loves his little girl. Sh . . . sh now, my jewel. We won't tell Mother about your bad dream or she may stop you looking after the lambs and you like looking after the lambs don't you, my maid? It'll be our secret. I promise I'll never tell . . . now you promise too . . . you don't want Mother to be upset, do you? You don't want to hurt her, do you? We'll keep your bad dream a secret and I'll see about getting you a pony at the next horse fair.'

The ewe was in labour for twenty-four hours and it ended with Father throwing her into the high-sided knacker's pick-up truck.

'You should've got the vet in to that ewe,' said Mother.

'First loss is best loss,' said Father.

'You've started your courses, I see,' Mother had said to Janet. 'Don't make a fuss, girl. Put that sheet in to soak before you go off to school. You'll have to wear one of these. You can take one with you for a change at dinner time. Wrap it up well and don't let anyone see. It'll happen to you every month from now on. I expect you'll have pain, I always do. It's a cross we women have to bear. You don't have to tell anyone . . . it's not something to talk about.'

During the next three years Janet missed a lot of schooling . . . what with her painful periods and the housekeeping and helping Father outside. She couldn't wait to leave school.

'Father's little helper,' Mother used to call her.

The neighbours in the high, dour dale thought it nice to see a father and daughter working harmoniously together. The two of them spent long days out on the moor . . . feeding up and checking stock, mending banks, clearing the drainage ditches. They stayed out all day.

At dinner-time Janet would unpack their baggings in the sunshine of hidden heathery hollows or in winter and bad weather in snug hay-bale nests high within the tin field shelters. Then they'd lain together and played their special game, which by the time she was fourteen, Janet had come to look for and enjoy.

Janet seldom left the farm. Mother always did the shopping. 'Janet? Shop? She's no more money sense than that cat, that girl. No one would credit she was nineteen. You've spoilt that girl, Father.'

Mother often said, 'There's no call to waste petrol and hard-earned money on trips to town. Not now that we've paid so much for a big colour television. Mind you a lot of the stuff they show isn't fit for Christians. Rubbish, most of it. All that fighting and bad language and a lot of its downright dirty. We don't like that sort of thing, do we Father? We can turn it off when we want to. We know where the "off" switch is. There's no need for it is there? We're not ashamed to be thought a bit old-fashioned about such things, are we Father?'

It was never the custom to the folk who live up on the high fells to pay visits.

'We keep ourselves to ourselves then no one's got any reason to know our business. They'd all dearly love to

113

know how much we've got in the bank, and that'd be the only thing which would bring neighbours sniffing round,' said Mother.

The family went to chapel every Sunday. Janet liked going to chapel. When she was only thirteen she'd been asked to teach the little children their Bible stories in the chapel schoolroom during the preacher's sermon. She liked being with the little ones. She could talk to them without her face going red.

'So nice to find a well brought up, quiet girl to whom we can entrust the innocent babes,' said the chapel trustees to the preacher.

Janet had never been into a pub. Good Primitive Methodist families are total abstainers.

She didn't go to the Young Farmers' Club because they had discos and girls who go to discos smoke, wear make-up, drink, are common and get into trouble, according to Mother.

Janet did go to the doctor's . . . often. She had trouble with her periods, with rashes and she was nervy . . . just like her mother.

The doctor put Janet on the pill . . . 'it's just to help make your courses more regular and less troublesome,' Mother insisted. 'Don't you get any ideas. It's unfortunate that it's the same pill as . . . well, anyway, don't you go getting any ideas about young men. The day you leave my door to go down the aisle you'll go as you should be . . . not like that Smetherham slut down at Nadderswater . . . eight months gone she was . . . and looking like farrowing any moment . . . '

Father laughed. 'Bed 'em before you wed 'em, Mother. It's a good farmer's motto. What use is a barren cow to a farmer? We was three months sure of our Daniel as I remember . . . '

'That'll be quite enough, George,' said Mother sharply. 'You know I can't abide that sort of talk.'

Janet would have liked to have asked the doctor why she went red in the face when people looked at her but she didn't dare to. Just sitting in the surgery waiting-room made her face flame. The doctor might have some clever way of knowing about her, about her wickedness, about her secret games with Father. He might tell Mother about it and that would kill her. Father always said that knowing would kill Mother. Janet didn't want to kill her mother.

She often wished she could make it up to her Mother, who always seemed to be so unhappy. Nearly always Father was bad tempered with Mother. Janet did all the housework so that Mother could get out whenever she wanted to. Mother went out every day, shopping, to WI meetings, to the Women's Bright Hours, and her new hobby was going on day coach trips with Mrs Driver. Janet was glad that Mother had a friend.

Father was hardly ever bad tempered with Janet. Sometimes, when she'd upset Mother, Father spoke roughly but Janet knew that he was doing it to keep the peace and that he didn't really mean it. Janet always knew that Father loved her.

Only when Janet was less than eager to play their special game did he get cross and then he never said anything very much ... he would just turn away sadly, deeply disappointed, and wouldn't speak to her for hours afterwards, even when she begged him to tell her what he wanted for his dinner, and cried and told him she was sorry.

She'd have to promise never to vex him again and he'd look straight at her as though she wasn't there and his coldness would freeze her tears. She knew that she would do anything to make him look at her again with a smile in his eyes. She knew that she would die if he always looked at her in the way that he looked at Mother.

On some special days, when Daniel was working away on Aunty's farm, and Mother was off on a mystery tour, Janet would serve Father his favourite dinner, settle Aunty in her room and leave the washing up till later. On those days Father took his nap upstairs and he liked Janet to keep him company in the big brass bed.

Trapped by unscalable stairs Aunty would cock her listening ear upwards, nodding her head in time with the song of the bed springs. Aunty would shake her head when Father came down but she kept her counsel. Father's often promised threat to send her to end her days with strangers in an old people's home kept her tongue so still that everyone came to believe that the stroke had robbed her of her speech.

Janet loved it when Father took her to market with him. It was so exciting.

The drovers shouted crude jokes and obscenities to each other as they cracked their thick sticks down onto the backbones of the terrified beasts while cramming the store cattle into holding pens. Sometimes a beast would lose its footing on concrete made slippery by the rich mixture of excrement. It would bellow as its fellows trampled on it. Sometimes an excited, confused heifer, gripped by uncontrollable need for a bull, would mount another cow and the drovers would laugh and whistle and gleefully beat her down.

Sometimes, accorded the last useless dignity of a pen of his own, an aged bull waiting to be bought by the pie-makers would be standing head down, humbled in slack-balled indignity.

Janet would climb up and sit astride the smooth bars of

the pens, grip their coldness tightly between her thighs and rock with the excitement of it all.

At dinner time Father would push their way into the packed and steamy wooden hut which served as the market canteen to buy their tea and pies. Squashed on a wooden bench Janet would squeeze her buttocks together and rock. She tried not to . . . she tried to sit still . . . she would go red in the face with the effort.

'Stop fidgeting girl, do, or you'll have us all on the floor.'

Janet always stared dumbly at the floor. She was terrified that people would notice her red face. If they got a chance to look into her eyes then they would know all about her. Mother always said that what you think shows in your eyes, you can't hide it . . . if any of the men looked at her they would know what she was thinking . . . would know what she wanted . . . would know that she was wondering if their strange weight would feel like his when they pressed themselves into her . . . would know that her stomach was lurching and aching for the wanting of it.

If they found out what she was thinking they would go home and tell their wives and the wives would name her as common and then no one would ever marry her. Market was a torment of excitement to Janet.

'She doesn't need to go looking to go away,' Father would say whenever the subject of marriage was brought up by Mother. 'She's got all she needs at home.'

'That girl's got to get out and meet more people or she'll never get a husband. She's turned twenty. She'll be on the shelf. She'll make a good farmer's wife, I've brought her up to it proper,' said Mother. 'Although what I'll do without her I don't know.'

'You'll never want for anything, my little bird', Father would say to Janet. 'Don't you go upsetting Father by looking at those louts. They'll never treat you so well as

Father does. Look at home before you look away. He'll never let any harm come to you. He'll always look to all you need. Don't you ever leave Father.'

When Janet was twenty-two the doctor gave her tranquillizers for her nerves. They were just like the ones he'd given Mother. He also said that Janet should go out and mix with people of her own age.

So Daniel was told to take her to the Young Farmers' Club with him. He didn't want to take her. He was courting strongly and it was easier to get along if Father didn't know exactly what he got up to when he was away from the farm.

'She's too young yet,' said Father. 'She's young for her age. Give the girl time to grow . . . she's got all she needs here. She's shy. It's not kind to push her out.'

Today is a special day. Janet is twenty-two and three weeks old. Mother who hasn't been going out lately, has taken a risk and gone down to town to shop.

'Don't you get up to anything while I've gone,' she said as she went.

Today is the day that the crack in the shell becomes a hole. Today is the day on which the chick, unsteady on its feet, its down bedraggled, knowing both too much and too little, will struggle out through the hole which is too small. It cannot get out without cutting itself on the jagged broken edges. The gosling chick has no choice but to use up the last of its fast dwindling strength on its desperate venture or die.

Before she leaves home Janet climbs up to the fell, up to one of the secret places which look down over the farm in the treeless dale. She has to say good-bye to her old pony.

This done she sits for a moment in the warm, sheltering, ring of stones which is all that is left of the walls of a neolithic house. The pale sun warms her and she closes her eyes and lifts her face to it in worship, just as her lambs in the field around her do without being taught.

She hears, close by, the chatter of the stream which is full of its February self. Despite the early sunshine she knows its waters bite cold. As a desperate child of twelve she had once stood in it before dawn, she'd stood in it lower down where it runs by the barn. She had stood in it until the cold numbed the pain between her legs while she tried to wash away the blood which trickled out of her.

Janet lies back on the sheep-nibbled grass and day-dreams. She plans who she'll have for her bridesmaids and what her wedding-dress will be like. She dreams of wearing make-up and nail varnish and having long blonde hair and going to pubs and discos and having a good time. When she leaves home she will be able to be sophisticated . . . her bottom will no longer wobble in spite of her squeezing it up tight all the time . . . high-heeled shoes will make her legs look longer . . . perhaps she will be a model . . . her face will never go red again once she leaves home . . .

But sneaking into her day-dreams are memories. Janet remembers that it was near here that Father had first caught her up by one wrist and one ankle and swung her round and round, her short cotton skirt flying out like a turkey tail. She had flown, up into the sky and down towards the brushing heather and she can hear it now, hear his strong deep laugh and her screams laughing and crying, dizzying and flying, frighteningly, wonderfully, dangerously, safely, anchored to his strong centre.

And now in this souring day-dream she is wearing such a beautiful white wedding-dress as he holds her, helpless, as he used to do to tease her, with one of his big blunt red hands at his long arm's length. He's chuckling as he always did at her helpless fury. And she flails pathetically at him with small child's fists clenched at the ends of short wind-milling arms.

And worse now, the chuckles she can hear are mixed with his grunts of effort as he'd held her, stretched face down, over the kitchen table, pinioning her neck in his vice-grip while with his free hand he'd torn down her skirt and knickers baring her bum.

Janet had cried out and begged her mother to stop him, but without a word Mother had reached around Father from behind him and undone the wide leather belt he always wore to support his back. She had put it into his hand.

It had been Mother who found out that Janet had been going to the pub with Daniel and his friends instead of to the Young Farmers' Club meetings. She'd triumphantly told Father that Janet had been seen by Mrs Driver's husband wearing make-up and drinking and she had been seen too in the car park with her blouse undone and her skirts around her neck, carrying on shamelessly with that diddycoy boy Smith, the one that did the banger racing.

In the village school hall the children get over excited and forget to sing sweetly. The teacher is preoccupied with the demands of the National Curriculum . . . she's contemplating early retirement . . .

When I first came to this land I was not a wealthy
   man.
So I got myself a daughter I did what I could
and I called my daughter 'No Better Than She Oughter'.
But the land was sweet and good. I did what I could.

'You've got to do something about that girl, George. She's getting herself a reputation. She'll never get a husband with a good farm if she loses her reputation. You've always spoilt her. It's your doing. Now you must do what you should have done long since ... she's wanton, she'll be ruined going round like a whore of Babylon ... in car parks in front of people ... with young men ... any man ...'

The puny picador cunningly goads the powerful bull until the beast, driven by the terrible burning in his balls, charges to destroy, destroy ...

Janet remembers clearly that Mother stood and watched with her arms folded. Janet knows that her mother was pleased ... that she'd watched with a queer look on her face. A sort of pleasured, revengeful, excited look. Janet knew that she deserved what was happening to her but she begged her mother to stop him.

'Mummy, Mummy. Stop him, Mummy. Oh please. Please stop him!'

Father had swung his arm and shouted over and over again, 'Jezebel. Whore. Faithless filthy whore.'

Mother had not tried to stop him.

That happened three terrible weeks ago. Janet has begged and begged for their forgiveness but Father refuses to have her anywhere near him. If she comes into the kitchen, even if he's eating, he leaves the house.

Mother finds it's rather pleasant to cook and serve Father's meals now that he refuses to eat anything touched by Janet. Mother, strangely, is softer in her manner towards Janet these days.

Janet can't think of anything she can do to please Father, so she collects up all her tablets and Mother's too and swallows them, washing them down in handfuls with water from the stream. But Mother finds her in time and makes her swallow mustard and thickly salted water which make her vomit so Janet lives.

Mother has had to cancel her holiday in Scotland with

Mrs Driver so as to stay at home to keep an eye on Janet just in case she tries it again. It was very awkward. Mother had to pretend that Aunty was too ill to leave.

'I've had to give up my small pleasures to keep you alive. If I get ill it'll be at your door. I hope you're pleased with yourself, my girl.'

Janet knows that Father will never forgive her. She knows that her mother will never help her. Janet knows that it's her own wickedness which has spoiled everything, knows that she deserves Father's wrath, deserves to be shut out from his love.

Shivering, Janet goes down to do what has to be done.

She closes her suitcase with a struggle, clutches her bulging plastic bags and goes down the steep stair. She forgets to latch the door and leaves Aunty in a draught.

'Janet? I want a drink. I want a drink.'

'Good-bye, Aunty,' says Janet. 'I'm going away. Don't worry. Mum and Dad will be back soon. They'll see to you.'

'You're a selfish, wicked girl. You've grieved your father. Your wickedness will kill your mother.'

'Yes, Aunty,' says Janet. 'I'm sorry.'

When Father and Mother come home they find that the fire's out and that Aunty's wet herself and ruined the new armchair they bought for her.

'Where's Janet, you old fool?' shouts Mother, shaking Aunty till her eyes rattle.

'Gone,' says Aunty.

'She's done it again,' shrieks Mother, 'I shouldn't have left her alone. She's dead for sure. We'll be disgraced.'

'Packed her bags and gone,' said Aunty.

'What? What's that?'

Mother rushes upstairs to check.

'She's taken all her clothes . . . and she's taken her savings book. You've got to do something, Father. Go after her.

Bring her back. You've always spoiled that girl. You've brought this on us. Who's she gone off with, that's what I want to know? She'll squander all that money, you see if she doesn't. What'll people say? She's in trouble. That's it. She must be in trouble, in the family way. Well, she'll not bring her trouble back here. I'd die of shame. How could she do this to me? She's better dead. Dirty. Dirty that's what she is. It's all your fault. You've always been too soft with her . . .'

'Don't take on so, Mother. I'll go after her. I'll find her, don't you worry, I'll find her. I'll fetch her back. She'll feel the weight of my arm when I find her . . . Don't you get worried up so . . . I'll bring her back.'

'She's not coming back here. I'll not have her in this house again, do you hear? Not after what she's done to me . . . running off like this, spoiling her chances . . . making the neighbours think we haven't brought her up proper . . . it's not as though we've not always given her everything. No she'll never come back here, only over my dead body . . .

'She's done it to kill me, that's why she's done it . . . she's trying to kill me. She'll kill herself. It's in your family, no one in my family has ever done such a thing. No. She's made her bed. She can lie on it.'

Mother starts to hit at Father.

'She'll squander all that money in pubs. Two thousand pounds she's got in that pass book. She's not fit to have it . . . How will I manage without her? How will I look after Aunty on my own?'

Mother is screaming now, 'How will I do all the washing by myself? You know that I'm not strong enough to stream the sheets . . . You've got to do something. How could she do this to me? She's wicked. Bad. Bad. Bad. She's gone off like a bitch on heat . . . She's just like you . . . you can't think about anything else . . . always at me you'd be if I'd let you . . . as if I wasn't a good Christian . . . She's gone off like a sow looking to go away . . . '

He stands, clumsy and dumb in the blast. He looks down at the twisting face and sees hatred, jealousy, disgust. A frail wisp of a memory, buried deep, drifts up and fails to resolve.

Hadn't there once been a moment when he and this woman had lain together and he had pleasured her . . . so long ago now that he can't be sure? Since then they had lain separately, side by side, wooden in their marriage-bed. Flesh had brushed flesh only by accident. Lonely he'd been. Always lonely, lonely. Until his little lass, dear little lass, had given him her love . . . Now life would be as bleak as the bare acres to which it had been bound.

Janet enjoys her first week in the factory. She can't stop chattering. She is told off for it but she still can't stop. She wears lots of lipstick and sparkly pink eyeshadow, she wears tight jeans with her stiletto-heeled red sandals. She paints her finger nails bright red . . . and her toenails too. Janet gets a car, gets drunk and crashes it. She goes to a different doctor and gives up the tranquillizers. Janet goes to the pub every night. She gets a boy friend, gives him up and finds it's easy to get another one . . . finds that men like her . . . She moves out of the YWCA and shares a flat with two other girls who have lots and lots of boy friends who come in every night.

One evening she drives to Lancaster and waits in the wine bar for Daniel and his girl friend. Daniel doesn't want to do it but he takes a letter home for her.

Dear Mum and Dad,
I hope you are well. Please don't worry about me. I am quite all right. I would like to come home and see you one day. Please give my love to Aunty. I hope Father isn't too mad at me. If he wants me to I'll come back and help

with lambing. Please send a message by Daniel when it is all right for me to come.

Hoping this finds you as well as it leaves me.

Your loving daughter,

Janet. xxx.

Daniel brings no return message.

For Mothering Sunday Janet goes to the flower shop and spends a whole week's wage on a gorgeous arrangement of silk flowers and has it delivered to the farm. She waits a week and then, on market day, drives home. She hopes to make it up with her mother but she is out.

'Who's that?'

'Hello, Aunty,' says Janet, 'it's me.'

'You're a wicked fallen creature. We've been praying for you, and they have been up at the chapel too. Everybody knows all about the wickedness you've done to your poor Mother. The shame of it's killing her. You're fallen, you're a shameless hussy wearing make-up and smoking and going into pubs.'

'Did Mum get the flowers?' asks Janet.

'A Jezebel you are. You're a wicked creature. The devil's got you for sure. Flowers? Flowers? You won't get round her with flowers. She'll never have you back. Not after what you've done. Shaming her in people's eyes. Making people think you weren't happy at home. Running away because you're in trouble. You're a wicked, fallen creature. The Devil's got you for sure. You won't get round her with a few flowers . . . she threw them straight on the fire.'

Charred petals lie red as blood drops in the ash of the unswept hearth.

The square, barely furnished meeting room is quiet as the panel of two women and one man rustle their way through the patient's notes. They have met, as the law requires, to consider the appeal by a female patient against being detained under a section of the Mental Health Act and treated against her wishes in a mental hospital.

The panel have a lot to read in the half hour before the patient is brought before them. They have to read the Consultant's Report, the Nursing Report and the Social Worker's Report.

PATIENT RECORDS .... CONFIDENTIAL

Patient ....Janet Mary Cookson.
Date of Birth.....................20.04.1960.
G.P. ....Evans and Coldridge, Lancaster.
Admission Date ....18.07.1990.

ADMISSIONS HISTORY

Voluntary.......02.06.1982	Discharged herself ....04.06.1982.	
Voluntary.......30.10.1983	Discharged herself ....06.11.1983.	
Sectioned........12.12.1983	Discharged to hostel ....09.01.1984.	
	Left hostel ....10.02.1984.	
Sectioned........20.09.1984	Discharged to lodgings ....02.06.1985.	
	Left lodgings.......................11.10.1985.	
Sectioned........18.06.1987	Ind. living............................21.11.1987.	
Sectioned........18.07.1990	Subject of this appeal.	

The charge nurse and the doctor have spoken to their reports and they beg to be excused for they are very busy. The chairwoman thanks them for their attendance. They leave.

The chairwoman speaks, 'We've met before, haven't we, Janet? May I call you Janet? The question is do you think you could cope if we lift the "section"?'

The social worker speaks unbidden, 'I know Janet wants

very badly to come off it. And she has made a great effort this time. She's attended most of the group sessions and has tried to see her Mother from time to time. She won't agree to going home and refuses medication, but I think we must respect her wishes.'

'The consultant doesn't seem to be so sure. There is a history of suicide attempts.'

'Oh him!' Janet who had not so far uttered a word screws up her face as she speaks.

'Don't you get on with Dr Wyatt, Janet?' asked the retired RMN (the man on the panel) who is sitting on the chairwoman's right.

'He's a man. He's got red hands.'

'I think Janet relates better to women, don't you, Janet?'

Janet looks at her social worker suspiciously. She's learned that words are weapons and is checking to see how the question is loaded.

'Er . . . sometimes,' offers Janet cautiously.

'Janet. I may call you Janet? Have you anything you would like to tell us? If you like, your social worker can leave too if you can speak more freely without her being here.'

'Er. No . . . thank you. I like her. I . . . er . . . want to come off. I think I can. I'm much better now . . . I've tried very hard . . . I want to get a job with animals . . . or children. I'm good with children . . . '

The man on the panel, a retired nurse, leans forward and says, 'I see. You've haven't been able to keep jobs for long in the past. And your illness and your police record will make it difficult for you to get a job with children, but perhaps a note could be made for Rehab that you'd like to work with animals. You would be with animals if you live at home. Your father writes that he would be glad for you to go back and live and work with him at home. Are you quite sure that you wouldn't like to do that? You don't seem to be very good at looking after yourself. Your father and mother both want you to go home. Your father says here that he'd buy you a car so that you could get into Lancaster for treatment. They love you very much.'

Janet shakes her head. 'I don't get on with m'dad. I don't want to be like him. He's got a red face and I hate it when my face goes red, it makes me feel like him . . . I don't want to be like him . . . he's a dirty old man . . . '

'Is there anything else you want to ask any of us?' the chairwoman breaks in hastily.

Janet shakes her head again.

'Well, er, thank you . . . if you could just wait outside while we consider your case we'll let you know what we decide as quickly as we can.'

'Thank you,' said Janet politely.

The patient and her social worker leave the panel to their *in camera* discussion.

The woman on the chairwoman's left, who has not, up till now, said anything, now says angrily, 'She's obviously unfit to go out. She's totally vulnerable, she'll get into trouble and be back in three months. And it shows how far from normal she is to dislike a doctor just because he's got red hands!

'And I noticed his hands while he was here, they aren't red at all. And all that stuff about her father, poor man, he's a good man you know. On the parish council and a chapel elder. And she's so promiscuous . . . It's only a miracle that she's not on drugs or got Aids. Just look at her confidential history . . . are the patients tested by the way?'

They flip through the thick folder of documents . . . has had twenty jobs most of which she has lost through absenteeism caused by drink and depression . . . She has lived in thirteen bedsitters and a series of old caravans . . .

She admits to over forty sexual partners, usually much older men ... two abortions ... emotionally labile and can be violent ... presently unemployed and probably unemployable ... unco-operative ... refuses all medication ... refused family therapy ... late adolescent onset paranoid delusions ... developed into full-blown schizophrenia ...

'You see what I mean,' she says triumphantly. 'It's a very sad case. I don't see that we can let her go. For her own sake. She's a danger to herself.'

'That's all very well, but given the good reports from the ward and the social worker a refusal would be hard to justify before the Mental Health Act Commissioners,' said the retired RMN. 'What do you think, Madam Chairman?'

'Well, the consultant isn't so keen to have the section lifted ...' ventured the chairwoman.

'Is he ever?' snorted the retired nurse.

'Well no, I grant you that. Not often. Yet I rather agree with him. I don't feel that it's right for her to come off just yet. I don't know. Not getting on with your father's no good reason for locking someone up! I feel she should stay on the section but it's a very paternalistic decision on my part ... hard to justify legally. What do you want then, Jim?'

'Oh I agree, reluctantly. She should stay on.'

'OK. So let's have her back in. What are we doing, I wonder, running down this hospital when the Janets of this world so obviously will need to keep on coming back ... Ah, Janet ... do sit down ... now what the panel has decided for you is this ...'

Occasionally Janet meets her mother in a cafe and they have tea together. She steadfastly refuses to meet her father, who sends his love each time and always offers to take her back. He says that he'll buy her a car if she wants one. Janet will never say why she won't go home and her mother can't understand it. As she always says, 'It's so odd because they used to be so very close.'

A student comes to the country school to do her teaching practice. She's keen on music and wants to teach the children some new songs. Her supervising tutor has impressed upon her that all teaching material must be relevant to the lives of the children. She thinks the words of their favourite song are sexist and she doesn't like them to sing it.

What could be better than the signature of the farming programme?

Oh-oh, what have you got for dinner Mrs. Bond?
There's sheep in the meadow and geese on the pond.
Dilly Dilly, Dilly Dilly, come and be killed
For you-oo must be st-uffed and my po-or stomach
    filled.

The children know the tune and sing it well enough. But . . .
'Miss. Miss. Can we sing the funny one now? Please Miss. You know the one about the farmer and his land . . .'

The fledgling gosling which fought its way out of its hard, loving shell is scooped up by kind hands and put into a sheltered environment where it will be safe from predators . . . the ark has a nice dry warm box at one end and a wired in run so that the goslings can live as naturally as possible and peck at the green grass which will sustain them and add variety to their diet of dry 'growers' pellets.

The farmer's wife is meant, each day, to move the ark across the field (as recommended by the manufacturers) but unfortunately it is a bit on the heavy side and she has a lot of other jobs to do. The grass inside the run is scoured and soured by the goslings' puddling feet.

One gosling pecks persistently at the wooden sides of the run, remembering dimly that once before it pecked its way through to life. Its compulsive tapping goes quietly on, disregarded.

At the proper time, in June, the farmer and his wife stand and look down into the run.

'Well, Mother, as usual you've done a proper job with these. They'll make a fine sight in the orchard under the old trees. I'll hang up t'fox I shot t'other day, its stink will keep t'others away. Now that one's a strong young male. Ther d'you see him? We'll keep that young bucko. He can tak on from the old stock gander . . . the rest can go off 'oven ready' to the Michaelmas sale.'

'Oh look, Father', said the farmer's wife sadly, 'there's one there come to grief.'

'Oh yes . . . Aha, I see what it's done. It's stuck its head through a small hole in t'wire and hung itself . . . silly little goose.' And he went off shaking his head and chuckling at his little joke.

ALTERNATIVE CURRICULUM

Anne McKay

Anne McKay was born in Manchester and is married with five children. Since gaining a B.A. degree and B.Ed. she has worked with mentally handicapped adults as well as teaching English and drama. Anne has now given up full-time work in order to spend more time writing.

ALTERNATIVE CURRICULUM

You can go on the Alternative Curriculum at my school for all sorts of reasons. It doesn't mean you're thick. It's a special curriculum for people the system has failed in one way or another. You get more attention paid to your individual needs and you are taught things you want to know, not things you don't need, but you can still have homework and take exams if you want to. You also have privileges the mainstream kids don't have, like being allowed to keep your coat on in your base room and having an electric kettle and being allowed to brew up whenever your base tutor lets you. You can also have biscuits with your tea whereas the mainstream kids get put in detention just for chewing gum. You go out in the community a lot and you don't have to go in the gym, you do Outdoor Pursuits instead or sometimes you can go to this club where they have pool and darts. It's good. There are only thirteen to a class and we have our own prefabs away from the main school block.

I went on the AC because my Mum was in a bad road accident, then she had a stroke so I missed nearly all of the third year. She is off the hospital list now and she can move about but she gets dizzy spells and she can't talk very well and also it's left her agoraphobic so she needs a lot of looking after and Ms Friar who is Head of Alternative Curriculum Strategies thought I might not be able to manage the GCSE coursework just yet. She said I should give the AC a try during fourth year to see how I get on, particularly as there is always an imbalance and she desperately needs more girls. I said I would, though I would like to go back on the mainstream in the fifth year if my Mum keeps on improving.

There are only seven tables in our base room and we have red bucket-seat chairs but they hurt your bum after you have been sitting on one for about an hour. The tables are at the front in the Working Area. At the back there is carpeting on the floor and some black padded seating units round a coffee table. This is the Informal Area where we sit for Personal And Social Education or to play cards or Connect Four. Also Ms Lucas, our base tutor, uses it to hear Robert or David read. We are allowed to decorate our base room so we have put sugar-paper displays on the window-walls for privacy. I sit at the right-hand back table just below Karla's poster of sexually-transmitted diseases and my mate Erica sits next to me. There are two tables in the middle row for Karla and Clare and Nicky and Robert, but Nicky is hardly ever in. On the left-hand side there is Muktadir's table at the front and behind him there are two tables pushed together. Craig, Paul, Antony, Darren and David squash up at these. David is supposed to sit with Muktadir but he can't because Muktadir's breath makes him puke. There is nothing racist in this. Paula should sit at the table in front of Erica's and mine but she leaves home regularly and can be missing from school for weeks on end while the police are looking for her.

She sometimes tells us about the weird characters she meets under cardboard boxes at the back of the Arndale Centre or in Piccadilly Gardens. Sometimes she goes begging with them and catches fleas or worse and once she saw a knifing. Listening to Paula makes you realize that there are some very deprived people around, very disadvantaged and inadequate. I would have a fit if I thought I could end up like that. The boy that got knifed lost the use of one of his arms afterwards. It was in the paper.

We do these Letters of Credit. We do some in school and some in the community. For example, we do this one where we are given our bus fare and sent out in pairs to make our way to Manchester Airport or Central Reference Library or Manchester Town Hall. We are given a little slip of paper to take with us which must be signed by an offficial at the airport or the library or the Town Hall to prove we actually went there. When we went to the Town Hall we couldn't find an official to sign our slip so we asked this woman who was queuing up to see somebody about broken tiles on her roof and she signed it. She said she was a householder so it was all right. A few weeks after we had done this one we were given a certificate each which listed our achievement. It said on it that we had demonstrated an ability to:

a) select the correct bus, going *and* coming back, and
b) communicate satisfactorily with the driver thereof, insofar as this is necessary to secure our journey and furthermore, it shows that we are able to:
c) locate a predetermined landmark.

The certificates look very impressive. They are on thick, best-quality paper and the writing is the kind with loops and fancy flourishes. Ms Friar says that by the time we are ready to leave school we should each have at least fifty such certificates, neatly bound in a blue folder ready to show to prospective employers along with any other bits and bobs on our Record of Achievement. She says they are a useful alternative to GCSE certificates but I am not sure about this and I think I would rather have the GCSE ones which are what employers ask for in all the job advertisements. I have never seen one asking for Letters of Credit. Ms Friar says that employers are in the process of being informed of alternative means of assessment and will know all about them by the time we leave school.

The Letters of Credit form very positive statements about us, Ms Friar says. They list what we can do, not what we cannot do. Our Department of Alternative Curriculum Strategies goes for Letters of Credit in a big way. You can get one for doing virtually anything. I once looked down the list in Ms Friar's office and there were things like Making An Illustrated Wall Poster, Using Bus And Train Timetables, Assessing Social Change In The Mid-Nineteenth Century Through A Study Of The Literature Of The Period and Making A Short Video Film. Ms Friar has written a lot more since and there are hundreds to choose from now. They are not graded, they are all of equal worth but some are harder than others to cater for the widest possible ability range. Some teachers get special allowances for writing them, not just in our school but in some others as well. Ms Friar writes for our school. She wrote the one for boarding a bus to reach a pre-determined landmark and it is very popular. I quite fancied the one about social change but another school wrote that and Ms Friar is having difficulty getting hold of it.

It is agreed that they are a good thing. The mainstream kids don't have them. Karla got one for making her illustrated poster of sexually-transmitted diseases just before she got pregnant.

She is a fool, she let Wayne Bannion from the fifth year go all the way without a condom. It is not as if Wayne doesn't know about condoms. The way they keep on at us about the subject you would have to be deaf and blind not to know, but Wayne is like all the boys, they say it's not manly and that you lose all feeling wearing one so it's hardly worth the bother of doing it when they really mean they are not sure how to put it on properly and they are scared it might split or plop off at the crucial moment, making the girl laugh at them. Why are boys so obsessed with looking a fool? Look where it can lead. Karla is waiting to be transferred to a special school for expectant schoolgirls and it could all have been avoided if Wayne had practised a bit beforehand in the privacy of his own bedroom.

I don't ever want to have a baby. My sister went suicidal after she had our Lee and he had to be put in a foster home. She goes to see him but she says she doesn't feel as though he is hers any more and he calls this other woman Mum even though the woman tells him not to.

On the AC our timetable is flexible and tailored to our individual needs by Ms Lucas who is great mates with Ms Friar. Ms Lucas walks round with a plum in her mouth but on the whole she is all right. She should be stricter with Robert, though. The other morning she was taking registration and we were in the Working Area which is where we are supposed to be, ready to start our lesson as soon as registration finishes, all except for Robert who was having a massive sulk, sprawled out on the padded seating in the Informal Area. She ignored him for as long as she could so as to avoid confrontation and give him the chance to sidle into his seat of his own accord, but then the bell went for the end of registration and he hadn't moved and she had to be up on the third floor of the main block taking fourth-year Set Two French. She went and sat on the end of the seating near Robert's feet and we all watched. Robert just turned his face to the backrest, away from her.

'Do you want to tell me about it, Robert?' she coaxed.

'No,' he muttered.

'You can't stay here,' she said. 'Mr Gilbert will be along in a minute and he won't be pleased to see you stretched out here . . . '

'He can fuck off.'

'Pardon?'

'Nothing. I'm not staying here with Gilbert, I'm going.'

'Where will you go?'

Silence.

'Do you want to go and work by yourself in Ms Friar's office?'

More silence, not quite so frosty. He started swinging one foot which with Robert's sulks is always a good sign.

'Do you want to come with me and sit at the back of Set Two?'

'Might as well.'

'Come on, then,' she said with a glance at the clock on the wall. 'I'll leave a note for Mr Gilbert.'

Robert moved himself and even got his *World Perspective Made Simple* textbook and his exercise book out of his boxfile. I suppose he felt he could afford to be generous with her.

'Borrow me a pen, Miss?'

'Wait until we're up there.'

She should not keep giving in to Robert, it just makes him worse. I'll bet he didn't do any work at the back of Set Two. I'll bet he just sat there chewing the end of her pen and I'll bet she didn't say anything. Robert really annoys me at times. Everybody's got problems, it doesn't give you the right to behave like a baby. So what if his dad knocks him about? He's bigger than his dad, he could put a stop to it if it's that bad. If it's *that* bad he could clear out. There are plenty of places to go, Paula could tell him – and I don't mean cardboard boxes. She knows other places. But I don't think Robert was in a mood that day because of his dad. I

140

got a whiff of his feet while he was sprawled out behind me and I noticed the black ring round the inside of his shirt collar when it fell open as he pulled himself up. No washing was getting done at his house, and still isn't. It's obvious what's wrong but there's nothing anyone can do about it so what is the point of sulking? But you can't say this to Robert, he wouldn't listen.

Anyway, it was probably just as well that he wasn't in Gilbert's lesson, the mood he was in. You have to be very careful with Gilbert. He hates teaching AC kids but he has to because of contractions in staffing ratios. He is always telling us this and how wonderful his fifth-year GCSE History Set One is, he is in love with them. I don't know why we have to have Modern Studies at all, our curriculum is supposed to be alternative but it is a compulsory subject so everyone has to have it.

Muktadir always looks out for him coming across the yard from the main block because no one else will do it. Muktadir is so quiet you would think he was dumb but he can draw like an artist. He can do you any cartoon character you care to name. He wants to be a commercial artist or an animator when he leaves school so he spends a lot of time drawing cartoons. Ms Friar says she will write a Letter of Credit specially for him as soon as the yoke of writing the *Guide to Alternative Curriculum Strategies for Head Teachers, Inspectors and School Governing Bodies* is off her neck. He usually stands on Paula's table as you can see the door out of the main block clearly from the strip of window above the sugar-paper there. It is not very nice having his sweaty crotch practically in my face but I ignore it by writing my name in tiny fancy letters on the inside back cover of my exercise book.

Gilbert has two moods, one of them disgusting but safe and the other one deadly serious. When he is in his safe mood we know about it before he has both feet through the door because the rigmarole is always the same.

'Right!' it goes. 'Coats off! Ciggies down socks . . . '

Then to one of the girls, usually Karla, ' . . . or wherever you like to put 'em.'

He expects the girl to blush and she does, murderously.

Then it's, 'Get those hands were I can see 'em, you dirty, disgusting lot!'

Then he'll point a finger at David or sometimes Muktadir, and it's, 'Wipe that right hand, boy, before it touches that pencil!'

The boys have to titter and the girls have to keep their eyes down, otherwise it doesn't stop.

Then Craig will give him a cheeky grin and say, 'Slumming again, sir?'

Gilbert rolls his eyes at the ceiling and says something like, 'And what precise pearls of wisdom are we waiting to receive in that vast space between our ears this week, eh?'

Then we know we are all right. The lesson will be long and boring but bearable. We know that Gilbert will give us a worksheet instructing us to fit one-word answers into gaps in sentences. The words we have to choose from will be printed in a list at the bottom in the order we need to choose them. We know that when we have finished putting in the words we will have to copy out the whole thing in our exercise books for handwriting practice but we also know that Gilbert will take his copy of *The Guardian* out of his briefcase and leave us alone.

When he is in his deadly serious mood we are in trouble.

'Slumming?' Gilbert thunders. 'Good God, boy, this is a school, not some sleazy taproom! You're here to learn!'

We know that he has been marking his GCSE Set One's history coursework and comparing it with the worksheets he writes for us and that it has made his professionalism ache. He thinks we are all thick but it is his worksheets that are thick. Robert would have copped for it for sure if he had been there.

Gilbert came in with a face like concrete set in fury, whipping these blank maps of the world on to our tables right away without a word. Then he punched a much larger version on to the blackboard with Blu-tack and stood in front of it, glaring at us. He picked on David.

'Come out here – you, boy – and point to the continent of Asia!'

Poor David. Those blank, white land masses sitting there on the board, giving nothing away, waiting for a sacrifice. David knows what Asia is like. Half his street's Pakistani and he watches films about drug running. He could probably give a talk on the opium trail. He pointed to Africa.

'I don't believe it,' Gilbert said, too quietly. There was this awful pause while we waited for the rest.

'I just cannot believe that in this day and age, in a civilised post-industrial society, there can exist any person over the age of five who cannot distinguish between the continents of the world. The thickest of the thick could pick out Asia if asked, but not you. Yours must be some peculiar sub-species, possibly of alien, extra-terrestrial origin, *not* to know where Asia is!'

Big, thick veins stand out like stalks on his neck when he starts shouting and he showers you with spit. He is supposed to be important because he writes textbooks in his spare time but he has the manners of a pig. David tried to go back to his seat out of the way but Gilbert stopped him.

'Come back here! I didn't tell you to sit down.'

David is five feet one inch tall, three inches smaller than the next-smallest boy. Ms Lucas says he hasn't properly started his growth spurt yet, but that this is nothing for him to worry about.

'Try again, Miss Mary Jane, and this time put your brain in!'

All the boys tensed at this, expressions as tight as barbed wire. You could almost feel the monster coming out of the silence they made and climbing the wire, heading for Gilbert. Gilbert felt it the instant the words were out of his mouth, you could tell by the look in his eyes.

'Come on, lads, you can see me at Break if you're desperate for a football, I'll lend you one. Just give David here his brain back, will you? He needs it.'

But no-one laughed. We just sat there looking at him and David stood there looking from the map to the floor, then he let David go and picked on my mate Erica instead. It makes you sick.

'Erica, come out here and give us the benefit of your superior knowledge, will you, dear? Show us where Asia is.'

He is always picking on Erica even though she always gets all the work right. Erica went out and pointed to Asia but Gilbert wouldn't leave it at that.

'Excellent,' he said, but he was using his sarcastic voice. 'Erica knows where Asia is. Well, you would, wouldn't you, dear.'

'What's that supposed to mean?'

She is no coward, my mate Erica. She might be a warrior queen in a different time and place.

'Oh, I beg your pardon, wrong continent. You're African, not Asian. Can you show us where your homeland is?'

'I come from here. Manchester.'

'No, dear, I mean your place of ethnic origin.'

'My what?'

144

'The land of your ancestors. Oh, come on, for god's sake! What's your name, girl?'

'You know my name, what are you asking me for?'

'Erica Timba. Tim . . . ba. You can hear the beat of the bongos in that name. Point to Africa.'

'What did you call me?'

'I didn't call you anything. Don't you know what a drum is?'

'You said bongos.'

'They're drums. Look, never mind, just point to Africa.'

She looked at him but she didn't say anything. Gilbert is our school's nominated senior teacher in charge of promoting racial and sexual equality so there is nothing to say.

Gilbert gave up after that and filled in the rest of the world's blanks himself and we copied from the big map stuck on the blackboard on to our blank maps and then we put the missing words in a geography worksheet he gave out. I whispered to Erica that she should tell her dad about being picked on but she whispered back that there would be no point, even though he is built like a fork-lift truck and could make mincemeat out of Gilbert. Erica's dad would be too scared to come into school. The booky smells and the long words the teachers use would make him feel light-headed. Some parents are like that. Clare's mum had to come in once ages ago to explain why Clare was wearing red plastic sandals instead of regulation black shoes and she had to have half a bottle of sherry first. My mum doesn't come in either but that's because she is not well, not because she is frightened.

Ms Lucas is not frightening anyway. She likes us. She volunteered to be an AC base tutor right at the beginning when our school asked to be picked to have extra money to start up an Alternative Curriculum. The school was picked and Ms Lucas says it was an exciting new experiment in the early days. This was a bit before my time. When Ms Friar came to our school Ms Lucas wanted her to be an AC base tutor as well but Ms Friar had already got tied up with maths initiatives. She didn't join the AC until after we had had the big visit from the Inspectors and Headmasters and all sorts of VIPs from all over the place who said it was a splendid step forward and the blueprint for schools in the future. There is a display of photos of them going round the prefabs on the wall just inside the main entrance. It is a bit dingy and frayed at the edges now. The extra money was only to fund the first three years which is why we can't buy equipment now, Ms Lucas says.

She brought Robert back at Break that day but he didn't stay. It was one of the days when Ms Friar had to go to one of her meetings or courses or some such like instead of taking us for Practical Arithmetic and we knew our lesson would be covered by another teacher who probably wouldn't know us, so Robert went round to the toilets at the back of the AC prefabs and then took off for the park. He didn't come back until dinnertime.

Those toilets haven't been raided for ages so there will probably be a swoop soon. Morris, our Head of Year, knows about the man that lives in the flat over the video shop opposite the back gates and the rumour is that the police are watching him, waiting to catch him red-handed. I don't do drugs so I keep well away. It only takes a few minutes to walk across our yard and round the side of the main block to the science labs and use the toilets near there. Only the idiots and the inadequates go behind the prefabs.

Ms Friar is going on more and more in-service training courses these days. She is in charge of Alternative Curriculum Strategies but she doesn't teach many classes any more as she has to spend a lot of time writing about it. I don't think she knows as much as Ms Lucas because you could not pull the wool over Ms Lucas's eyes but Ms Friar doesn't even realize when you are doing it. She still doesn't know the Dim Game. In this game you have to pretend not to understand something simple so that the teacher has to go on explaining patiently over and over again. It can be very funny watching them tearing their hair out trying to find clearer ways to explain. Ms Lucas saw through it very early on and some teachers you wouldn't dare try it with because they would either give up on you and give you copying to do or they would explode. Some teachers have a very short fuse. But the boys still do it sometimes with Ms Friar. David and Darren did it yesterday with a student and it was so funny that we all joined in.

It was a rare day and a real treat. Student teachers do not usually practise on AC classes because our special individualized timetables are too complicated for them to handle and the Headmaster is worried we might put them off the job. Yesterday, though, there were more teachers off than usual and the student was given to us.

'I had expected fourth-year Sociology Set Three,' she told us, twisting her worksheets round her fingers. They had little pictures all over them. She must have spent ages making them.

'Do you take Sociology?' she added, looking hopeful.

We said we didn't and her face crumpled.

'We usually do Practical Arithmetic in this lesson, Miss,' Darren said.

'I think I can manage that,' she said, looking relieved. She smiled but not for long.

The Dim Game horrified her. She started talking about re-writing the guidelines for student teachers and saying how it was a good thing we'd have left school by the time the National Curriculum worked its way up to the fourth and fifth-year as we'd have been crucified. After a while it was painful watching her turn puce in the face as her brain shot into overdrive searching for meaningful explanations of simple sums so we told her about the game and she took it very well but she was still giving us pitying looks.

'Why don't we do a poster instead, Miss?' said Clare.

'Oh? What sort of poster do you have in mind?' said she.

'Free choice, Miss. You know – Aids, Stop Smoking, Drug Abuse, that kind of thing. We've got plenty of sugar-paper and felt tips in the cupboard.'

'Yeah,' Craig chipped in, suddenly coming to life. 'I'll do you my skeleton with the United scarf, Miss.'

'Craig always does his skeleton, Miss,' said someone else.

'Hmm. Do you know enough about these issues to be able to cope? I mean, they're very complex, serious issues . . . ' she looked embarrassed. 'Er . . . won't you need reference books and things to help you?'

'Oh, no, Miss,' I informed her. 'We do these all the time.'

It only took a minute for everyone to get organized and once we'd started and she was walking round making her helpful suggestions you could tell she felt good, like a real teacher. We didn't give her any aggravation, we thought she was funny and sweet. She stopped at Craig's poster and had a good look.

'Well . . . it's very nice but it's not really a poster, is it?' she said with a delicate frown.

'It is, Miss,' said Craig.

Craig has got one of those flat baby faces and wide-spaced eyes and eyebrows so fair you can hardly see them. Some people think this makes him look lovable but when you have to be in the same base room with him day in and day out, suffering his farts exploding round you all the time, you tend not to agree. Ms Lucas once tried to shame him into exercising more control over his bodily functions by spraying him with her Impulse every time he did it but it only made him worse so she had to stop. She said it was too expensive an experiment, even though it was only Impulse, especially as it was not working.

'I suppose it's a start.'

I think the student was trying to be kind. I think she thought Craig looked lovable as he had not farted near her up until then.

'What is the message going to be?'

'What, Miss?' asked Craig.

'The message. What will the writing say?'

Craig just gave her a blank look. 'Nothing. It's finished, Miss.'

I think she was trying to decide whether he was really very clever and having her on or simply as thick as he appeared to be and I don't think she could make up her mind. She pressed on with a bright, forced smile.

'Well, can you explain it to me? Tell me what it means?'

'It's a skeleton in a United scarf, Miss.'

'No, I mean, is it symbolic? Is there a message here about the dishonoured reputation of football in this country today? The skeleton representing violence and death brought to the game by a minority of hooligans bent on destruction? Or does it represent the demise of the ordinary genuine fan whose pleasure in watching the game has been destroyed? Is this what it means?'

You should have seen Craig's face, it was a picture. He was gazing up at her with utter fascination.

'Something like this?' she prompted hopefully.

'Yes, Miss,' said Craig.

He lapsed into an awkward pause while she studied his picture in more detail then he said, 'It stands for United, Miss. It's a skeleton in a United scarf.'

'He can only do skeletons, Miss,' someone told her. 'He can't draw nothing else.'

When she came to mine she got excited and picked it up and started gushing over it. It was very embarrassing, really.

'This is really good,' she insisted. 'You've used really startling imagery here. It's quite harrowing.'

I'd done a tree with a bit of a face on it. It was lying on its side, hacked down by an axe and it was gasping painfully for breath. Money was spilling out from the hacked-through base and out of great big wounds I'd put on the trunk. Near the tree was a huge coffin. Big fat generals and politicians and rich people were scooping up the money and running with it into the coffin which was slowly closing. I hadn't got round to doing the words for it.

She didn't ask me what it meant, she just bent closer and whispered.

'You've got a brain in your head, why are you in this class?'

I told her about missing the third year and that I might be transferring to mainstream to do GCSEs in the fifth year.

'But it's a two-year course with a hefty coursework load ... has anyone talked to you about it?' she said with a frown.

I told her what Ms Friar had said. She straightened up and I didn't catch what she muttered, something about sacrificial lambs on bandwaggons, it didn't make sense.

'Pardon, Miss?' I said.

'I wish you luck,' she said and gave me a funny glance before she turned away.

Just before the bell went she asked Craig if he knew what a case study is and would he mind if she did one on him? He said he didn't mind.

'I'll talk to your Ms Friar, she's still in charge of you I

think – or has she already taken over the introduction of the National Curriculum?'

Fancy asking Craig.

'What, Miss?'

'Something the Head was saying to her when I went to his office this morning . . . Never mind, it doesn't concern you. I'll sort it out,' she promised, and Craig sat there grinning after she'd gone, thinking he'd been singled out for stardom.

She must have fixed it up because he kept going on about how she was going to interview him this morning in Outdoor Pursuits. In the old days kids from our school used to go away for a week to a hut in the Lake District to learn things like abseiling but there have been a lot of cost-cutting initiatives so now we abseil from the third to the ground floor in the mainstream block down the central stairwell. It can sometimes be fun. All the AC classes join together and are split into groups for Outdoor Pursuits and one group does abseiling, another does Pre-Driving and so on, then after four weeks we swop round. Craig and his farts always end up in my group, unfortunately. I do get away from him in Options when you can choose to do Practical Car Maintenance or Practical Parentcraft or Practical Home Economics but as I am doing the Practical Home Economics I am not with Erica either as she goes to the creche at the local FE college. Ms Lucas has got us a deal with Tesco's whereby we can go in and study the products on the shelves to do price checks and additive checks. She is trying to clinch a similar deal with the Co-op so we can do comparative price checks and additive checks but so far they have not seemed keen.

Anyway, I was glad when dinnertime came as I had had as much as I can take of Craig's showing-off and farting. I go home for dinner but I had lost my Pass Out so I had to go to Morris's office for a new one. You are not supposed to leave the school grounds without a Pass Out. Everyone ignores this and goes to the chippy but my Mum likes me to keep things legal. Morris is all right except he keeps trying to uncover cases of incest. He is a bit perverted that way, so are some of the other Heads of Year. Morris wants us to regard him as a father-figure and friend. He is in charge of pastoral duties and we are his sheep.

'You can talk to me about incest, anything,' he tells us. 'Anything at all. You won't shock me. You can't tell me anything I haven't heard before. I'll help you. It's what I'm here for. Incest, drugs, pregnancy, child-battering, incest, anything . . .'

You would think he was in a competition to find the most dirt.

'And how many cases of incest have you uncovered this week, Morris?'

'Oh . . . three or four.'

'Ha! Beat you. I've uncovered six, so there. I claim the merit mark.'

He whistled some old tune from the Sixties while he wrote the Pass Out.

'How is your mother keeping?' he asked me.

'She's not too bad,' I said.

I wanted to ask him about something but Ms Lucas came in, talking to Ms Friar, so I didn't hang around.

' . . . and I can't get a straight answer out of him regarding our AC's future, post-bloody-National Curriculum . . .'

She shut up when she noticed me and looked a bit embarrassed about the swearing. I couldn't fathom Ms Friar's expression.

I have to get my mum's dinner and see that she is all right. It is no good leaving it to my sister, she's hopeless.

She says she is not on tablets any more but I think she is, she's always like a zombie these days. The social worker tried to get my mum a nurse but she can't even get a Home Help let alone a nurse. They are like gold, the social worker said. My mum was told she has adequate care within the family unit. And she has, I see to that. I'll never let them put my mum in a home. I wanted to ask Morris about how you cure agoraphobia.

I would like to find out if you can do a work placement at the airport when you are in the fifth-year as I would really like to be an air hostess when I leave school. I know you have to be above a certain height and below a certain weight but I hope they will still take you if you are not especially pretty.

I am a very good attender. I haven't had any time off since I started the AC School which is not too bad, you can have a laugh with your mates and it stops you brooding. The only thing I really hate is when we have Assembly in the hall and we all have to stand up and sing a hymn. We make a bloody awful noise and if the Headmaster doesn't think it is loud enough he makes us sing it again.

Apart from that things are all right, really.

THE BLACK SHEEP

John Moy

John Moy, an export manager from Chelmsford, took up writing when he picked up his entry form for the Ian St James Awards. He is married with two children.

THE BLACK SHEEP

PROLOGUE

The night was overcast and moonless, and from a distance the car was almost invisible as it cruised slowly along the ridge above the village, showing sidelights only.

As it reached the copse above Hywel's barn, it turned off the road and continued into the trees. The lights were extinguished, and the car could no longer be seen.

Two dark-clad figures emerged, crossed the road and climbed the low wall which bounded the home pasture. They made their way swiftly and silently down the hill, approaching the first houses of the village from behind. By the light of a shaded torch they consulted a map, confirmed the identity of their objective, scaled the garden wall and gained the rear of the house. In a matter of moments they had expertly let themselves in and had begun to search.

They were interrupted by the sound of boots on cobbles from the street, mingled with the soft panting of a dog. A tall figure appeared at the front door. Keys jingled, and the door opened. The two interlopers emerged hurriedly from a rear window, crossed the garden and half-climbed, half-vaulted the wall into the meadow beyond, to melt, phantom-like, into the night.

The dog ran barking into the house, directly to the rear window. The tall man followed, and, finding the window open, looked out across the lawn. All was silent. He shrugged, scolded the dog, then went to the kitchen to put the kettle on.

It seems an incredible thing, looking back on it, to lose a coffin at a funeral.

How did it happen? Well, to be honest, I'm still not quite sure. One moment everything was going smoothly, a lovely send-off, in fact, or so people were saying. The widow was grieving beautifully, the family was looking all sorrowful, the friends were talking about all the good times and saying what a great fellow old Dai was and all that, when suddenly the younger Griffiths boy, I think it was, shouted out – shouted, mind, and at a funeral, too – that there was no coffin in the hearse.

Then we all noticed that the pall-bearers were standing over the hearse looking bemused and not moving a muscle, and there they were: wreaths, sprays, floral tributes of all kinds, and under them, nothing.

Well, as you can imagine, this caused no end of consternation. Young David Griffiths was still sounding off, wanting to know where old Dai had got to, so his father fetched him one around the ear, and quite rightly, too, so some said.

Old Dai's widow started screaming fit to bust, and the minister went off for Constable Roberts.

Well, now, you can't have a funeral without a clergyman, so folk started to feel a bit better, the minister's departure having taken the urgency out of the matter, so to speak. Mind you, the widow didn't feel like that about it. She was just inconsolable; kept insisting that her Dai had got to be found immediately, and so had the minister. She was in no mood to listen to reason.

Well, Huw Griffiths sent his eldest off to fetch Bethan and Mary, and they took old Maggie Jones, the widow, home for a cup of tea. Then the minister came back with

Constable Roberts, who started asking all sorts of damn fool questions, like when the deceased had last been seen. I had to remind him that Dai had been laid out all the previous day, and that he'd been nailed down that very morning.

That sent him off after the undertaker, who, incidentally, was beside himself. Seemed to think that his professional standing was compromised by this fiasco, as he called it. I couldn't see, myself, what difference it was going to make, and I said so. After all, Owen is the only undertaker in Aber Dowlan, and whatever people might choose not to do, they certainly have to die.

After a while standing around in the cemetery wondering what to do next, people started to remember they'd got a funeral reception to go to, and what with the memory of breakfast receding into oblivion, they began gravitating towards old Dai's place.

I suppose we have to regard the arrival of Mr ffitch as the second strange thing to happen that morning, although Dai's disappearance was really nothing compared to this, and I'm sure it was driven from most folk's minds immediately.

Now, Mr ffitch was English, but that was not all. He was also a solicitor, and, as if that were not enough, he spelt his name with two small 'f's. Seems he'd come all the way from London to see Dai, and when he found out Dai was dead, he wanted to know when it happened, and when we told him the body was missing, he wanted to see the death certificate.

Now, Wyn, Dai's eldest, reckoned as how he'd put it in his bureau drawer the previous day, but when he looked, it wasn't there.

Well, after a few minutes scratching his head, Wyn declared that he had no idea where it was. He was quite embarrassed about it, I could tell.

Oddly enough, Mr ffitch didn't seem very surprised. Just nodded sagely, as if such things were only to be expected. Then he addressed the strangest of questions to Wyn.

'Has anything unusual happened here during the past, say, twelve hours, Mr Jones?'

'Well, Mr ffitch, my father's body has vanished. How unusual a thing do you want?'

'Let me be more specific. Has the house been broken into?'

'Bless you, no. There hasn't been a burglary in Aber Dowlan since . . . ' Wyn's voice tapered off as the memory of his nocturnal walk returned to him.

'You've remembered something, Mr Jones?'

'Well, I don't know, really. It's just that Shep played up a bit last night, or rather this morning. About two o'clock, it was. He's usually so well behaved, you see, coming from a long line of sheep dogs and all.'

Well, Wyn related as how he'd stayed up to watch over his father, and had started to feel real melancholy. So he took Shep for company and went for a long walk.

Well, when he'd got back to the house Shep had started barking and carrying on, and also, Wyn had noticed that a window had been left open.

'You didn't attach any significance to this at the time?'

'Well, of course not. You surely don't think we've had burglars, do you? There isn't even anything missing, as far as I can see.'

'You're forgetting the death certificate.'

'Now who would want to steal that?'

'And your father's body?'

Wyn looked at Mr ffitch in absolute astonishment. I don't think it had occurred to him that old Dai's body might have been stolen.

'But Dad's body was still here when I got back from my walk.'

'My guess is that you interrupted them, obliging them to hide up somewhere and return later.'

'But we actually placed the coffin in the hearse.'

'Well, of course you did, and you seem to have forced the thieves into stealing the coffin from the hearse. They couldn't have relished that.'

'But we never took our eyes off it from the moment we left the house.'

'Come now, Mr Jones. You must have, if only for a moment. We're dealing with very determined, professional criminals, not magicians.'

'But why would anyone want to steal Dad's body?'

'As I said, I'm sure it was the work of professionals.'

Wyn looked as though this reply hadn't really helped him very much.

'Do you have proof of death now that the body is gone, Mr Jones?' Mr ffitch said this as though he attached great significance to it. Wyn stroked his chin thoughtfully, but didn't answer. He seemed to be having difficulty coming to terms with things.

Well, anyway, Mr ffitch insisted on being shown the window in question, and it didn't take him and Constable Roberts long to find plenty of footprints, in the garden and in the house, that didn't belong to any of the occupants. What's more, they led straight over the garden wall into Home Meadow. That's when Constable Roberts called in the CID from Brecon.

What a turn-up. The funeral was all laid on, but no one had any idea where the body was, and here was this stranger asking all sorts of questions, and being very reticent as to his reasons.

Not twenty-four hours previously, the entire village had

filed past Dai's remains, so nicely laid out, he was. I must say, Owen does a lovely job; and now it seemed we weren't even able to prove he was dead.

Then Evan Evans that keeps the grocer's spoke up.

'What do you want proof of death for, Mr ffitch? After all, when a man's dead, he's dead, and that's really all there is to it. It don't hardly make no difference whether you can prove it or not, does it?'

'Would that it were that simple, Mr – er – Evans, is it not? I not only need to prove that Mr Jones is dead, I also have to establish the exact time of death.'

'Mr ffitch, you surely don't suspect that he was, well, done in, do you?'

'Certainly not. And anyway, the point is irrelevant.' And so saying, he took himself off to the Shepherd and Flock, where, as we soon learned, he booked a room for an indefinite period. It seemed that Mr ffitch was going to be around for a while, and there was a great deal of conjecture as to why.

When news of all this got around the village, especially the part about murder being irrelevant, folks started to treat Mr ffitch rather more circumspect than they would an ordinary Englishman, so to speak. I don't think the poor man ever quite understood why the whole place just closed up on him like that.

THE GHOST OF EPHRAIM HUGHES

She had definitely heard it. That name. The name that hadn't been whispered in Aber Dowlan for more years than anyone could remember, except perhaps just occasionally, to warn erring youngsters of the fate that awaited the dishonest and the dissolute.

Ephraim Hughes. The black sheep, the reprobate who had been disowned by his father when scarcely more than a boy.

Mr ffitch had been talking to his office in London, from the telephone in the little room behind the bar at the Shepherd and Flock, and Gwen that works the telephone exchange had been listening in to everything as usual, so as to have plenty to gossip about later. Of course, nobody minded this time, Mr ffitch being English and all.

She didn't understand very much of what was said; it was almost as though they were talking in code, she said, and perhaps they were. Gwen is no fool, but then I doubt if Mr ffitch is, either, and he may very well have realized that someone was eavesdropping. Then again, he was a solicitor.

Anyway, that name made her sit up, I can tell you. Ephraim Hughes. In our village, that's almost like swearing.

Well, old Geraint Griffiths worked it out. It was the year following the bad winter, when every hill farmer hereabouts lost half his ewes. Terrible to see, it was, or so they tell me, all those frozen woolly bodies being dug out of the snow. Broke strong men's hearts, so it did.

That would make it, according to Griffiths, nigh on sixty years since Ephraim left, practically chased from the village, he was, or so the old folks say.

I'd always believed he was dead, and there were those who would swear the likes of him must have died long ago, probably in prison. When you got right down to it, though, nobody really knew. I suppose there weren't many who were old enough to remember him.

I did get the impression that old Griffiths knew a bit more about Ephraim than he was letting on, but he didn't seem to want to talk about it.

Well, after that, Mr ffitch became the object of more

circumspection than ever. People treated him almost like a leper, and at the same time kept following him around, wondering what he was going to do next.

Then the story broke in the local press. It seems some young eager beaver in Brecon had got wind of the goings-on in Aber Dowlan, and had been most intrigued about the arrival of a London solicitor. He took the trouble to check what calls were going in and out of Mr ffitch's office in London, and found there were a lot of foreign calls at the time.

He had somehow managed to find out where they were going, I suppose these journalists have their methods, and after that it was easy, since the whole story was common knowledge in America.

Yes, America. That was where Ephraim Hughes had ended up, all those years ago, and he had died last Monday, the same day as old Dai, having first made and lost several fortunes, married and divorced no less than three times, and got up to all sorts of other scandalous pranks, by all accounts.

At the time of his death he was worth, so the paper said, around five million dollars.

LAST WILL AND TESTAMENT

There was a great deal of speculation after that as to why Mr ffitch was in Aber Dowlan, why he was so interested in old Dai, and what was his connection with Ephraim. There was also a lot of wild talk about the money, and who it would go to.

What had been forgotten over the long years was that Dai and Ephraim had been firm friends up to the time that Ephraim had left Aber Dowlan, and of course Dai had probably never reminded anyone, considering Ephraim's notoriety.

Well, you get snoopers in every little community, but in Aber Dowlan there are one or two who have elevated snooping to an art form. Thanks to these stalwarts the rumour started, and persisted, that Ephraim had left all his money to Dai.

Not surprisingly, the rumour tied Mr ffitch in with the matter, and the relatives laid siege to the poor man in his room at the Shepherd and Flock. They had heard the sound of two coins rubbing together, and that was enough for the Joneses.

Finally, the truth of it started to come out. Although the money was left to Dai, there was apparently some problem handing it over to his widow. It seems that it was all to do with those three ex-wives that Ephraim had in America.

More than that we couldn't discover, as Mr ffitch was playing his cards very close to his chest. He'd learned a thing or two since he arrived.

Now eventually, of course, Mr ffitch had to take Wyn into his confidence. He's Dai's eldest, and head of the family, like. Not a pushy type at all, very quiet sort of chap, but in the end, he had to be told.

Mr ffitch called at Wyn's house, and he was there for something like an hour and a half. Well, Evan Evans got wind of it straight away, and he arrived at Wyn's place as Mr ffitch left.

Evans was a very different kind indeed. Pushy, all right, and what he lacked in intelligence he more than compensated for in ambition. The grocer's shop had served generations of villagers, and now he had all sorts of fancy ideas about wanting to open a supermarket, like they have in the big towns, only he didn't have the money.

The thing is, Evans was married to a Jones. Bethan, her

name was. Nice little thing. Used to fancy her myself once, when we were young.

It had always suited Evans to make the most of his connection with the Joneses, they being better off than he was, and I have heard certain members of the family complain from time to time that he behaved as though they owed him something.

Anyway, what it amounted to was that Evans saw Ephraim's will as a chance of getting his hands on some real money.

From the moment that Evans got hold of Wyn, he kept him to himself almost twenty-four hours a day. Of course, I knew he was up to something, and I could guess the sort of thing it was. I could see the greed, plain as day, in his piggy little eyes, but it wasn't till later that I found out exactly what he was planning. But then, of course, I didn't know what was in the will, something that Evans had found out quite a lot about from Wyn.

Dai had been named in the will as sole beneficiary, so there was no argument about it, provided he had survived Ephraim, if only for a few minutes. Otherwise, it would all go to Ephraim's three ex-wives.

The newspapers had reported that Ephraim had died on Monday afternoon, whereas there were a dozen witnesses to the fact that Dai had lasted well into the night, so Evans was quite convinced that Dai was the rightful heir, and that the money should now go to his widow, which meant, of course, that Wyn would have control of it.

The other thing that Evans now had confirmation of, and which we had all guessed anyway, was that Mr ffitch had been retained by Ephraim's executors.

Evans had made up his mind that the disappearance of the coffin with Dai's remains, and of the death certificate, had only one possible explanation; someone who stood to gain from Ephraim's will had stolen them both, with the purpose of making it impossible to prove that Dai had survived Ephraim.

A week after the funeral, as people were still calling it, the local paper ran a follow-up story, in which they reported that the ex-wives had launched a joint suit to try to get the will quashed.

Evans had a wild imagination. Old Maggie had taken to putting flowers on the empty grave, just as though Dai were really buried there. It had a memorial stone and everything, and you would never suspect that it was anything but a real grave. That's when it struck him. Where could Dai's body have been hidden? Why hadn't the police found it? Could it be that the thieves had interred Dai's remains in his own grave? The idea seemed so reasonable to Evans that from then on there was no shaking him. That was where the body was, as far as he was concerned, and it had to be got out for a proper post mortem, before it was too late.

THE GHOULS OF ABER DOWLAN

Evans was not looking forward to the interview with the magistrate at Brecon, but even he could not have guessed how badly it would go.

He'd taken Wyn with him, of course, Wyn being the next of kin, and having the legal prerogative, so to speak.

The magistrate looked at Evans as though he did not much like what he saw.

'Now let me get this straight, Mr Evans. You want to open a grave because you think there might be a body in it?'

'It does sound a bit strange, don't it? But officially, you

see, Your Honour, the grave is supposed to be empty.'

The magisterial countenance fixed Evans with a steel-blue gaze, evolved through long years of dealing with persistent offenders. Evans shifted his weight self-consciously from foot to foot.

'What do you mean, supposed to be empty? Has there been a burial, or hasn't there?'

'Well, actually, no.'

'So where are the remains of the deceased?'

'They're, er, missing. Stolen, we think.'

'Have you reported the matter to the police?'

'The minister reported it, the day of the funeral, to Constable Roberts.'

'And?'

'Well, they brought in a Chief Inspector from Brecon.'

The magistrate's cold, blue gaze descended another degree or two as it bored into Evans with renewed vigour. 'I see. And this is presumably not satisfactory?'

Evans really didn't know how to answer that one. I suppose it was an unfair question, really. His silence brought a further question from the magistrate.

'And now you expect me to issue an exhumation order for a deceased who has never been buried?'

Evans smiled weakly, but said nothing. What was there to say?

'Tell me, Mr Evans, do you suspect foul play?'

'Eh? That is, pardon, Your Honour?'

'Is there any reason to believe that the deceased did not die naturally?' There followed an embarrassing silence. Wyn had by now turned beetroot to the tips of his ears, and was wishing for the ground to open and swallow him.

Evans had lost the use of his tongue altogether, so it was Wyn that answered.

'Ah, no, Your Honour, no. I don't think so.'

Embarrassed and feeling very foolish, Wyn took Evans by the arm, made his excuses in faltering tones, and slunk out of the court house. Within five minutes, Evans had his tongue back, and was volubly complaining that the magistrate was not open to reason, and that some other solution would have to be found.

Young David Griffiths had been watching the cemetery for days, ever since the funeral. The memory of that sting around the ear still burned, and he had no intention of forgetting it.

He had been sent to bed at half-past eight, and had sneaked out of it again, his bedroom being on the wrong side of the house for grave-watching. He had then secreted himself in the loft, which had a small window with an excellent view over the cemetery. A bolster was doing duty for him in his bed.

He had done very well to work things out so far, but it must be said that he had missed his mark. He had expected to catch the criminals who had stolen the body, in the act of putting it back. In the event, he did not.

Nevertheless, he was not disappointed. At about one o'clock in the morning he caught himself dozing slightly, and then he realised what it was that had wakened him.

There were lights in the cemetery. Torches, or something like, and the sound of muffled voices, whispering to each other furtively. Then he noticed the softer, more sinister sound of shovels biting into soil.

Now, this was just the sort of thing he had been hoping for, but this didn't prevent his imagination conjuring up images of ghouls and demons. Nevertheless, the lad sneaked downstairs in his robe, pulled his wellingtons on over his pyjamas, unbolted the back door, and silently let himself out into the night. He then hot-footed it directly to Constable Roberts' house.

'But you see, Constable Roberts, we aren't really grave-robbing, because this isn't really a grave, seeing as how old Dai was never buried.'

Evans stood in the grave, shovel in hand and piles of earth all around him, caught red-handed and defending himself against the law. Next to him stood Wyn, and even by the light of Constable Roberts' flashlight, his face showed bright red to the earlobes.

'Well, if that isn't a coffin, I should like to know what is.'

He shone his light down into the grave, where the two men were standing. Through the earth, polished wood was just visible, and the surface on which they stood resounded to their booted feet.

'Ah, yes, well, I must admit that on the face of it, it does appear to be a coffin. The question is, which coffin? After all, the one that Owen made for Dai was never buried, was it? And by rights, shouldn't be here at all, should it?'

Constable Roberts started to look quite concerned about his chances of getting a conviction for grave-robbing, despite the evidence of his eyes.

'Are you quite sure this is old Dai's grave?' he asked, not very hopefully.

'No doubt about it,' said Evans, shining his torch on the brand new headstone.

'What what's in the coffin, then?'

'That, Constable Roberts, is what we should all like to know.'

Well, the coroner was got out of bed, and the Chief Inspector came from Brecon, and it was old Dai's body, all right. It wasn't difficult to identify, but it was apparently going to be impossible to determine the time of death, the cadaver now being too old.

Dr Thomas was quite definite that Dai had passed away late on the Monday night, as he had not been dead more than a few minutes when he examined him at about half-past ten. That was all we had.

TIME AND TIDE

Evan Evans now started to pursue Mr ffitch quite relent-lessly. His feeling was that the time of death had been established, and that the fact of the body having been stolen proved that some ruthless people were after Ephraim's fortune, and that this should therefore be handed over to Maggie forthwith. Mr ffitch tried very hard to avoid him, but in a small place like Aber Dowlan, it simply wasn't possible.

Then we heard from America that the wives' suit had failed, and the will had been upheld. That did it. Evans was now worrying the life out of everybody: Mr ffitch, the coroner, the magistrate, and anybody else who failed to get out of his way, dragging round with him poor Wyn Jones, whose face was now more or less permanently scarlet. Evans could now see a very real possibility of getting his supermarket, and perhaps even a whole chain of super-markets, and he wasn't going to let anybody's feelings stand in his way. Consideration for others never was his strong point, anyway.

Finally, the hearing he'd been agitating for came about, probably despite his efforts.

It seems that the purpose of the hearing, officially speak-ing, was to establish whether a crime had been committed, either with respect to Dai's death, or the disappearance of his body. It was held in the coroner's court, and what was of such inordinate interest to Evans was that they were going to have to establish the cause, and more importantly the time, of death. Evans reckoned that once a court had pronounced on that, giving it legal validity, so to speak, the executors would have to hand over the money.

The first witness was Dr Thomas, who confirmed the cause of death.

'Who was present when you examined the deceased, Dr Thomas?'

'Well, there was just the family. Mr Jones was taken quite suddenly, you see, and although I came immediately, he was dead by the time I arrived.'

'So that would be who, exactly?'

'Well, Mrs Jones, and Wyn, Dai's son.'

'I see. And at what time did you arrive?'

'I'd say about half-past ten.'

'Did you manage to establish the time of death?'

'Not exactly, no. But it was about half-past ten.'

Evans was in the public benches, grinning from ear to ear. We now had official confirmation of the time of Ephraim's death as 17.23, and it seemed very clear that Dai had outlived Ephraim by a safe margin that nobody could argue with.

Evans had seated himself directly behind Mr ffitch, and he now leaned forward, and whispered loudly: 'Doesn't seem to be any doubt about it, does there, Mr ffitch?' Gloating seemed to be Evans' favourite pastime, and he was enjoying himself now. Then Mr ffitch wiped the smile off his face.

'On the contrary, Mr Evans, it seems to be very close, and a great deal depends upon what the other witnesses have to say.'

'I don't see that, myself, Mr ffitch. 17.23 is twenty-three minutes past five in the afternoon, isn't it?'

'You are correct, Mr Evans.'

'Then Dai lived hours after Ephraim died.'

'Not so, Mr Evans. You have forgotten the time difference.'

'The what?'

'Eastern Standard Time is five hours behind GMT. Mr Jones and Mr Hughes died within minutes of each other.'

Evans blanched, white as a sheet, he went. Then he heard the coroner's clerk calling Wyn Jones to the witness box.

'Now, Mr Jones, where were you at the time of your father's death?'

'I was with him, Your Honour, the whole time.'

'And did he, in fact, pass away quickly, as Dr Thomas has suggested?'

'Mercifully, yes, he did.'

'Mr Jones, I am very sorry to press you over what must be a most distressing memory . . . '

'Oh, that's all right, Your Honour, you have to find out, I know.'

'Thank you, Mr Jones. Can you tell me, please, exactly how sudden was the death? Was it a matter of a few minutes?'

'No, Your Honour, it was just seconds, just seconds . . . ' Wyn's eyes were looking glazed, and I suppose he was back in his own parlour on that Monday night, reliving the death of old Dai. A tear appeared at the corner of his eye.

'If you would prefer, Mr Jones, we could adjourn for a few minutes.'

Wyn came to his senses immediately. 'Oh, no, it's all right, really. I was just thinking, that's all,' he said, starting to turn red.

173

'Very well, if you feel able to carry on. Now, can you tell me the time at which your father passed away?'

Evans had not really caught up with events, but his dull mind had grasped the point that the fortune was in danger. All at once the penny dropped. I saw it happen, plain as day, the exact moment when he realized what Mr ffitch had meant about the time difference. His ashen face went whiter yet, and he caught his breath. I think the whole court must have heard it.

Ephraim had died at twenty-three minutes past five, and if Mr ffitch was right about the five hour time difference, which no doubt he was, that meant twenty-three minutes past ten GMT, just about exactly the same time as Dai.

'Well, I can help you there, Your Honour. I remember it as being about half-past ten myself, the same as Dr Thomas, and the reason I remember is this; when dad was struck, he was standing before the mantelpiece, just knocking out his pipe in the hearth.

'First, he grasped his chest, then, as he fell, he grabbed at the mantelpiece, and he knocked the old carriage clock into the hearth.'

'And did the clock stop?'

'Oh, yes, Your Honour. It fell right hard onto the stones, and I don't think it will ever go again.'

'And what hour did the clock show?'

'Just twenty-eight minutes past ten, Your Honour.'

A broad smile spread across Evans' unprepossessing countenance. Wyn had no idea of the way he'd kept Evans strung up, because nobody had pointed the time difference out to him. Besides, Wyn being Wyn, it was the loss of a father he was thinking of, not the acquisition of a fortune.

Evans could hardly believe his good luck. He'd been badgering Wyn for days about the use of the money, about a chain of supermarkets throughout South Wales, and now it was actually going to happen. Dai had managed to survive Ephraim by five meagre minutes.

'And so you are quite certain, Mr Jones, that your father died at exactly ten twenty-eight in the evening?'

'No, Your Honour. Ten eighteen.'

'But, I thought you said . . . '

'I said the clock showed ten twenty-eight when it stopped, and so it did. But we always kept that clock ten minutes fast, so as to avoid being late for chapel.'

A strangled cry emanated from the public benches, followed by a loud sobbing, and an usher was instructed to escort Evans from the court.

Upon their arrival back in Aber Dowlan, Wyn and Mr ffitch walked together to the Shepherd and Flock. They were chatting amiably enough, and seemed to have struck up something of a friendship. I think that Mr ffitch had realized what a really genuine sort of chap Wyn Jones is. One of the best, I'd say.

When they got into the inn, they found Evan Evans waiting for them.

'But Evan, what did I do? I only told the truth, and after all, I was under oath.'

'What did you do? You ask me what did you do? You just gave away five million dollars, that's what you did. There was no need even to lie, you could just have kept your stupid great mouth shut, that's all.'

'Evan, I don't understand this at all. We've been getting on so well this last week or two, you and I, and now, quite suddenly . . . '

'Been getting on well, have we?'

'Why, yes, you've been an absolute rock to me since Dad died.'

'Yes, I know. Putting up with your inepititude and trying

175

not to swear. Licking the boots of the Joneses, just as I've always had to do. Well, I've finished with you now, boyo. You've given away our chance to be somebody, given away my supermarket, just through sheer, brute stupidity.'

Now, Wyn was still completely perplexed by all this enmity, until Mr ffitch pointed out to him that there were only five minutes separating the two deaths. Poor Wyn. He was already pink from the collar up, and now he turned magenta.

'Well, Evan, I'm sorry about your supermarket, really I am. I know how bad you wanted it, but we couldn't go into court and lie, could we, even if I'd known?'

'You're stupid, stuck-up hypocrite. You give my super-market away, and then you expect to be commended for your honesty? I can see where you inherited your brains from, boyo. You're about as bright as that idiot father you've just tried to bury.'

That did it. There's no doubt that Wyn had a genuine regard for old Dai, for his gentleness and honesty, and I believe he felt the kind of love for him that we all should feel for our fathers.

Anyway, Wyn went perfectly scarlet, only this time it wasn't embarrassment, it was anger. I don't think any of us had ever seen Wyn angry before. 'Now you listen to me, Evan Evans. Call me stupid if you like, and you may be right, but don't you insult my father's memory.'

Still Evans hadn't the sense to hold his tongue.

'You think you can get out of it like that, do you? Insult your father's memory? I shouldn't hardly think that possible. It's well known that your Mum and Dad were married just six months when you were born.'

I must admit to a feeling of satisfaction at the crunching sound as Wyn's huge fist made contact with Evans' nose.

Well, there they all were, gathered in the Temperance Hall. The entire Jones family and their spouses, including Evans, who had evidently come to gloat. Odious man.

Mr ffitch was sitting at a desk on the platform, with his clerk beside him. He read from a prepared paper the details as to when and where the will had been drawn up, and it seems it was more than twenty years old. Then he got on to the will itself.

'"I, Ephraim John Hughes, being of sound mind . . ."'

There was a nasty little snigger from Evans on the 'sound mind' part. It seems he realized he had burned his boats with the Joneses, and anyway, nobody could see them inheriting now. The reading of the will was just a formality. He was still nursing two beautiful black eyes, and they didn't seem to have improved his character any more than his looks.

Anyway, Mr ffitch went on reading the will in his upper-class English accent, and the whole thing was altogether more complicated and difficult to follow than anybody had expected. When he got to the last clause he slowed down, and weighed upon his words in a very suggestive fashion.

' "Notwithstanding the foregoing, which shall retain validity should the attested die without issue, the full estate shall pass to the progeny of the attested, should such an heir exist at the time of death, or in the event that more than one such heir shall exist, the aforesaid estate shall be divided equally among such heirs, the estate or portion of the estate to be held in trust by the executors in the case of any minor heir, until majority be attained." '

Mr ffitch now turned directly to old Maggie, her son Wyn and old Geraint Griffiths who was sitting with them, he being the only non-relative present.

'What this means is that the entire inheritance would have gone to Mr Jones, had he lived, and that since he did not, it should be divided equally between the three Mrs Hugheses, providing there are no children. Mr Hughes' will specifically allows that any offspring shall have precedence over all other claimants.

'The executors have satisfied themselves that no such heir was fathered by the deceased on any of his three wives, and they know of no other progeny of the deceased.

'If no other heir can be found, it will be presumed that the three Mrs Hugheses are the rightful beneficiaries under the terms of the will.

'Now, Mrs Jones, I understand that you may have a contribution to make.'

Maggie had aged visibly since Dai's death, and she looked very small and helpless, there between Wyn and old Griffiths, both big chaps, flanking her like two sentinels, as though they were afraid she might be in mortal danger.

Perceptibly, she straightened herself up in her chair, looked Mr ffitch straight in the eye, and announced:

'Yes, Mr ffitch, I do have something to say.'

She seemed to have come to a decision, crossed a line that was irrevocable, and the years fell away from her as she rose and faced her late husband's family. 'What I am about to tell you now, I once promised Dai never to breathe to a living soul. It's hard for me to do, but I think he would understand.

'Ephraim tried to save us the pain of this moment and of whatever might follow, but unfortunately, Dai did not live long enough, and his good intentions came to nothing.

'Whatever you may have heard about Ephraim, I can assure you that most of it is untrue. He was not a bad man, and he was more sinned against than sinning; and neither was he driven from Aber Dowlan. He left of his own accord.'

The Joneses were fidgeting in their seats, bored by all this ancient history, and uncomfortable as well, about having their attitudes challenged. At this stage, they simply wanted to be told that they had inherited a fortune or, if that were not possible, as now seemed to be the case, they wanted the whole sorry business over with. To tell you the truth, I believe that one or two of them were beginning to get rather annoyed.

Maggie Jones' next statement at least took care of their boredom.

'Ephraim does have an heir. He is my son, the man you all know as Wyn Jones.'

The effect of this bombshell was beautiful to behold. All those sanctimonious Joneses, suddenly feeling their respectability being cut away from under them. This was just too close to home. The head of the family was not really a Jones at all, and his mother, the respectable widow, had conceived a child on the wrong side of the blanket.

Very distinctly, though, you could hear the pennies dropping as one Jones after another realized that this scandal might very well mean that the five million dollars were coming into the family after all.

Evan Evans's face was a picture. First he leered horribly, enjoying the discomfiture of the Joneses, and particularly of Wyn. Then, as realization dawned, his jaw dropped, and he began to show an emotion close to panic.

Maggie had sat down, and Geraint Griffiths was now facing the massed Joneses.

'You all know me as a neighbour, and as an old friend of Dai's. What you may not know is that I am also an old friend of Ephraim's, as was Dai.

'Maggie here was Ephraim's sweetheart, long before

most of you were born, but Maggie's father wouldn't consent to the match, insisting that Ephraim was a bad lot.

'Dai had always loved Maggie, and so, after Ephraim left for Cardiff, meaning to get a ship and work his passage to America, Dai asked her to marry him. He knew she was carrying Ephraim's child, but it didn't make any difference. Like I said, he loved her.

'When Wyn was born, he was passed off as premature. I don't think anybody believed that, with him being such a big chap and all, nearly eight pounds, as I remember, but I think there were those who accepted him as Dai's. Anyway, they didn't say anything to the contrary.

'Maggie's father wasn't deceived. He couldn't say anything, but from that day on, and for the rest of his life, he never missed an opportunity to blacken Ephraim's name.'

The entire Jones clan was having difficulty with so many revelations, but my heart went out to Wyn. I found out later that he had only known about all this himself for a few days, Maggie having confessed it to him when it was realized that Dai hadn't lived long enough to inherit Ephraim's estate. He had hardly slept in all that time.

He stuck by his mother, though; sat there beside her the whole time, coloured up brighter than ever before, right to the tips of his ears.

Well, it turned out that Ephraim hadn't even known when he left that Maggie was pregnant, and by the time he had found out, she was already married to Dai.

So the legend died. The hell-raiser was an ordinary man, vilified by the resentful father of a young girl.

After that I got quite curious about Ephraim, having looked on him as the black sheep ever since I was old enough to understand such things. I was fascinated by the way he'd been turned into something he never was, and wondered what else we'd had wrong about him all these years.

First chance I got, I buttonholed old Griffiths.

'You know, you could have knocked me down with a feather, hearing you and Maggie Jones talking about Ephraim as a real person, so to speak, not just history. I must admit that I hadn't realized there was anybody still around who had known him.'

'Well now, Emlyn, my boy, that's because you're one of the younger fellows.' We both laughed at that. I'm not of Geraint Griffiths' generation, he and Maggie must be around eighty, and Ephraim too, for that matter. That was old Dai's age when he died. No, I'm not of their age, but I'll never see fifty again.

'Of course, what surprised me most was finding out he wasn't the villain he was made out to be. Was that really all the work of one man?'

'Oh, yes, entirely. Hatred is a terrible thing. It made old Hywel, Maggie's father, quite bitter by the time he was done. Of course, he couldn't tell anyone about Ephraim being the baby's father without bringing disgrace on himself and his family, and so he just blamed Ephraim for everything else he could think of. After many years had passed, the belief grew up that Ephraim had been disowned by his father and chased from the village. In fact, he was an orphan.

'He'd gone into farming on rented land over at Waenrydd, the most marginal and exposed in the area, that being all he could afford.

'Well, he was unlucky. His first winter as a farmer was the worst in living memory, and he lost his entire flock. Everything he'd worked so hard for was gone. He was ruined.

'On top of that Maggie's father wouldn't acknowledge

him; said he was a foundling, which wasn't true. He simply didn't have any money, and that was the real reason.

'Ephraim decided that nothing would ever go right for him until he got away from Aber Dowlan, so he took himself off to try his luck in America. I believe he would have taken Maggie away, too, after he'd got himself settled, but she couldn't wait for him, on account of her condition.

'Old Hywel ran Ephraim down for years, blamed him for everything from Llewelyn's rick fire the previous year over at Pencelli, to young Olwyn Davies' inexplicable baby, and I'm quite sure he was already gone by the time that child was conceived. And anyway, he never had anything to do with the girl.

'The years passed, then the decades, and Hywel kept looking at young Wyn and hating Ephraim. In fact, he died hating him. Terrible thing, that.

'After all that time, there were precious few around who remembered the truth, and two of those didn't dare say anything.'

'Maggie and Dai. Yes, of course. It would have shamed them and their son – Ephraim's son, that is. And now it's all come out because of the five million dollars that Ephraim tried to leave to Dai.

'Tell me though, what sort of a man was Ephraim, really?'

'Well, he was a good friend, and that's a fact. He went without sleep night after night, that terrible winter, trying to save his ewes. Looked really ill by the time he'd finished. But when he knew he'd lost them all, and the bad weather continued, he turned to and helped his neighbours, digging other men's sheep out of the snow, and putting his own heartache to one side. He was a fine man.'

'And what did he look like?'

'Well, he was a big man, strong but gentle. A quiet, mild

sort of a chap. And he used to get embarrassed easily.'

'Really?'

'Oh, yes. quite comical it was, sometimes. He couldn't hide it, you see. He used to go bright red, right to the tips of his ears.'

THE FACE
OF AN ANGEL

Deborah Parker

Deborah Parker trained as a doctor at the University of London but knew she always wanted to write. Now busy writing her first novel, Deborah works as a freelance medical journalist and lives in Yorkshire.

THE FACE OF AN ANGEL

It is mine to avenge; I will repay.
In due time their foot will slip;
Their day of disaster is near
and their doom rushes upon them.
                    DEUTERONOMY 32:35.

Matthew laid the metal instrument carefully in a bowl of antiseptic, unscrewing it so that its jaw dropped noisily shut. He turned on the water using his elbows and the tap extensions and slowly, meticulously, he washed his hands, scrubbing with a brush at his fingernails and underneath his wedding ring. He ignored the body laid out behind him until he had finished washing and had written a few notes. Then he turned, catching her still struggling with her under-wear.

'Well, Mrs Richardson, I think we better have you in for a little operation. Just to have a look and see what's going on in there.'

'Oh.' She straightened to look at him, leaving her tights wrinkled round her ankles.

'Nothing to worry about. We just pop a little telescope in through your belly button and have a look around. You'll only need to be in for a couple of days. My secretary will make an appointment for you to come into the private wing.' He smiled and returned to his notes.

'What do you think is the matter, doctor?'

'Well, now, it could be a number of things, we really need to have a look before we say for certain. I'm sure it's nothing to worry about.'

She hesitated. She wanted him to reassure her.

'I'll see you again in the hospital, then, Mrs Richardson. Goodbye.'

She didn't dare to ask. She picked up her bag and went to get off the couch, forgetting about her tights. She stumbled momentarily, then pulled them up too rapidly, laddering the right leg.

'Damn!'

'Sorry?' The doctor looked up.

'Nothing. Nothing, just my tights.'

'Ah.'

Perhaps it was cancer after all, she thought.

As a child he had been much admired. His father's lady friends had said he had the face of a little angel. It was true that his skin had been unblemished and creamy-smooth, his hair a mass of soft blond curls. The ladies admired his looks, thinking he was a little girl. That embarrassing mistake had ceased with puberty, although ladies continued to admire. His hair was still as blond, but straight now and cut short. His body was lean and elegantly dressed, his long bony fingers jutting from immaculate cuffs. His face was built square, but he had an intelligent look. Intelligent, except for his eyes, which held quite another promise.

Vanessa had met him first when she had had a D and C. A 'scrape operation', her mother had called it, making her feel sick. She had seen Matthew in the clinic and then again on the ward. He was a kind man, with a charming smile. He had explained carefully what they were going to do to her, that he was sure there was nothing seriously wrong, that she would be able to go home after just a day or two. She was impressed.

Nonetheless, she was taken aback when introduced to him over cocktails three weeks later. It was most unnerving, she explained to her friend Elizabeth, to watch hands which had so recently probed such private flesh now proffering a bowl of cocktail nuts. Elizabeth was sympathetic, but only to a degree. Anyone with a gynaecologist as desirable as Matthew Potter should abandon modesty.

Vanessa had been transfixed by those hands all evening. They should have been ugly, with their long bones only barely covered with skin, but they had a grace of their own. He moved them slowly, showing off the perfectly manicured nails, and gesticulating just a little as he spoke. They had mesmerized her and it wasn't long before he was holding her face between them, smiling down at her.

They had achieved a very proper courtship, quite befitting the daughter of a knight of the realm. Everyone said they made a lovely couple, Vanessa petite and blonde, Matthew tall and fair. They had matching suits made for their engagement photos and smiled perfectly, confident in their looks and in one another. Matthew's eyes gleamed still from that picture on their bookshelves.

Vanessa was a virgin on their wedding night and Matthew was cautious with her, soothing her quietly before delving into the secret places of her body. Afterwards he snored, holding her forcibly close, even in sleep.

Her life settled into a new routine. Matthew would kiss her at breakfast and read the front pages of his paper. In the evening he kissed her on his return and ate, usually in silence, before reading the back pages of his paper. At the beginning of the week he would discuss with her when he would be on call and check the dates that they were going out or entertaining. Often he came home late, but he always

189

telephoned to warn her. She understood this, she was a surgeon's daughter. Sometimes he bought her flowers or other little presents, a scarf, a pair of earrings. Once he came home with glinting eyes and took her outside to show her a new car. A little sports car. For her.

Two or three times a week, when he wasn't too tired, he would move his hands across her body and climb on top of her. It was pleasant. He was considerate always. But in the daytime, she would lock herself in the toilet and cry.

She continued to work. Matthew did not object. She enjoyed office life and sometimes, when Matthew was on call, she had girfriends in for the evening, laughing over glasses of wine. With them she discussed the ways of the world, politics, crime, her old joys and sadnesses, her hopes. Matthew would never be drawn on such subjects. He half-listened to her when she recounted tales of torture in South America and when she wept over the death of a friend's new-born baby. He held her for a few minutes and kissed her, carefully turning the subject to supper, or the weekend, or a film they might go to see. She felt perhaps her concerns were insignificant beside the responsibilities and distresses of his job. But he would not speak about his work either. He said it would bore her, that she wouldn't understand. Her mother said he didn't want to bring his work home with him, that it was a subject best avoided.

On one occasion only his work intruded into their home. A woman called Richardson began to ring the house, trying to contact Matthew. She was distraught, but he refused to speak to her. He said she was a patient, neurotic. There was nothing wrong with her, but she was terrified she had cancer. Vanessa tried to reassure her, but she wanted Matthew. He would not discuss it further nor answer the phone. After a while the woman stopped ringing.

Vanessa did not understand her own unease. She had a good husband, a beautiful home, a job she loved. She sat in an unruly corner of her garden and counted her blessings. But something was missing. Something she could not pin down.

She had presumed that marriage would bring with it that special closeness so evident in the lives of her married friends and sister. She thought that something in the act of lovemaking would draw them into one another's confidence. Matthew was always attentive, always thoughtful. But there was no intimacy, only politeness.

It began the night of his appointment as a consultant. He had succeeded with the help of Vanessa's father.

He came home very late and very drunk. Vanessa was waiting for him in the lounge. The car engine made a churning noise, stopped as the tyres squeaked against the drive. His usual grace was gone, his movements heavy and slow. The door slammed and he dropped his case in the hall. Vanessa sat immobile. His figure, stooping slightly, appeared in the doorway. As he came closer his face, red and distorted by a smile, formed itself into familiar features.

'I got it.' His voice was astonishingly controlled.

'I was worried.'

'You needn't have. Everyone said I'd get it. Your dad reckons they'd made up their minds before the interview.'

'Oh, yes. I mean, no. I wasn't worried about that. Well, yes, I was. And I'm glad you got the job. Very glad. You deserved it. But I meant, I was worried because you're so late. I thought something might've happened. And you hadn't phoned.'

'It didn't finish till late. Then we went to celebrate.'

'You could have phoned.'

'For heaven's sake, woman, I cross perhaps the greatest

hurdle of my career and you moan because I didn't phone to say I'd be late. I'm always late.'

'You always phone.'

'Perhaps I'd better stop that then.'

'Didn't you think I might want to know whether you got the job?' Her voice was quieter now.

'I wanted to tell you myself. Come here.' He reached out for her, lunging almost, with his right arm. She flinched, instinctively moving away. His co-ordination was poor and he caught a picture frame, knocking it to the ground.

'Shit,' he looked at it for a second then moved towards his wife again. 'I said, come here.'

'Matthew, please, you're not sober. Let's talk in the morning.'

'I don't want to talk.'

His face was screwed up with intent, the eyes small, like pigs' eyes, shining black. He moved closer to her, cornering her between his body and the wall. She could not account for her fear. Afterwards, for a time, she put it down to her worry and his drunkenness. His arm stretched out, his long fingers wrapping round her wrist. His grip tightened as he drew her towards him, his eyes fixed, without blinking, on her face. She resisted, trying to retrieve her arm, but he pulled harder, squeezed tighter, forced her into his arms. He kissed her, open-mouthed until she was nearly drowned by his face.

He brought her to the floor, still holding her arm, and stripped her. He was triumphant. He pushed into her so hard that it made her cry out. There was no one to hear, but he stifled her, holding a cushion across her mouth until he had finished. Then he collapsed beside her, half-dressed.

In the morning he had risen, bathed and dressed by the time she came downstairs. He made no reference to the previous night, no apology, no explanation. Her mouth was sore and her wrist was growing livid spots where his fingers had dug in. He breakfasted, read the paper, kissed her as usual. When he had gone she went into the lounge. All was in order. The cushions plumped and ready, the furniture in place, no mark on the carpet. As if nothing had happened. Except that the picture was missing, the photograph of Matthew as a baby, the black and white print of the plump, angelic infant with pale curls. It took her a while to find it. The frame was bent and the glass had broken, scraping the picture. She put it away in her desk, locking the drawer, sweeping up the glass. Then she went to work.

They had conceived their first child. There had been no time for the precautions about which Matthew was always so insistent. Everyone was delighted. A new job and a new family, they said, how delightful, how well organized. Vanessa tried not to hate the child growing inside her. It was not, she told herself, the child's fault. It was wrong to punish it. Her bruises faded, but her belly grew, a vast reminder of its beginning.

Matthew gave the impression of the proud father. Privately, he never spoke to Vanessa about the child, except to express his disapproval when she continued to work throughout her pregnancy. He gave her clinical advice and had her checked regularly at the hospital.

It was about this time that Vanessa discovered what was wrong with their sex life. Lovemaking had resumed as normal the week after the child's conception. Perhaps it was the contrast that made her realize, or just her heightened awareness: he had no passion. Sex was a clinical procedure, the careful satisfaction of a need.

Matthew Potter's son was born on 24 October. Healthy, screaming and pink. They called him Nathaniel. Vanessa was glad it was a boy. She had a better excuse to keep her distance. A mother was expected to be close to her girl child, but a boy was different. She refused to breast-feed, claiming her own inadequacy as protection. Matthew finally gave in.

Throughout her pregnancy, Matthew had been kind, if more obviously distant. The trouble started again when Vanessa returned to work. Coming home late one evening, she found him waiting for her in the study.

'Where have you been?'

'I'm sorry, we've got a lot on at the moment. I had to stay and help out.'

'Had to? I see. And what about your son?'

'He's fine. Pascale takes care of him.'

'You think she replaces a mother's care?'

'I didn't say that. But he's quite safe with her.'

'You think so?'

Something in his voice made her look at him more closely. 'Has something happened, Matthew? Is Nat all right?'

'I don't like you calling him that. Nathaniel is fine. But he might not have been.'

Vanessa sat heavily on a chair. 'Matthew, really. Don't frighten me like that.'

'You should think about these things before you go gadding off doing whatever you please.'

'I was at work. I wasn't gadding anywhere. Pascale can always contact me there.'

'How the hell do I know where you were? You could have been off spending my money. Or gossiping with your silly women friends. Or maybe you've taken a lover.' His head jerked up. Vanessa blanched.

'Is that it? Have you got a little man stashed away somewhere?'

'Don't be ridiculous. I wouldn't . . . I'd never . . . You

194

know I believe in faithfulness. For heaven's sake Matthew, I've just had your son.'

'But you don't seem very interested in him. Perhaps you don't like bearing my children.' He had risen from his seat, was pacing in front of the fire. 'Perhaps you'd prefer somebody else's.' He turned to her. His face stopped her breath. He came over to her, wrenching her from the chair, holding her by the shoulders.

'Please, Matthew. There's nothing to fight about.'

His fingers were sinking into her flesh. He held her, staring into her face, shaking her every few seconds, just a little. 'Would you like another baby, Vanessa? Would you?'

The shaking was hurting her head. Her voice came in spurts between the shakes. 'Well . . . yes . . . of course . . . But perhaps . . . we could wait . . . a while . . . I mean . . . Natheniel's not very . . . old.'

'No. And he needs his mother. So do I.' He stopped shaking her and bent instead, kissing her, violently at first, but then more gently, until finally he pulled away and sat down.

'I don't like you going out to work. There's no need.' His voice was flat, calm now.

'I know. I'm sorry. I'll try not to stay late again.' She could not bear to lose her job as well.

She went upstairs to change, but stopped short on the landing, gripping the banister. This time Matthew was completely sober.

She was more cautious after that. She tried never to be late when he was home. If she was she would phone from the noisy office to tell him so. She fitted her shopping trips and meetings with friends into the day or on evenings when he was away. For a while there were no more outbursts, but odd things began to happen. Small bruises appeared on her back and thighs where she had no recollection of hurting herself. Matthew began to wake her in the morning by pinching her hard on the arm or buttock, until she learnt to wake before him. When they made love he would bite her, not little nips, but whole mouths full of flesh, hurting her and drawing blood.

One Sunday, returning early from church, she found him rummaging through her wardrobe. He said he was looking for a lost pair of shoes, but when, later, she came to hang up her dress she realized he had been searching her clothes, emptying the pockets, going through her bags. After that he searched her desk and chest of drawers. She moved her precious things to the office, said nothing.

Elizabeth, her friend, had married an American and lived in New Mexico. When she returned to London for a visit she rang to ask if she might stay a few days. Vanessa agreed without hesitating. She was delighted at the thought of a reunion. She took some days off work. Matthew was furious.

'You might've consulted me. This is my house.'

'It's our home, Matthew. You know Elizabeth. I thought you'd be glad to see her.'

'I have a very busy life. I don't want the little peace I have disturbed by people inviting themselves to stay.'

'But we have a lot of people to stay. I never thought you'd mind.'

'Well, I do. We don't have guests during the week.'

'Yes, we do . . . '

'I don't want some strange woman prowling round my house all day when I'm not here.'

'She's not strange, Matthew. Anyway, I'm taking some days off work, so she won't be here alone.'

'I see. Days off work. She is privileged.'

Vanessa let it rest. When Elizabeth arrived, Matthew

hardly spoke to her. He came home earlier than usual all week and sat behind his paper.

'Is Matthew all right, Vanessa?'

'Oh, he's just tired. He's working very hard at the moment.'

'He doesn't seem very pleased to see me.'

'It's not that. He just gets a big funny sometimes.'

Elizabeth raised her beautifully arched eyebrows.

'I think he's just jealous of me spending so much time with you.'

'Jealous? But that's silly. We hardly see each other now. And it's not as if I was a man, some long-lost lover or something.'

'No.'

'Is something the matter, Vanessa?'

Vanessa drew breath. She had to tell someone. She wanted to. 'Liz, does Kirk ever go through your things?'

'Go through my things? How d'you mean?'

'Well, looking through your clothes, your letters. As if you were hiding something from him.'

'I should hope not. I'd have something to say to him if he did. Why? Is Matthew checking up on you?'

'I think so. I found him a couple of times going through my wardrobe and my desk. He said he'd lost something, but I don't know. And I keep finding things disturbed, not where I left them.'

'Does he think you're having an affair?'

'Maybe.'

'Are you?'

'No, of course not.'

'Of course. I forgot you're religious that way. Have you asked him what he's doing? Told him to stop it?'

'I don't think that would do much good. He'd just get angry.'

197

'So?'

'I don't like to make him cross.'

'Good God, Vanessa. You can't have a marriage without making each other cross sometimes. You just make it up afterwards.'

'Yes.'

'Well, then?'

'I don't like making him angry. He frightens me.' Her voice was very quiet now. Her head turned away.

'Frightens you?' In a rush, it occurred to Elizabeth. 'Is he beating you, Vanessa?'

'Not exactly.'

'Not exactly? What the hell . . . ?'

Elizabeth took her weeping friend in her arms, soothing her and frowning. It seemed to Elizabeth that Vanessa must have got things out of all proportion. Matthew was not an unreasonable man.

In bed at night Matthew began to ask her what she had done each day. What she and Elizabeth had said, where they had been. He would not accept simplistic explanations. He wanted detailed accounts of every minute of the day. That was when he suggested she keep a diary. A diary for him to read: everything she did, everything she said, everyone she met, each day. She hoped he would forget it, thought it was just the product of Elizabeth's visit. Perhaps what he really wanted was another child. Perhaps that would reassure him.

Esmé was a beautiful child, blonde and always chortling. Perhaps because she had chosen to have her, perhaps because she had a daughter, Vanessa was drawn to the child from the moment the pregnancy was confirmed. She could not have been more wrong about Matthew. He was convinced the child was someone else's. Vanessa's delight served to increase his fears. And his rage. He did not touch her during the pregnancy, but after her six week check, he sent the nanny away for the evening and took Vanessa upstairs. Deliberately and without explanation he put her across his knee like a child and beat her with the sole of his shoe. He placed the marks carefully so they were invisible when she was dressed.

One afternoon her boss asked her to see him. He was polite but firm. Her husband had talked to him at length, outlining the strain that work was putting on her now that she had two children, explaining that she did not want to let people down by leaving, although she longed to be at home. Vanessa protested, but her employer persisted. Eventually he admitted that Matthew had expressed a fear for her mental health if she continued to work, that he had given it as his professional opinion that she should give up. They were letting her go.

Stunned, not even tearful, she wandered home. She dropped the private contents of her desk into a litter bin outside the tube station. The house was still in chaos. They were having an extension built and the lounge was full of concrete dust and tools. A large iron girder stretched across the floor, waiting to support the second storey when a hole was knocked in the supporting wall. The builders had disappeared. They knocked off early on a Friday. She stepped carefully over it and went to stand at what remained of the window.

The garden was quiet and warm. The nanny had taken the children out for the afternoon. Toys lay strewn across the lawn, Nat's miniature tractor turned on its side. The laurel bush rustled a little as the breeze took it, dancing light off its shiny leaves. A tiny sparrow was creating furious clouds of dust as it bathed in the dirt.

Behind her the house creaked gently, making its familiar family sounds. Water gurgled in the upstairs pipes, the fridge whirred busily in the kitchen. The Sanderson walls, the painted cornices, the tasteful furniture. Her home. Her prison. She felt stifled, crushed. She was powerless. She took a long breath and let it slowly out. She would fuse with the house, become a shadow, a decorative accessory. He would whittle her life away over the years, until she faded into nothing.

A frown crossed her face. The tamarisk tree had been pruned. It was her favourite part of the garden, overgrown and wild with the irregular, pink-blossomed tree overhanging the lawn. She liked to sit in the shade and read. It irritated Matthew. He said it was untidy and made it difficult for the gardener to mow properly. And now all the beautiful, feathered branches had been lopped back to short stumps. It was wounded, its amputated limbs sticking forlornly into the air.

Damn him, she thought. Damn him. I will not let him do this to me. He has no right. He has destroyed my tree. My beautiful tree. He hurts all the harmless things. He hates everything he doesn't fear. How dare he mutilate my tree and lock me up inside this doll's house?

She did not move from the window. She still stood there, gripping the sill, when Matthew returned.

'Hello, sweetheart.' He came across to kiss her.

She moved her face away, still staring into the garden.

'Is something the matter, Vanessa?'

'You could say that.'

'Whatever is it?' He put his arm across her shoulders, but she jerked it away.

'Don't touch me.'

'What has upset you?'

'You cut down my tree.'

'Now, really, I didn't cut it down. I asked the gardener to prune it. It was so untidy. It hung right over the lawn.'

'Look what he's done to it. Look.'

'It'll grow back. It'll be much neater now, that's all. There's no need to make such a fuss.'

'I liked it the way it was. You knew that. Why didn't you ask me first?'

'It needed pruning.'

'Like I need to be at home?'

'I'm sorry?'

'What gives you the right to tell my boss to give me the sack?'

'I did no such thing. I merely explained to him the strain you were under.'

'My work has nothing to do with any strain I am under.'

'Of course it does. Look at you now. You're all het up.'

'That's not because of work.'

'You may not think so . . . '

'But you know better.'

'Yes.'

'You told him I was going mad.'

'No. I said it wasn't doing your state of mind any good trying to work and be a good wife and mother.'

'What gives you the right?'

'I'm your husband. I care for you.'

'If you cared one iota for me you would have consulted me before having me dismissed.'

'I knew you'd object.'

Vanessa stared at him, incredulous. Then she strode back across the room, stepping over the girder, to get at her bag. She took out a cigarette.

'Vanessa. You have given up smoking.'

'I've restarted.'

'Now, look here . . . '

'I'm not a child, Matthew. I'll do what I choose. And I shall find myself another job.'

'You will not.' The colour was rising in his face, the eyes shrinking into dark spots. His long body grew taller when he was angry, so that his head stooped over, like a vulture. He was spitting his words in a low, hissing voice, 'You will stay at home where you belong and look after your children. They need you. I need you. Here.'

'You don't need me here. You just want to be able to keep tabs on me. What are you going to do? Bribe the nanny to spy on me maybe? Or the gardener?'

'You are paranoid.'

'Oh. So you're going to have me locked up now. In the attic, perhaps? A second Mrs Rochester?'

'That's enough. I work extremely hard to look after you. I've bought you this beautiful house, a nice car, lovely clothes. A good many women would be grateful. But not you. Oh, no. What do I get in return? I get a selfish, vicious wife who doesn't love her children, let alone her husband. Who flits off to some insignificant little job as an excuse to deceive me. Well, I won't have it.'

He began to cross the lounge, slowly pacing towards her, keeping his gaze fixed on her face.

This time she felt no fear. She was furious. She wanted him to hit her, to release her, so she could strike back, so she could wound him as she had wounded her tree, so she could chop off his arms and break his malicious face into a thousand pieces.

He came closer, almost within reach now, a thin smile hanging on his mouth. Behind her, Vanessa's hand closed over the crowbar the builders had been using to knock down the wall. Matthew reached out his right arm, his long fingers stretching to grab her.

For an instant, her vision dimmed. Her eyelids twitched

madly. When she refocused, he had gone. His pink, piggy face had disappeared. It took her an instant to realize where he was, what had happened. She hadn't heard him fall. He had tripped on a bag of concrete, fallen sideways, splitting open his head on the iron girder.

She stood over him. His face was dappled grey, blood oozing through his hair. His eyes were still open, but wide now and gaunt. Irregular breath sputtered from his mouth. She watched him, setting her mind to remember, then she raised the crowbar high above her head.

He was in intensive care for weeks. At first it was very much touch and go. No one was prepared to commit themselves. But Matthew was not the sort to be defeated. It became apparent that he would live, although with what degree of disability no one knew.

Vanessa visited every day. At first she was emotionless, shocked, preoccupied with the mechanics of organizing the children, getting to the hospital, talking to the doctors, running her household. Then she began to enjoy Matthew's dependency – on the machines, on the nurses, on her.

He recovered sufficiently to sit in a wheelchair. They kept him in hospital for rehabilitation, to improve as far as possible the use of his right side. He was often impatient, angry with his useless limbs. He could not move either arm or leg and his mouth drooped at the corner. He saw no point in exercises when he saw no improvement. He demanded to go home.

Vanessa had a special bedroom and bathroom built downstairs. There was, at first, suggestion of a chair-lift for the stairs, but she refused this. It was no trouble to have him downstairs and alterations were already in progress. Silently she was delighted at the thought of a space which would be beyond his reach. She reorganized the house and applied for a new job, on the grounds that they would need the money. A plausible explanation, although not strictly true.

Ian McInnes, a colleague of Matthew's and an old friend, had sorted things out at the hospital where Matthew had worked. His clinical career was over, but he could continue to lecture and teach, and perhaps also set up some research once the Richardson problem was over. Vanessa had known nothing about this, but it seemed the distressed woman who had telephoned the house so often was a private patient of Matthew's. She was accusing him of professional malpractice. Something personal, Ian said. Vanessa did not investigate any further. He would have to be cleared before he could take up the teaching post.

Everyone commented on Vanessa's resilience and courage. She never lost her temper with her invalid husband, even though he shouted and threw things. She helped him every day to bathe and dress and eat. She even helped him in the toilet. And she did a full-time job and looked after her children. She was a remarkable woman.

Vanessa enjoyed it. She learnt to shift nimbly away from his left arm which would lash out or grab at her. She ignored the tantrums and abuse, even in public. Especially in public. She taught the children to be careful. Every day she trotted off to work and every night, when she had put Matthew to bed, she would retreat up the stairs to her own room. She knew he could do most things for himself if he tried, but it did not bother her.

She reinstated the angel-faced photograph in the lounge, buying it a new frame and painting out the scratch. The cherubic looks smiled out at their lopsided successor, like the picture of Dorian Gray after his death. Sometimes, when he rattled the wheelchair impatiently into her thigh, or the long fingers of his left hand grasped her wrist too tightly, she wondered if things would have been better if she had let the crowbar fall onto his head. On the whole, she thought not.

MATTIE AND CLYDE

James Roberts

James Roberts was born in London and educated at the Latymer School and King's College, Cambridge where he read Arabic and Persian. Since the age of 16, James has frequently studied and travelled abroad particularly in France and The Sultanate of Oman. He is presently studying law in London.

MATTIE AND CLYDE

In East Anglia, they often say that the wind which scours the Fenlands all winter comes straight from Siberia. Of course this is by no means impossible, although it could just as likely have been churned up over the Baltic or in the North Sea off the Goodwin Sands. Siberia is merely a convenient shorthand for the coldest inhabited place in the world. Staring out across the silent flat fields, with their breath turning to steam and only the rooks punching holes in the silence, perhaps Fenlanders can feel a special chilly affinity with the exiles of the tundra.

But if the wind had really come straight to the Fens from Siberia in January 1944 – and that winter was as cold as any – it would have had to creep up behind the backs of the Red Army on its steady westward march, comb through the sufferings of Poland, skirt around Switzerland – a rocky island of peace in a sea of war – and at last blow past the grey concrete boxes of the Atlantic Wall defences; an epic journey to be made before it could ice the beet fields over like a bloody-minded pastrycook, freezing the ditches into solid muddy stone. But this would have been just another epic journey in an epic time, a cruel wind in a period of cruelty of mythic proportions.

In 1944, the greater part of East Anglian farmland had been devoted to the production of all the sugar beet it could be coaxed to churn out. It is easy to picture the producers of cane sugar; they live under a hot sun, are probably given to spontaneous singing and dancing, and the blackening between the teeth brought about by the incessant chewing of their produce only serves to accentuate their guileless smiles. But the farmers of sugar beet have less to smile about – try chewing raw sugar beet some time if you want to see your teeth fall out – and never more so than in the chilly misery that prevailed in the fifth winter of a world war. On weekdays in tiny villages like Harport Magna, the ancient streets saw few faces emerge red and puffing through the mists. The farmers and their wives preferred to stay hunched around their fires when there was no good cause to visit the village store; most of the labourers had been replaced by Italian prisoners who stood around in their camps, homesick and blowing on their hands. The silence of the streets was further muffled by the fogs that rose off the fen, filling in the dark spaces between all the rickety houses. Only the church stood clear of the whiteness, like an expensive ornament there hadn't been quite enough cotton wool to wrap up completely. It was the oldest structure in the village, the bequest of a wealthy thirteenth-century merchant in an age when the bestowal of a church showed off the status that flashy cars display today. By the time morning had slipped into afternoon and the fog cleared a little perhaps, the streets were deserted and silent, remaining so until the evenings when a few troops from the army camps nearby might venture out to swallow watery wartime beer, half-heartedly singing songs to the accompaniment of an off-key piano.

Cold mornings, quiet afternoons, lonely evenings and early nights: these were merely the sections of Miss Sefton's daily routine. Every day at eight-fifteen she bicycled in from her cottage a mile or so away to open the sub-post office. She entered through a back door – it wouldn't do to enter through the front-door before the shop was opened –

brewed tea on a gas-ring in the parlour at the back, then unlocked the door just as the radio squawked out the nine o'clock time signal. The Rector used to say that the bells above Miss Sefton's shop door were a far truer timepiece than those in the church tower, which, in any case, had been silenced for the duration of the war. Some thought that the vague possibility that they might one day be needed to ring out an invasion warning still existed.

Very little disturbed Miss Sefton's morning vigil in the post office; she sold a few stamps, might cash an occasional postal order from sons in the Forces, put the man from the main office in his place when he came to pick up the village mail with some cheeky and quite unnecessary remark. Then, at two o'clock precisely, she closed the shop, ate the little parcel of lunch she brought from home in the store room at the back of the shop, and reopened at four, pulling back the dark curtain she had made herself for the front of the post office grille. In the afternoon sessions, she would only leave her perch on a high wooden stool to dole out sweet rations from the tiny selection of confectionery she could obtain in war time, held in rapidly emptied jars on high shelves at the other side of the shop.

But after eating her lunch and perhaps brewing a further cup of tea from the carefully dried leaves of the morning pot, perhaps from two-thirty until a quarter to four in the afternoon, Miss Sefton did the work that earned her the regular vote of thanks at the end of the harvest festival and Christmas sermons. Barely giving a thought to the cold religious mustiness and damp chill, she swept out the village church daily, arranged new flowers and cleared out the dead stems, brushed down the vestments weekly and starched the surplices once a fortnight; she was, in short, a pillar of the community. That was the phrase the Rector most often employed. And when her work was done, Miss Sefton would kneel and then, when that position became too uncomfortable, sit a while in front of the war memorial, really nothing more than a brass plate set into the wall, where she daily laid the best and freshest flowers donated from various churchgoers' gardens.

Miss Sefton's faith was a conventional one, untroubled by doubt or dogma. She attended services as a matter of course, belonged to a generation where the church had not yet faded out from the pattern of weekly life like the colours of the tiny flowers embroidered on the kneelers. But, above all, the church was a quiet place to sit a while, far from the tinkling of the shop bell and the constant mention of outlandish names and places fought over on the BBC News. And here, where the dust motes floated in and out of the beams of coloured light from the shabby stained glass windows, she felt closest to Reggie, although his only presence there was in the black letters cut out from the burnished brass of the plaque, just under the inscription about no man having greater love, right at the top of the list, mind, what with his having been made an officer just before the end.

Miss Sefton was well aware that tens of thousands of girls, women now, had lost men, no, boys, just as she had in the Great War. But how could a general and obvious truth like this help to ease the grip in her chest she felt when she thought of him? When she had been a young girl, she had imagined that expressions like 'a wound in the heart' were only meaningless codes for romantic novelists. She had been able to smile at the thought of such shameless old clichés having the dust blown off them once again, until the morning Reggie's mother had told her that the boy wouldn't be coming home again. 'Coming home again.' Those were the words she'd said. She hadn't been able to utter the final punctuation of 'dead' or 'killed', not where her own son was concerned.

Matilda and Reggie had first met in the hot summer of 1914. He was tall with neatly combed down blond hair and, at least to a country girl like Matilda, seemed to have something of the air of a slick city boy, even though she knew very well that they'd grown up in the same village; 'masher' was the word she'd laughingly applied and he'd smiled knowingly. Reggie certainly didn't mind a joke, but he felt himself made of rather sterner stuff than that, not at all the sort of chap who hung around on Saturday nights in front of the Corn Exchange in town. But it was true he'd set out from this rural idyll, he said, and held a position in the largest and finest millinery emporium in Ely. But even we tradesmen, he added with a confident smile, have a responsibility as members of the first generation of this twentieth century to attend to the burgeoning arts and sciences that would make our age the opening of a great new civilization. He promised to bring her a novel by H. G. Wells from the lending library when he next came home.

Miss Sefton, or Matilda, as it's more appropriate to call her before she became a pillar of the community, was not so much flattered as captivated by Reggie's attention. True, she was only a little dazzled by his having assumed the responsibility of promoting the cultural triumphs of a brand new epoch, or whatever the phrase he used was; perhaps her remaining in the village far from the city lights of Ely had kept her horizons limited. But, above all, she admired his obvious difference from the other village boys; he seemed to see further than a life of ploughing, poaching and breeding children, spent his free time at night-school rather than guzzling beer and shouting insults at old women who tottered past with heavy baskets. When she asked the girls who had been his class-mates in the village school – many of them were by now married with children – what they thought of young Reggie Vernon, they said he'd always been one of the bright ones, teacher had wanted him to go to the grammar school in town, but his mam had made him find a job to bring some money in, seven kids and the father gone gallivanting away a year or two back. It was clear he wasn't cut out to be a farm labourer, so he'd taken the weekly bus into Ely and come back proud as punch, found himself a place as trainee counter-hand at Dobson and Sons, the milliners. And had she ever seen such lovely hats as they have in the windows there?

Their courtship ran its course slowly, made all the slower by Reggie's absence from Sunday evening to late Saturday afternoon. It amounted to little more than twenty-four months or so of Saturday teas together, sitting side by side in church and walks in the lanes after Sunday lunch. Reggie refused to stop in the lane that village lovers traditionally frequented, walked through with Matilda on his arm and his head only turning to nod a greeting at old acquaintances who were satisfied with courting as their parents had done. Instead he would lead Matilda to what they considered a stream, just a large ditch really that nature had taken over, where he would mutter a poem about knowing a bank where the wild thyme grew. On those afternoons they would sit among the ferns holding hands and Reggie would talk about the great future now just a little postponed by the War, which was in any case a necessary purge of retrogressive forces. Matilda hoped that Reggie's bright new future might include their being married and living safely together in the privacy of the hygienic dwellings for artisans he was always talking about. She wondered if the reason that she failed to see this new age of scientific glory as clearly as her young man might be because of her not having the benefit of night-school in Ely; sometimes she worried he might tire of her if she didn't keep up with his learning. On other days there were afternoons when Reggie spoke of these things and she felt like a mother listening to her tired but happy child babble about the day's excitements. Then Reggie would subside a little and lie back with his head in her lap, the greatest physical closeness they ever achieved. Occasionally they heard a rumble in the distance and wondered whether it was thunder or the guns in Flanders.

A year or so later, when it had become clear that the war was not going to remain a formal matter to be dealt with between professionals, Reggie started to feel uneasy about his not yet being in the army. He knew the war to be the crusade of civilization and progress against barbarism and had told Matilda stories of what the Huns did to Belgian babies that made her flesh creep. Also, although he did not say as much, several customers had asked Mr Dobson, in Reggie's hearing as they intended, why he hadn't yet released a sturdy young man like that to go to the Front.

Reggie first raised the matter on a Sunday morning at home. His mother, a tough woman whom hard times had made tougher, listened in silence at first, then slammed the *Sunday Pictorial* down on the table, sending bread crumbs dancing across the grimy boards. 'Join the army, join the bloody army, there's nothing but that rubbish in every newspaper I read. Look at this,' she commanded, indicating a full-page illustration of Britannia with her arms outstretched, ' "Mothers of bloody England send your sons today!" You'll wait until you're sent for, my lad, not a moment before.' The youngest child, a girl of four years or so, began to cry quietly at this unexplained explosion of anger, and Reggie's two immediately younger brothers, both farm labourers, smirked stiffly, not unamused to see Reggie put in his place for once. Mrs Vernon snorted, then resumed her reading of the newspaper, which featured a detailed account of a particularly bloody murder and suicide in the back streets of Huddersfield.

But Reggie did not have to wait very long before he was sent for. The magnitude of his leaving for the army was too great for them to grasp at first. They had already become used to his long absences from home during the week; his mother was kept busy looking after the younger children, and Matilda had already started to help the old village sub-post mistress to release another man for the army. The extent of the upheaval only dawned on them one afternoon when Reggie came home in uniform, on embarkation leave before joining a draft for the Front. Reggie's mother and Matilda were vaguely aware, though country women and not exposed to the patriotic madness of the towns, that they were supposed to be proud of having their man safely clad in uniform at last; not wanting to lose him, as the song put it, though really rather thinking that he ought to go. But no one present on that day found much to say; when Reggie went at last to say goodbye to his old school friends not yet called upon, his mother and Matilda wailed in each other's arms.

Reggie and Matilda took their usual stroll on Sunday afternoon and sat in a meadow. The thunder, or guns, were silent that day. Reggie spoke rather less of the course of progress and civilization than usual. Matilda thought that he might be clinging to her tighter than usual for need of comfort until he tried to feel her body through her Sunday clothes. Before his conscription, his belief in what he termed free love had only been a theoretical one. Perhaps the banter – dirty talk, he once would have called it – in barrack rooms between less innocent young men and more likely soldiers had put such ideas into his head. Matilda fought him off, but gently, eventually stood up and threatened to go straight home if he didn't stop that instant. But it seemed wrong to be angry with him on their last day together, and they were soon settled back chastely on the grass of their river bank. All the same, Matilda was a little disgusted. She had hardly expected this of the boy who brought her books each week from the library in the town.

One might have expected that the Western Front would make short work of an innocent like Reggie, but this was not the case. After the losses of the Somme offensive and the difficulty in finding candidates of sufficient calibre – reading and writing well were at a premium – he was promoted to sergeant within a few months. Night-school clearly brought benefits Reggie had never imagined. After a period of rest and training they returned to the trenches, where a young officer, still pining at the loss of a romantic friendship with a younger boy at his public school, found – caught would not be quite the right word – Reggie reading Shelley in a dug-out, and befriended him. Please believe that their intimacy was as innocent as that between Reggie and Matilda; more so perhaps. The lieutenant's parting gift before his transfer to a staff posting behind the lines was the dubious favour of recommending Reggie for a commission.

Reggie came back once again to the village after an accelerated officers' training course at Sandhurst. He wore his new uniform with a different air, haughtier and rather more patronizing towards Matilda and nobly condescending towards his family. Matilda was uneasy with him, felt he treated her now more like a younger sister, or perhaps his consort in the career of knight errantry he imagined he'd embarked on. She felt confused; never before had her future seemed so uncertain. Nor did their formal engagement, their marriage to await the end of the war, make prospects seem clearer. It was hardly a surprise; they had both long seen it as an impending part of their future, though one they left undiscussed. But in 1917, even girls from backwaters like Harport Magna knew that engagements to soldiers were no guarantee of living happily ever after. And what about Reggie? Had he seen enough of the true nature of his shining new age at last to have learned to keep silent about the brilliant futures awaiting all mankind, and to try to take hold of some prospect of personal happiness for himself? Perhaps he even felt that he required the status of having a fiancée as part of a second lieutenant's kit, a pocket-sized photograph to show his new brother officers in the mess, and a damned good excuse not to join the drunken parties that set out to the French brothels reserved for officers only. And so, Matilda felt, that was that. She was an engaged woman at last, would marry one day if the war did not last for ever. It was of little comfort when Reggie left, waving a handkerchief from a railway carriage window, that his mother said, 'There, it's an ill wind, as they say, that blows no good. This war's made a toff of my son and a gentleman to be your husband.' Reggie survived long enough to be killed in action in 1918.

What comfort was there for Matilda in being not quite the widow of a provisional gentleman? Although Mrs Vernon had prevented her son from joining the army for as long as she possibly could, Reggie's death prematurely enrolled Matilda in the ranks of the women who had lost their men just as permanently as if she had lived to be a village widow. She had made the transition from girlhood as young Mattie to the staid aridity of Miss Sefton without passing a happy interval of womanhood.

When Reggie first began his elegant courtship of Matilda, his mother had been a little stand-offish towards her. This was not only the jealousy to be expected of a mother at her son's attraction to another woman; Reggie had taken on a paternal role at home when his father had left, and it seemed to Mrs Vernon that she was on the verge of losing the man in her life a second time. But a life as tough as hers fosters common sense in those it doesn't polish off altogether. Even before Reggie was killed, she had quite taken to Matilda. The girl had started visiting the Vernon household in her spare time and helped to look after the younger children. Mrs Vernon quickly began to appreciate and then depend on her company. After the loss of their beautiful young man, too terrible to discuss overtly over the piles of ironing and pots of steaming tea, Matilda began to spend more and more time there. The Vernon household spent the early 1920s dominated by the twin matriarchs, proud of their womanly practicality in feeding farm labourers who ate in silence, a little sheepish and guilty at not having been blown to pieces in the war like their sainted elder brother. When she was not busy at the Vernons, Matilda found herself taking over more and more responsibility at the post office, where the sub-post mistress was becoming patently unable to cope with her paper work; copper-plate handwriting was fast becoming less important than the maintenance of accurate accounts. Then the Rector persuaded the dear old lady to retire, and no one was at all surprised when Matilda was appointed as her successor. And the strong young man whom she had replaced 'to free him for his country's service'? He had travelled now, seen something of the world, lost a foot in Mesopotamia – bloody careless of him, he used to joke – and had no intention whatsoever of returning to a dump like Harport Magna. He was quite content to live off the widowed licensee of a pub well located near the Liverpool docks.

*

The years flowed by sluggishly and solidified into history. Was it her appointment as sub-post mistress or some change in her features unnoticed by Matilda that inspired the villagers to rename her Miss Sefton and treat her with new respect? The adjustment was as sudden as if there had been a meeting at the village hall to decide the matter in her absence. Miss Sefton; at twenty-five an old maid who had lost her one true love in the Great War and settled down to become a widowed virgin. She was as much a respected village institution as the Rector or the Doctor.

But with the decencies of mourning observed, why had Miss Sefton not found a new love to accompany her through the drowsiness of village life? No, there were so few men left unmarried, even without the war having taken the best of them away, and Miss Sefton was certainly not about to throw herself at some mucky-fingered ploughman when her fiancé had been an officer, if you please. Those sons of the wealthier local families who had survived the war and might have been fit for her new station in life spent little time in the village; when they visited they were hardly likely to court the sub-post mistress. Miss Sefton finished by admitting to herself that Reggie had only been a temporary gentleman, and that whatever else the war had changed, she was unlikely ever to be invited for tennis parties or the cocktails she read about in the magazines at what passed for great houses in the district. Miss Sefton never bobbed her hair, wore short dresses, or rode the pillion of a young man's motorbike. She knew herself to be an Edwardian, took refuge in maintaining the dignity fitting to such a relic, and devoted her main attentions to the forethought and care that the efficient functioning of a village post office demands.

The Fenlands reek of history, just as they reek of decaying vegetation at certain times of the year; history, however, does not rot in the damp. Romans, Saxons, Vikings and the Dutch irrigation engineers have all planted hobnailed sandals or boots there, and the mud has swallowed their imprints for ever. When the Second War of Miss Sefton's life began, great wooden army camps appeared like a new strain of rectangular fungus, full of foul-mouthed men in damp khaki battledress that never quite dried out. Then came the American bomber crews, men as handsome as the film stars seen at the cinema in Ely; their beautiful teeth were the talk of the village. And they had money to spend; at Christmas they had given a party for children of the English orphanages, in a brief interval between bouts of creating more German orphans. But from 1943, huge camps had begun to appear, fenced off and secret in their obvious preparation for the Second Front. Every day and nearly all night, enormous green trucks roared in and out, splashing mud and filthy water over the grass verges and flower-beds by the sides of the roads; through openings in the canvas-topped backs, the villagers occasionally caught a glimpse of dirty, raw faces under steel helmets. The Mayor's ad hoc committee for co-operation did its best, but the villagers simply had to accept that their roads were too narrow for these roaring great vehicles, and that ruined geraniums might well be part of the price of winning a war. But such complaints ceased when the chance came to meet these soldiers at village dances. Then the Fenlanders marvelled at the evident wealth of a nation that could equip every private soldier with a shirt and tie like a prosperous farmer in church of a Sunday.

One afternoon in January 1944, Miss Sefton returned from her private devotions of sweeping the church and cleaning – wasn't there a hymn about that being a valid form of praising the Lord? – and staring up a while at the evidence that Reggie had once existed. She was worried that his face was becoming harder to recall to memory and promised herself that she would examine his photograph that evening. As always, she entered the post office by the back door, felt a little like an actress who must not be seen by the public before the performance began; then she pulled herself together. No, she was not a frivolous woman who might have such thoughts, but a responsible public servant. The day was darker than usual; although the year is supposed to turn at Saint Lucy's day, the lamps still had to be lit at four o'clock. She shut the door behind her and, approaching the counter, thought she heard a noise in the shop. But this was an old building, and everyone knows that ancient timbers creak in the damp like wooden ships at sea. And who would wish to burgle her sparsely stocked shop, break in to plunder the balls of string and a few dusty envelopes? But when Miss Sefton draw back the curtains that screened off the post office window, a rasping voice in a foreign accent hissed: 'Now put your hands up, lady, and you won't get hurt.'

Miss Sefton had to strain through her gold-rimmed glasses to make out the form in the darkness of the shop. It repeated its command. As she raised her arms above her head, the threat of violence having shocked her far less than the strangeness of the event, she could make out a shadowy form dressed in a long green raincoat, tightly buckled with the collar turned up to the ears, where it merged into a soft green cap. She focused on a set of small, nervous features, and then, following the arm extended towards her, on the pistol trembling in his two joined hands. The thought flashed through her mind of how different it appeared from Reggie's revolver that he had kept well oiled in a brightly polished holster at his side; 'a Service Webley', she remembered he had called it.

'Please, lady,' the apparition insisted – Miss Sefton had first to accustom herself both to the strange accent and the darkness in the shop before fully understanding – 'please don't make me do something I'll regret later. Put those hands up where I can see them. OK, that's better. Now give me all the loot you've got there.'

'And how can I with my hands raised in this ridiculous manner?'

Oh God, that was just what he needed – a snotty limey like you see in the movies.

'OK, you can put them down to get the money. But do it slowly and don't try anything smart.'

'There isn't much, it was all collected up yesterday.'

'Just take what's there and put it in a bag or something.'

Miss Sefton did as she she was commanded, and briskly stepped out from behind the folding section of the counter.

'Oh Christ, slowly I said.' The figure trembled perceptibly. He was far more alarmed at the sudden movement than his victim was by the armed robbery. He forgot the terse little speech, packed with the bravado and criminal language he'd picked up from the movies, even though he had been rehearsing for days now.

'There's an auto outside, a car or whatever. In it, I mean get in it, we're going for a ride. You and me. Come with me. Now please.'

'Do you seriously expect me to leave the post office unmanned?' No regulations had been issued to instruct sub-post mistresses how to deal with armed robberies. Miss Sefton was, however, inspired by the spirit of service that had possessed her since 1920.

'Just look on this as an unexpected vacation. Put a sign in the window saying you're closed for the day.'

'But I've never closed when there was no call to. No, not even with good cause.'

'Lady, a forty-five in the guts is the loudest call you're ever likely to hear. Now come on.'

Miss Sefton wrote a note on the blotting pad on which postal orders were usually filled in to the effect that she was unwell and would return the next day. The man in the green raincoat stepped outside to start the car.

'Young man, I believe that's the Doctor's car.'

'I don't care whose it is. Have you got the money?'

'Oh no, I left it in the shop. And I haven't locked up yet.'

Miss Sefton disappeared for a few moments and then re-emerged with a small cloth bag, jingling and lumpy with copper and silver coins. As the bells above the shop door tinkled, the man realized that she could just as easily have barricaded herself in the shop and called the police, or have escaped through the back door. Cursing himself for an amateur, he pulled his face into a snarl and hissed: 'Get in.'

'I can only hope you have considered the gravity of your action in robbing the Royal Mail and taking another man's motor car.'

'It's going to be mine for a while, and you and I are going to take a ride in it.' He felt a little more at ease now. At least the words were beginning to sound right.

His name was Joey Shanahan and he came from Chicago. On the first night in training camp back in the States, he and his new comrades had sat on their beds in their underwear – the heat had been stifling on that summer night – and exchanged details of names and home towns. Joey told his new comrades in arms, the guys he was supposed to live and fight with and depend on, that they could call him 'Clyde'. His choice of nickname never stuck; after a few days they renamed him Shithead Shanahan instead.

There was something grotesque about the man's aggression. He was short and puny, but was forever trying to push into mess-hall queues. Another of his unwelcome habits was attempting to borrow money on every pretext; when his hints of menace had failed, he would lean over and wheedle at you with his stinking filthy breath right in your face. But his initial attempts to establish himself as a dominant figure failed miserably and group cohesion took over just as basic training intended. The drill-sergeant became used to hearing that Private Shanahan had blacked his eyes slipping over a bar of soap in the shower once again; the less physically inclined of the intake, some of them college men, found more subtle means to defend themselves against him, and Shanahan's normally grubby kit frequently became even more than usually shabby just before inspections. Once again he found himself without friends, and the platoon members focused their newly found team spirit on making his life unpleasant. When they decided he was responsible for a mysterious series of minor thefts, they gave him a beating that left his ribs sore for days. Even the most kindly ex-seminary student was prepared to admit that Shithead Shanahan deserved everything he got.

Who was to blame? It might have been nature that made him short and wiry with nasty, pinched little features, like a race of dog bred specially for some particularly unpleasant task, although that could just as easily have been the exterior reflecting what was inside. His early life had not been easy; when he was born his father had been a clerk in the Chicago slaughter-houses, came home each night smelling vaguely of death like other boys' fathers but with no blood under his fingernails. His mother stayed at home and took in sewing, and each night they ate supper together like a family taken from a Norman Rockwell illustration.

Joey played out on the streets like other boys, but never got to join the gangs that grew out of the different nationalities, Italians, Irish, Germans, Bohunks. He went to the movies alone each week to see the latest picture about the exploits of the real gangsters like Paul Muni and Jimmy Cagney. When the manager ordered out whole rows of unruly boys, Joey remained sitting as calm as a duchess, absorbed in the picture. On the streets it seemed that something was not quite right about him; he was too well dressed, too well fed, his folks made sure he ate right and never played truant from school. Apart from the occasional rotten vegetable lobbed at him from across the side of the road as he made his way home from school, he wasn't even paid the compliment of being thought worth tormenting. Joey got home, was given milk and cookies by his mother, and dreamt of homes that stank of bootleg hooch, where under-fed children in rags were beaten and abused by their mothers' latest lovers. Then Joey would sit for hours in his room and read about the criminals he knew were secretly behind every deal that was made in the city.

When Joey was twelve, his father announced that they were going to move out to what he called the country; the Depression hardly affected a man with his skills, and house prices were falling with the lack of demand. Now Joey could meet some nice new friends out there among the lakes and forests. Wouldn't that be fine? Joey smiled at the father he wished he could bring himself to despise. Inside, he decided to grasp at the chance to recreate himself in the image he desired.

Woodland Park was a suburb slotted between a lake and the woods. The Shanahans moved into a small house that shuddered when the freights on the adjacent railway thundered past and Joey went out to explore the streets as if he were entering a foreign country.

He might have been disappointed by the rows of tract houses and the Sunday streets full of churchgoers, if his

226

father had not told him of an event that took place some ten years or so before. According to a neighbour, Bonnie and Clyde had sped past that very same corner you go past each morning on your way to school, and old Mr Eisenbaum had then been able to tell the police chasing them which way the gangsters had gone.

Bonnie and Clyde. Of all the heroes glorified in Joey's pulp fiction, they had most securely taken hold of his imagination. The handsome man and the beautiful woman who had not paused to live the lives of dreary old saps in suburbia, but had taken charge of their lives, stolen cars and lived off the fools who were willing to settle for a life of slavery in a factory or office. Joey examined the turning in the road for tyre marks that might have been holy relics; the thought that his idols had once passed this way filled him with pride in the locality. From now on, though Joey by day at home and at school, he would remake himself in the image of Clyde Barrow, speeding across a sleeping America, his foot down hard on the gas towards yet another victorious battle with the forces of dull righteousness.

The throttle on the Doctor's black Austin was stiff, and when he forced it down the car jerked forward in convulsions.

'Young man, please take a little care.'

Joey began to wonder whether he had done the right thing in taking this old lady along. He was sure that the hostages, that was the word, that the real Clyde had taken were less of a pain in the butt.

'I can't see a thing in this goddam fog.'

'That is all the more reason to drive slowly.'

Clyde narrowly avoided running the car into a ditch and they continued forcing a way into the darkness. Where was he going? He had to admit that things might have been easier for a gangster who had all of the sunsets in the mid West to disappear into or a Canadian or Mexican border to make a run for. He decided to ask the lady where they could hide.

'Hide? You can't hide for ever anywhere. Sooner or later they'll come and find you, and things will only go from bad to worse.'

Clyde knew she was right. He began to wonder why he had let his fantasy life take over so completely. Life in barracks was miserable, and the invasion his unit was being trained for didn't seem anything like the sort of gun battle that had fascinated him at the movies. He thought that if only he could get away and – what then? Rob a bank, drive away and find some haven of peace where he could settle down on the fringes of legality, never have to march on a square again? He drove on, taking turnings at random. He should have run away from his life long before, should never have allowed the promise of home cooking and clean clothes each morning to drag him back from school each day. The fantasy of hitting the open road and living free had vanished now he tried to grasp it, and he realized that he was just another deserter. He wondered if he could be shot for his crime. Then the car jerked to a halt. Outside the steamy windows, he could just make out a bank of trees.

'What's wrong with this thing?'

'I should have said that we've run out of petrol.'

'Where can we get some more.'

'You can't without coupons, which I don't for a moment imagine that you have. The Doctor, of course, has a special supply for his work, which you seem to have wasted. I can only hope you're proud of yourself.'

Joey knew that he had to get away from the stranded vehicle; that was the first thing the police would look for.

A professional would have arranged for another getaway car to be placed here for his escape.

'Come on, we're getting out of here.'

'Where do you imagine going? We'll catch our deaths out there.'

'Anywhere. Somewhere we can hide for the night.' They got out of the car and looked around in the empty night.

It is difficult to say whether Miss Sefton would have been alarmed had she fully understood the nature of her predicament; she was a calm and capable woman in a crisis. But she had simply never heard of the desperate bandits and nicknamed Italians who had haunted Joey's childhood, had no idea of the implications of 'being taken for a ride'. She shivered a little in the chill of the fog outside the car, though.

Joey, of course, had no idea where they were. Miss Sefton was scarcely any the wiser. It was clear that they had to get away from the car, and stepped over a ditch and through the gap in a thorn bush. The steam from their mouths seemed to melt into the surrounding greyness, and they pressed on into the dark obscurity of a winter evening.

There was a sudden slight breeze that came and blew through the trees just then, scooping out the fog for a moment from the hollow in which they were standing. Joey shuddered a moment and pulled his raincoat tighter around himself. Miss Sefton shuddered also, but not from the cold. Her feet seemed suddenly rooted to the ground.

'Come on, we've got to keep moving.'

Miss Sefton had to force her legs to move forwards from the path. She knew precisely where they were now.

It was clear that they had driven around in circles on leaving the village; a driver who didn't know those roads intimately could not have done otherwise. But chance dictated that they had passed the lane where village boys and girls had courted long before another war, and blundered upon the path where Reggie had led Matilda over to their bower, that patch of ferns, to talk of civilization and progress but never love. The fog danced a little higher around Miss Sefton's elbows, and she walked on behind another male form in a military uniform that he seemed far too young to be wearing.

Yes, there could be no doubt about it now. They were approaching the ditch, the stream, whatever it was, the running water where Reggie had thrown broken twigs and Matilda had watched them float away. A warm prickle of recollection crept over her and drove out the cold from her body.

'We'd better stop here,' said Joey. 'No, better on the other side. They might hunt us down with bloodhounds.' This he had also seen in a movie about jail breaks.

He was a sloppy soldier, far more so than was to be expected. He had taken his small-arms training far more from Hollywood gunmen than from the constant repetitions of army instructors, thought the reiterations on the use of the safety catch necessary only for the hicks he was stuck there with. As they stepped across the water on slippery stones, he lost his balance and fell down flailing. As he hit the stream bed flat on his side, there was a muffled thump in his coat pocket. He sat on the wet gravel and gave out a moan from the back of his throat, far more from despair and frustration than pain. He had shot himself in the foot.

'Jesus Christ. Oh, Jesus Christ.' Matilda helped him out of the stream, half dragged him across to the opposite bank.

It was clear that they could neither go forward nor back. Miss Sefton knew that sooner or later the police would come after them, but thought it best not to point the fact out to the young man. There was no need to make an armed man desperate.

Immobile on the stream bank, they shivered, sat and then huddled together in silence. Joey put his coat around Miss Sefton's shoulder. In the strained light of the day, she could see his face was white. His lower lip was clenched in his teeth and colourless.

'Why did you do this?' The young man began to shake convulsively. No tears came, but Miss Sefton was rocked back and forwards inside the coat by his movements. After some moments he calmed down and tried to begin: 'You can't imagine, you just can't imagine . . . '

What? He would have liked to be able to describe the cold, the loneliness, the fear, the sheer desolation of belonging to a military machine that was gathering the strength to throw itself across the sea at a wall of concrete and barbed wire. In the world there were tanks and bombs and guns and a million ways to die but only one to be born, and Al Capone would never have got into this mess and not even Eliot Ness and the Untouchables could make a deal with him now. He was cold in this freezing country and would have given anything to be back in Woodlawn Park, or waiting for his Pa outside the slaughter-house, or best of all safe by the hot stove with a comic book while his mother thumbed her way through the *Saturday Evening Post*. But Joey did not have the words. He rocked and shuddered and muttered like a litany: 'You can't imagine, you just can't imagine.'

Miss Sefton held him closer to keep him still. The wound didn't seem too serious, everything would be fine soon enough if he didn't try to move. But however hard she tried to remember what she'd learned in first-aid classes at the village hall, her thoughts were elsewhere – everywhere. She thought of the clean-limbed sons and daughters she had once planned to have with Reggie as their contribution to the peopling of the new Utopia; if they had married after the Great War they could have had a son the same age as this soldier, but then he could have gone and been killed like Reggie had, only that was nonsense because Reggie's death had prevented their having sons and daughters in the first place. Then she thought of Reggie and wondered if he had died a hero; perhaps at the end he had crouched and trembled and there was no way that she could ever know if his courage was just an act for the benefit of his mother and her. After this there was some confusion, and Miss Sefton had to concentrate hard to clear her mind that was confusing place and time and the feeling of a man in her arms under the open sky again.

After an indefinite time, she became aware that the moon had appeared. The soldier had stopped moving, lost consciousness or drifted into sleep. Miss Sefton gently laid him back on a bed of brown and crackling ferns, and wrapped his coat around them as best she could. She slept little, but stared at the soft pink flesh of his closed eye-lids as she had once stared into Reggie's candid blue eyes.

A thumping of boots through the undergrowth an hour or so before dawn shook Miss Sefton out of her light doze. She stood up and saw a caped policeman approaching with two other men in steel helmets and raincoats similar to the sleeping boy's. When they made out her form in the mist, they blew a harsh note on their whistles, and the policeman stomped across the stream. Miss Sefton tried to quieten them for fear that they might wake the sleeping boy, but they didn't hear her concerned mutterings.

'Wake up, asshole!' bellowed one of them in Joey's ear, and then turned quickly to Miss Sefton and apologized for his lack of respect in a lady's presence.

Back at the road two American Army jeeps had parked alongside an English police car. The first two Military Policemen left Joey leaning askew against the hood of their vehicle with the weight off his leg, and were checking that Miss Sefton had come to no harm. Just as the English policeman was helping her into the back of his car to take her home, one of the Americans spotted Joey reclining against the hood of the jeep. He did not know about the wound in his foot, and took his casual posture to be an act of defiant bravado just typical of that little creep. He strode over, and cracked him across the belly with his billy-club. Joey folded over in the middle like the jack-knife he had carried in his pocket throughout his Chicago boyhood.

An American colonel came to apologize to Miss Sefton for this unfortunate incident. The authorities had decided it was best that it should not be publicized, no point at all in upsetting relations between two great allies and the friendship of two great peoples. Miss Sefton agreed, of course, and said that she hoped the authorities would not be too hard on a poor, downhearted and confused boy. The Colonel assured her that there were recognized channels for dealing with absence without leave and car theft, Shanahan wasn't the first and sure wouldn't be the last boy to go off the straight and narrow and there was no reason to worry about him. He would never come to trouble her again. Miss Sefton said that that would be a great relief, and smiled and offered the Colonel another cup of tea.

She had saved Joey from the far weightier charge of armed robbery by silently returning the coins to the locked drawer in the post office the next morning. In his nervousness, he had not even taken them from her. She could not, however, save him from the pain that followed the extraction of a .45 slug by a clumsy medic, the three-month

233

spell in the glass-house that followed, or the bullets that caught him in the stomach in the early morning of the following June, folding him across the middle once again as he ran forward across the sand of a Normandy beach. But Miss Sefton knew nothing of this. After the war she sometimes vaguely wondered what had happened to the boy who must have been sent to France before the war ended; then her thoughts would jump to Reggie like the words of a song on a cracked gramophone record. Occasionally she thought of drawing on her savings and going over to Flanders to visit her fiancé's grave. But no, she would think almost immediately, she was not getting any younger and should keep hold of any money she had put aside for her old age. There were now no brown strands at all to be seen among the grey hair she brushed out before bedtime, sitting at her dressing-table with the two vases of dried ferns cut from both sides of the stream placed in front of the mirror.

AN EVER FIXÈD MARK

L. V. Sheridan

L. V. Sheridan was born in Birmingham. She originally trained as an actress and worked in theatre and TV. She started to write seriously three years ago and is currently working on a novel, a collection of short stories and is collaborating on a children's book.

AN EVER FIXÈD MARK

A wistful smile strayed across Peggy's lips as she stood at the kitchen sink, drying her best china cups and saucers with a blue and white checked tea-towel that was, like Peggy, a bit frayed at the edges. Perhaps this time he might stay home for good. After all, he was no spring chicken any more. He couldn't carry on indefinitely being hauled up in court and being sent down. Not at his age. Besides it wasn't good for his health. He'd had a terrible cough ever since his last stay in the Scrubs. Perhaps she'd have him home for good now.

She looked out of the window anxiously, across the estate at the graceless blocks of grey concrete flats. A menacing slash of graffiti disfigured one wall and the fencing around the grass was broken in places. A small sapling, planted hopefully by the local council, fighting to survive repeated assaults by local children, reached out its scrawny branches to the sky. Peggy finished drying, shook the tea-towel carefully and hung it on a hook by the sink. Then she unrolled the sleeves of her best blouse and fastened the buttons at the wrist before checking carefully that her marcasite brooch was still securely in place at the collar. Oh she did so hope he'd like it here – wouldn't miss the old place too much. If it had been left to her she would never have moved but the man from the Town Hall had said there was no choice, what with all the redevelopment and that. Still it was clean here, and freshly decorated and the bathroom was beautiful but ... somehow, well it wasn't home was it? She smoothed the Nottingham lace tablecloth carefully and placed the cups and saucers on the best tray. She'd told him, of course, last time she went to visit, told him how to get here, what bus to catch and all that. She would have gone to meet him but he'd said 'no – do as we've always done. I'll come to you.' She sighed heavily. It seemed strange really when you thought about it, ending up here. Of course, they'd been bombed out twice in the Blitz, once in Whitechapel and once in Lambeth, but it was different then, people moved all the time but in the same areas, and it was all rented, none of these mortgages they all had today.

She moved across to the dresser and opened the cupboard door to check the contents. Six tins of best red salmon, three of tongue, three fruit salad and two bottles of his favourite sauce. He missed his sauce did Mo, when he was inside. She closed the door reassured. It was all there, she had forgotten nothing. That was all Mo asked for when he came home – a nice salmon salad with chips and a good strong cup of hot tea. She glanced nervously at the clock on the mantlepiece. Not long now ...

In the living-room she straightened the net curtains again. Outside, across the way, a young woman in a track suit, hair bleached peroxide yellow, hurried along pushing a pram and pulling a reluctant toddler by the hand. Strange how distant people were around here. Not a cheery good morning to be had from any of them. Not like the old place. Everyone knew all your business there, but not in a nosy way, just friendly like. You could fall down the stairs here and lie injured for weeks and no one would notice – or care for that matter.

It was queer really, all the things people could afford nowadays, all the money, never had it so good. Didn't seem any happier for it. Microwave ovens, wall-to-wall carpets and holidays abroad. Peggy took her handkerchief out of her skirt pocket and wiped her nose. It was a nice cambric hankie with a border of white lace and an initial 'P' worked in pink thread in one corner. She had seen them in the local supermarket last year, four in a box. So much nicer to use than those dreadful paper tissues. Still, that was society nowadays, use it up and throw it away. Why you only had to stand in the queue at the supermarket on a Saturday morning and look into the trolleys to see what sort of wives and mothers women made today. No wonder they didn't have any money to spare! Just bags of crisps, bottles of coke and frozen foods. It wasn't surprising half the children on the estate looked so pale and unhealthy. Some of them had never tasted fresh greens. And all that litter everywhere . . . she pursed her lips in disgust . . . not very nice. Years ago people took pride in their surroundings. They didn't seem to care any more today. She fingered the lace-trimmed nets at the window dubiously, hoping Mo would approve. The man in the market said they were best quality. Well, if they shrank at first wash she'd be there asking for her money back. Material today wasn't half as good as it used to be. Now that was good cotton lace she'd bought for their first home all those years ago. It lasted and lasted until she was sick of seeing it hanging there. Nice little house they'd had when they first married, all those years ago . . . just off Broughton Road, where the old cinema used to be. Nothing grand, just two up and two down, ten and sixpence a week. No bathroom, of course, not then, but a lovely little garden at the back filled with old-fashioned rose bushes. Mo loved his bit of lawn and his plants . . . had sort of green fingers Mo had. When he hadn't been inside, during the war and all that, when he was off duty from the fire service, he'd be busy down at his allotment. Mo's runner beans were the envy of the neighbourhood. One evening during the blackout, when the bombing was heavy and Mo was on call putting out that big fire they had at Regent Works over by the canal, a gang of lads went down to the allotment, goodness knows how they found it in the dark, but they did, and they stripped every plant bare and dug up his onions and all the cabbages and his carrots too. Mo went mad when he went down the next day. 'You can't trust any of the buggers around here,' he'd said. But food in those days meant a lot to people and it wasn't as if Mo kept it all for us, he always shared it around with all the neighbours. No, Mo could never stomach that kind of dishonesty. Say what you would, Mo was honest in his own way, he never stole off his own kind, that is. 'I might do a bit of burglary and a bit of petty larceny, but I only ever take from them that can afford it.' Peggy's soft brown eyes moistened. And he was generous too! When Mrs Marshall, who lived two doors away from them in Henry Street, when her baby died of TB and she had just put her husband and two daughters under the ground, he paid for a regular funeral for it. Only eighteen months old it was, pretty little thing with golden hair and big blue eyes. Mo took a bit of a shine to it, even talked of adopting it. He was so cut up when it died. Of course, in those days you thought nothing of kids – dying that is. Only half the babies born lasted until they were five. It was nothing to see a coffin being carried out down the path every month or so. Of course, after the war with the free orange juice and baby milk, things improved no end.

It was a nice flat but she wished it wasn't so bleak. The old place was cosy. He was used to it. There was so much concrete here and those dreadful lifts . . . sometimes in the mornings they stank! He wouldn't like that at all.

She'd bought a few pots of scarlet geraniums for the

240

small balcony, to look cheerful and brighten the place up a bit. Perhaps when he'd got himself settled he might buy some seeds and set a flower-box for the summer. It was a shame about the garden. Having to leave it all behind. She wondered what would happen to it. Ploughed in, she supposed. She sighed. All those lovely bulbs he'd set down when they first moved there – they made a beautiful show in the spring, just like the Chelsea Flower show – such a pity. And the dwarf flowering cherry – he'd bought that on their wedding anniversary, just after his release from Pentonville – a lifetime of memories in that garden. All gone, she shook her head – more's the pity. He'd been upset about his garden. She'd seen that when she told him but of course, if it had been up to her she wouldn't have moved. It wasn't necessary at their time of life. You got to know the people around you, you got settled, you knew where you were. Gem Street had suited them very well. The house wasn't posh but it was home and they were happy there. Last year they moved old Mrs Pottifer, from across the way at number eight. She was one of the first to go. Born there she was, all her family were and her sons and daughters too. Lived there all her life, she had. But they moved her all the same and she never got over it. Peggy met her daughter in Tesco's months later. 'Honest to God, Mrs Stevens,' she'd said, 'hand on heart, it's finished my mother. Lost the will to live she has ever since they moved her into that high-rise block!' Peggy shuddered. How cruel people were! People in authority, that was. And there'd been nothing wrong with Mrs Pottifer, nothing at all. Going on sixty-five she was, sprightly as the day, looked fair to make seventy until they moved her. Peggy hoped Mo wouldn't mope or get depressed or anything. She'd tried her level best to make the place as nice as she could, new curtains, a new rug for the lounge and new bedspreads from Marks and Spencer, all co-ordinating in a beautiful shade of blue. His favourite chair was waiting for him, near the fireplace, so that he could watch the telly in comfort. He liked to sit and watch television when he came home. They had a set inside, of course, but everyone had to watch and you couldn't choose the programme. Mo liked watching those programmes about wildlife and animals and birds. He loved animals, Mo did. They had a little pup a few years back called Beth, but she jumped the back fence one morning and ran out into the road and a bus went over her and since then they'd not bothered, although Peggy had often thought about getting another dog for the company like, when Mo was away, but she'd never got around to it. Mo said only a few months ago that when he'd got out, he'd go along to Battersea Dogs' Home and pick a dog up. 'Some poor little bugger stuck behind bars that nobody wants, waiting for the high-jump,' he'd said, but dogs weren't allowed in these flats, the rent man said. Peggy hoped Mo wouldn't be too disappointed. They could have a budgie though, if they liked, but Mo always said he hated to see anything caged.

There was nowhere to hang the washing either. Peggy missed that. There was something wonderful about freshly washed sheets blowing on the line in the wind. It was little things like that you missed in these flats. There was a launderette within walking distance but the clothes didn't smell really clean, and she hated using the same machines along with everyone else, and the place was so dismal, and the woman who did the service washes never smiled. No, Peggy much preferred doing her own washing at home and pegging it out to dry in the garden, in the sunshine. There was no real satisfaction in a trip to the launderette, none whatsoever. But then it was like the shops . . . in the old days you could slip round to the corner shop and get your groceries, and have a chat at the same time and catch up on the local gossip, and the shopkeeper treated you friendly like.

She hurried across to the sofa and plumped up the cushions for the umpteenth time. Oh, she did hope he'd like it here. She did hope he'd settle down all right. She bit her lip and surveyed the room critically. On the wall her wedding group in a gold-painted frame smiled down at her. Thirty-seven years together! Peggy pushed a worn hand proudly through her recently permed grey hair. Thirty-seven years! Still, when all said and done, it hadn't been so bad after all.

She remembered what her mother had said the evening before the wedding. 'You'll never know a day's happiness with that lad, our Margaret! Mark my words! He's a bad lot. Can't keep his hands off anything he can't – can't help it! It's in the blood. All his family's been inside . . .' A glimmer of a smile played across Peggy's lips. Of course, her mother had been right. Mo couldn't help it, he couldn't keep his hands to himself, not even when he tried. Not that Peggy condoned his ways and as long as she'd lived, she'd never laid a finger on anything that wasn't hers, but some of us are made different and there was no real wickedness in Mo, not like some of those 'psycho' what's-a-names they called them that you read about in the papers. Mo just went the way of his family; like her mother said, it was in the blood. Mo wasn't his real name, of course. He'd been christened Mortimer but no one ever called him that. He'd been Mo ever since he was six weeks old and she'd always been Peggy, except to her mother. Mo said she'd been born a Peggy and she was inclined to believe him. Margaret was far too stuffy and formal like. Not her at all.

Mo's mother was the only respectable one in his family. Plump and placid looking she was, with pale golden hair

243

always done up into a knot on the top of her head and pinned with a brown shell comb inlaid with mother-of-pearl. She had a strange way of walking, like a large goose. Peggy remembered, clear as yesterday, seeing her one day behind the fence in the garden pegging out the washing. This was before Mo and Peggy got together. Jimbo Stevens, he was about ten then, dashed down the path, behind his mother and dodged behind the coal-shed. Minutes later a fat constable, perspiring heavily, burst into the garden. There was a heated conflab between him and Mrs Stevens, who was all affronted dignity. The copper eventually exited, scratching his head and little Jimbo emerged from the coal-heap, grinning from ear to ear, his jersey full of apples! Mrs Stevens' caught Peggy's eye and she winked! Peggy didn't know which way to look, but she had to smile. What a family!

She had always had a soft spot for Lenny, Mo's father. He was a thin, quiet sort of man, always smartly dressed in a sports jacket and pale trousers. Very gently spoken. Her mother said he'd been inside when he was younger but he never went away when Peggy knew him. It was a bit of a mystery what he did for a living. He was in some sort of business with a chap called Wally. Mo said it was a jewellery business but he didn't go into details and Peggy knew better than ask. 'What you don't know, you can't tell,' Mo always said. It quite probably was jewellery, perhaps wholesale or something. Mother said most likely he was a fence. She would! Len gave Peggy a beautiful gold pendant on her wedding day. That was apart from the canteen of cutlery and the bone china tea-set.

Len was always generous. She'd never had such a beautiful thing in all her life. Set with garnets it was and she wore it with her wedding dress. Then her mother went and said out loud at the reception that it had been nicked! She'd never forgiven her mother for saying that. Oh the shame of it! She remembered Len's face as he went and fetched the receipt and handed it to her mother to look at. There it was in black and white: H. Samuel – *paid* the sum of eight pounds and ten shillings! Her mother looked right silly after that, of course, but it left a nasty taste in everyone's mouth. She had been so ashamed and never felt the same about her mother after that. It was like that with her sister Elsie. Just because she'd married a clerk in the local bank she felt it gave her the right to look down on Peggy and Mo. Didn't want to be connected with anyone who'd 'been inside'. Well everyone had a right to their own opinions and feelings and she and Elsie had never really hit it off together, so it was no skin off her nose if she wanted to keep herself to herself.

Apart from Jimbo and Mo there was Larry. Larry was into window cleaning. He had a good round and several lads to help him and then it got around that while they were washing windows, they were marking out houses and returning later on and breaking and entering. Larry went to France in the war, came back and sailed for Canada the same week. Broke his mother's heart, it did. He was her favourite son, Larry was. Ted, the middle lad, got married to a girl he met when he was on leave in Manchester. It didn't go off very well though and when he got three years for stealing from a warehouse, she up and left him, taking their little girl with her. She wasn't prepared to put with 'that' she told Peggy, even if she was! Poor Ted died of cancer in 1953.

Mo went straight for quite a while after they were first married. Then the war broke out and for a while it seemed he might be called up. Peggy couldn't sleep waiting for the letter from the Ministry of Labour to arrive. Then it did and he had to go but he was turned down, thank God, as his chest was weak and he'd had a couple of bouts of rheumatic fever as a kid. That was at the start of the war, of course, later they took every poor bugger they could get. Anyway, Mo was drafted into the fire service which meant at least Peggy didn't have to go through all the anxiety and worry that so many women did, what with their men away at the Front. Say what you like, it's women who always have to bear the brunt of everything. Men get away with it easy. She nodded. Yes, even her Mo . . . when all is said and done they were all like little boys, even the best of them. Mo had his good points, of course, she'd never say a word against him in public, not to anyone. He always saw to it that the rubbish was taken out and he never swore or used bad language or let her lift anything heavy. And when he was at home he'd always wash up on a Sunday after she'd cooked the roast. 'You sit down now Peg, put your feet up,' he'd say and he'd always jump up and make her a nice hot cup of tea when she got in from shopping or whatever. Not like some men she could name . . . 'Sit down . . . I'll make the tea love . . . ' on goes the kettle and the next thing you know it's steaming its head off and they're slumped in a chair waiting for you to hand them a cup and a plate of biscuits into the bargain!

No, he had his good points but sometimes of course it had been difficult for her, like the very first time when the police came to the house. Oh, she'd nearly died of shame! She'd learned to cope over the years with that sort of thing but her family had always been straight as a die. Respectable like. She felt awful too, going into the corner shop and hearing the customers whispering behind her back, but she held her head up high and didn't flinch . . . looked them straight in the eye. Just let them drop one hint . . . and she was ready for them. Just let them say one word against Mo and she'd go for them like a tiger. But inside it hurt because she knew he wasn't really bad, and she would have liked people to respect him like she did, but that's life.

You had to take the rough with the smooth and she knew what she was getting into when she married Mo. You had to take the good and bad in people and work it out from there. She'd not liked going to see him in prison either. They were very strict in those days; no open prisons like they have today and newspapers and books and all that sort of thing. The warders were down on you like a shot and they wanted to rub your nose in it and make you feel like dirt. But she'd never lost her dignity, or her pride. Always held her head high and they'd come to respect her, the decent screws had. But she knew that Mo was more of a man than half of them were, for all their uniforms and prying eyes. He had more heart inside him than those that went to church every Sunday, all togged up in their best. Hadn't Mr James, the last vicar at St Michaels, said as much? 'Mrs Stevens,' he'd said last time he called collecting for the jumble sale, 'Mrs Stevens, God says "In my Father's house are many mansions".' Not that she and Mo were regular churchgoers themselves. It wasn't easy for Mo, when he was always being up for breaking one of His commandments. Although, as Mr James said, the church is as open to sinners as to saints – much more so. Not a bad chap, Mr James. Peggy was sorry when he left. Went up to the coast, off Cumbria. Well he wouldn't find a large flock of sinners up there, she wouldn't think, but who knows!

She looked round the room. She was glad she'd had the gas fire installed. She was paying for it on the weekly, but she'd tell Mo she'd put the money by in the local social club savings fund. Mo wouldn't allow anything in the house on HP. He always paid cash. So, it was a little lie, but a white one. The electric heating here was clean but you couldn't get a real warm by it and it was very expensive, and the thing was he felt the cold, now that he was getting older. She worried about him. He'd got so much thinner of late. There was hardly any flesh on him. What with that and his cough . . . it wasn't good.

She'd told him time and time again that he ought to see the prison doctor and see if there was anything they could do to help his chest. She didn't say much but secretly his smoking worried her. She knew better than to ask him to give up his cigarettes. He wouldn't. Besides he didn't have many little perks. The occasional glass of beer down at the pub with a few of his mates on a Friday evening, and that was that, and he wasn't even as keen on that as he used to be. Now she couldn't nag him about his fags could she? In all fairness not really. He had cut down a lot just lately, and switched to one of those low tar brands but she'd read about lung cancer in the papers and it scared her to death. Sometimes when he coughed, the sweat seemed to spring out on his head, and he couldn't get his breath. It frightened her that did, more than she would like to say. Sometimes when she looked at him, her heart turned over. 'He won't make old bones . . . ' she could hear her mother's words, plain as yesterday. A cold shiver ran down her spine. He had to stay – as long as she did anyway! There was no way she could part with him, could carry on without him being there. People might smile, point out that he hadn't been there a lot of the time, and he hadn't, but that was different. Mo WAS there – safe in some prison somewhere or other, but he was THERE and Peggy knew that, and there was the comfort of visiting days. If Mo . . . well, she couldn't bear to think about it . . . if Mo wasn't around she didn't know what she would do. She really didn't – no use joking about it. She'd be finished. No one to keep the home going for, no expectation, no days to faithfully tick off the calendar every week ... whatever would she do? She'd have to make sure he went straight down to sign on with the local GP just as soon as he could. That cough of his worried her ... Thirty-seven years is a long time. She fingered the gold band on her left hand lovingly. It had never been off her finger, not once in all those years. It would be on her hand when they placed her in her coffin.

Of course, they'd had their ups and downs like any couple. Life isn't a bowl of cherries and at times it hadn't been easy. When they were first married and Mo went inside you didn't get social security like they do today, and Peggy had had to turn her hand to anything to keep the home together. It was a good way, in some respects, they hadn't had kids. Not that she wouldn't have minded a couple, but it wouldn't have been fair on the kids, not really, with their dad always away inside. But anyway, kids hadn't happened and as Mo often remarked, it was no use brooding on things that didn't happen, it was bad enough thinking about things that did. Anyway, they'd hung on together, not like today's lot, one sharp word or the potatoes burnt, and it was off out the door, that's that! Of course, he'd thumped her occasionally but only when he'd had a bit to drink, never when he was sober ... oh, never then. She'd give him that. She checked the clock in the kitchen again. What time had they said ... ten-thirty? She smoothed the tablecloth again, then wandered back into the living-room and perched down on the edge of a chair, picking at her nails nervously.

She looked up at her wedding photograph again. She'd chosen it all of course. It might have been different if she'd listened to her mother. Peggy had been a bright girl, bright enough to go to grammar school. After she'd left she'd taken shorthand and typing at evening-school and found a job in a posh insurance office. Her mother had been hoping

for much greater things. Peggy met Mo at the High Street
Palais de Danse one Saturday night. Her mother was livid.
'Throwing it all away on him,' she'd said! But Peggy had
made up her mind. There was something about him she
couldn't resist. Something deep inside her, reached out for
him, deep inside her heart, arousing a wild passionate
tenderness. Whenever she looked at him she felt it. She still
did. It was a strange thing when she thought about it.

She could have fought against it she supposed, but the
long and the short of it was she hadn't. Well what was the
point of it anyway? Not that she had ever really understood
her feelings for Mo or the reasons for her loyalty but
whatever you said about him, she loved him. Oh not in a
lovey-dovey, sloppy sort of way but in the truest sense of
being. She'd stuck with him through thick and thin and it
didn't matter how long he was inside Mo knew sure as
daylight, that when he got out Peg would be waiting for
him with a nice salmon salad and a nice hot cup of tea.
And that was something worth having. Mo said as much
and many a mate of his agreed. It wasn't every man inside
who could boast that his missus would be at home waiting
for him when he got out. No, today they were all too busy
getting dolled-up and going off with the lodger or a fancy
man. But Peg kept faith and Mo knew it. Not that she'd
ever looked at another man since their wedding day but
Mo had spelt it out. 'I'll break your neck if I find out you've
been up to something while I'm inside.' She'd laughed.
'Look at another woman and I'll break yours, Mo Stevens,'
she'd shouted back. And he hadn't . . . at least, not as far
as she knew. If he had, of course . . . behind her back . . .
she trembled, her heart constricting. Once, just once, she'd
found a scrap of paper in his jacket pocket . . . no she
wouldn't even think about it . . . ! She banished the memory from her mind, stamping it out of existence. Oh no . . .

not even the thought . . . she wouldn't be able to bear it. Her heart would break. Better not know, ever.

She saw a speck of dust on the teak coffee table and fled into the kitchen to fetch a duster. Mo liked a clean house, say what you will. Not that Peggy hadn't always kept things spotless but Mo had a knack of noticing if things weren't just so. She polished the table until it shone and tucked the duster back in the drawer. Oh, she did so hope he'd be happy here. It wasn't so bad when you got used to it. She hadn't liked it herself the first few weeks, but you got used to it after a bit and there was a nice little newsagents within walking distance where Mo could get his *Daily Mirror* and his packet of cigarettes every morning, and Mr Patel was ever so friendly, and ever so obliging, oh yes, very obliging indeed. Ten-thirty! Her stomach began to churn and waves of dizziness swept over her. God knows why! She'd been through it often enough before but somehow she'd never got used to these reunions, never learnt to cope. If he'd got straight on to a bus and the traffic was clear, he should be at the door in fifteen minutes time. She hurried into the bedroom and going to the dressing-table, opened a drawer and rummaged through it. Her fingers closed around a small bottle of Tweed perfume and she took it out and dabbed the stopper on her neck and behind her ears. Oh God, he'd be here any minute! She checked her hair in the mirror, eyes shining, her face touched with youth again. Oh, she could almost see him there, stepping off the bus, his gaunt figure hurrying along the pavement towards her, the familiar brown paper parcel clutched under his arm . . . She moistened her lips in readiness for his kiss, savouring the dryness of his cheek against her mouth and she laughed out loud. It didn't matter that he was tired and grey, that he was an old lag who couldn't keep his hands to himself, she loved him, would always love him. He was her Mo.

They'd weathered a few storms together, but they'd had their rainbows too! Yes, Sirrah!

A line of poetry flashed across her memory from her youth . . . a poem? A verse? No, a sonnet! Yes, that was it! A sonnet by Shakespeare, always been one for reading had Peggy. She remembered now learning it by heart at school . . . what were the words . . . ? Something about love . . . she stood still in the middle of the room, trying so hard to pierce the mists of time . . . trying to remember . . .

> 'Let me not to the marriage of true minds
> Admit impediments. Love is not love
> Which alters when it alteration finds,
> Or bends with the remover to remove . . .

She faltered, desperately willing the words to return. Oh, come on Peggy love, you knew it so well once . . . she closed her eyes tightly, concentrating with all her might.

> 'Or bends with the remover to remove:
> Oh no! it is an ever-fixèd mark,
> That looks on tempests and is never shaken . . .

She opened her eyes quickly. That was it! 'An ever fixèd mark'! She repeated the line to herself triumphantly. Of course, that explained it all. That was what her love for Mo was – an ever-fixèd mark! She understood at last.

The door-bell chimed hesitantly and she almost jumped out of her skin. Smoothing her skirt down, her heart beating ten-to-the-dozen, she ran into the hall, blushing like a schoolgirl.

A SEEING LESSON

William Walker

William Walker was born in London and educated at Cambridge. He later moved to Gloucestershire where he has worked as a public librarian, a porter in a radiotherapy unit and a night janitor. Although he has had a couple of magazine stories and travel articles published this is the first time in book form.

A SEEING LESSON

In 1939 the novelist Aldous Huxley, his sight failing, began to practise certain techniques of visual re-education. The Bates Method, devised by an American oculist of that name, involves such procedures as 'sunning', 'swinging', 'shifting' and (perhaps less felicitously) 'flashing'. In his book *The Art of Seeing*, Huxley records his own rapid progress: 'Within a couple of months I was reading without spectacles . . .' He has advice for those who dream of doing likewise. Achieve a state of 'dynamic relaxation' and you may be granted sudden flashes of normal vision, though these will be short-lived at first. This is not a book for someone hoping for a quick 'cure' from such stubborn ocular distortions as myopia (short sight) and hypermetropia (long sight). Even Huxley wore spectacles to drive a car.

The Art of Seeing is also of interest as an extended metaphor on the workings of the imagination – the patient building-up of a picture from existing, barely recalled fragments of experience until at last, without strain, focus is achieved and clarity prevails.

Huxley died in 1963. In the same year this happened. During the Easter holidays a party of schoolboys travelled to France on an Anglo-French exchange scheme. They were quite young – many were going abroad for the first time. In a photographic album labelled 'School', black-and-white snapshots record the event. Here is one of a bulky child leaning against the deck rail of a cross-channel ferry, squinting in bright sunshine. Plump in a gabardine raincoat he affects insouciance but looks a slob. His name is Chris Huggett and his picture is being taken by a friend, Paul Berry.

Now it is Paul's turn to be photographed. Here he is, in tortoiseshell spectacles which give him a studious air; he is solemn-looking in a bland way, a little too preoccupied with the future to be enjoying the present. His is not a particularly interesting face. They have just come from the Tea Bar, several decks below, and to have ordered refreshment in any kind of bar is a matter for satisfaction, even if it is only tea. The truth is that Chris considers his friend a shade immature, with slight priggish tendencies. These Chris does his best to ridicule. Paul is also what Chris's parents call 'highly strung' — there has been the odd emotional upset, and there will no doubt be a few more.

The exchange works like this. Every Easter the participating English boys spend three weeks *en famille* with their French 'partners', pupils at a lycée in Paris. In the summer it is the turn of the French boys to visit south London for reciprocal hospitality. Such an arrangement is sometimes applied to established pen-friendships, but in this instance they are not pen-friends; the scheme is newly enacted each year when a questionnaire is sent round asking about hobbies, interests, personal characteristics, diversions offered for the holidays (this as a way of identifying gross social incongruities). Some luckless schoolmaster — whether in Paris or London is not clear — has the task of identifying compatibilities and pairing off the partners. So in effect you have a three-week-long blind date with a foreign adolescent. This Scheme is not for the faint-hearted.

The party is being escorted by a teacher of French, Mr

Oakley ('Hearts of Oak', or simply 'Hearts'). He has been glimpsed behind a fug of pipe smoke in one of the other types of bar on the ship. Hearts is about forty-five with a ponderous sense of humour, and a teacher of English at the Lycée and his wife are to have the pleasure of entertaining him. He will remain on hand in Paris in case problems arise.

'The object of the exercise is to improve your French,' Hearts has told some of the boys in class, 'but watch out. Your partners will be trying to *perfect* their English,' and he guffawed at this (by now) familiar play on *perfectionner*. They tittered resignedly.

At the same time he added a cautionary note. Sometimes, it appears, the Anglo-French Exchange pair do not get on too well together. Sometimes things get a trifle strained. 'French boys can be arrogant little buggers,' Hearts said. 'If you feel like throttling your partner, try not to. Go for a walk on your own to cool down. Remember you're British.' (Can Hearts really have come out with a sentiment as crudely chauvinistic as this? Well yes, because even he has some slight sense of irony.) As they know the British – the English – and the French have spent most of history at war with each other, this portion of the advice seems dubious.

But you should not fret about the Frogs when you are thirteen years old on a sea-deck and the sun is shining and your friends are throwing bread for the screaming seagulls to catch as the unimpressive cliffs of an alien coastline loom up. Paul is now seated on a bench and has removed his glasses, putting them away in a crush-proof case before taking out a ballpoint pen and holding this about ten inches away from his eyes, in his line of sight to the ship's mast. With his free hand he now covers each eye in turn. He is getting curious looks. People wonder if there is some problem with the masthead and glance up at it nervously.

'So how's the Method?' Chris asks him after a while, in a sarcastic tone. 'How's the focusing practice?'

Paul frowns and abandons the exercise. 'Sometimes I think the Method is working,' he says, 'if it's a sunny day at the weekend. Then I seem to do without my glasses all right. But I have to put them on for school and my eyes get used to them again . . . Perhaps I'll try not to wear them in Paris.'

'You'll get run over,' Chris tells him. 'The traffic will come from all directions. Hearts says French drivers are maniacs.' Paul knows he is sceptical about the Method. Physics has an explanation for short sight – it occurs when eyeballs are distorted lengthways so that the focus falls before the retina. If you have long eyeballs, Chris simply cannot see that sunlight and a few exercises will shorten them.

Paul puts his spectacles on before they reach Calais.

Then it is Paris, the warm, sweetish air, the drive through darkling streets. The Lycée, the little gathering in the dining-hall for refreshments, the welcoming ceremony. The elaborate effusive speech in French by the *directeur*, followed by Hearts's stumbling embarrassing reply ('*Eh bien* . . . '). Their hosts are much too polite not to laugh at his jokes, or can it be his accent?

And the pairing off. They already know roughly who and what to expect. Paul is destined for three weeks in the company of Jean-Claude; there is said to be a country house in Normandy as well as the Paris apartment. Names are called out, boys step forward to greet their partners, hoping they are not the boys they most dislike the look of. A few will be unlucky, and here it is at least as much a question of what Jean-Claude will make of Paul as vice versa. Paul leaves accompanied by Jean-Claude and his mother, Mme

Marret. When Chris sees him again three weeks later the shadow of not-quite-his-fault will hang over him.

Chris's own assigned partner, Bernard, is two years older – some problems at the linking-up stage, or as Hearts put it, 'You were left over.' While the two left-overs are not, on balance, glaringly incompatible they are not strikingly compatible either. Their relations will remain polite rather than warm. Bernard is at a different stage of development; already he inhabits a world of subterranean coffee-bars, of motor-scooters, tennis and girls. Particularly tennis *with* girls, though his performances in the doubles games Chris witnesses are heartlessly mocked by the dazzling creatures he seeks to impress. His parents are resigned to his way of life. After some token attention to the 'sights' of Paris (Bernard pronounces the Musée de l'Homme in all its fascinating ethnicity 'disgusting'), much of Chris's holiday is passed in the Gauloise-turbid air of seedy basement dens, where the craze of the day, of the decade, is for a table-football game called *le babyfoot.*

His *babyfoot* improves. So does his French. Most usefully, he acquires a good deal of dubious adolescent cant-talk and Parisian street-argot, some of which will later baffle and infuriate Hearts when playfully introduced into an essay. If this were to be Chris's story we would elaborate on Bernard's Paris, but it is not. After the holidays they shake hands and say au revoir offering protestations of genuine mutual esteem. They give sincere expression to pleasurable anticipations of their reunion in London this summer.

Paul Berry goes to sit on the dilapidated stone bench in a corner of the garden, or what passes for one, at Le Cyprès. The eponymous tree is between him and the house so he does not feel too self-conscious as he places a hand over

259

his left eye and begins an oscillating movement with his head, inclining it to describe an arc that very briefly allows the sun to shine in his right (open) eye. Back and forth. He repeats this with his other eye. He knows moderation is important when you are Sunning; a little is beneficial, any more is bad. In the early days of the Method a few people interpreted Sunning over-enthusiastically and stared at the sun, with serious consequences. Now he decides to practise some Rapid Shifts, and here the possibilities of the cypress occurred to him yesterday when M. Marret took a shot at a rook high in its branches – the foliage detail would be ideal for 'analytical looking', which short-sighted people are supposed to do to get out of the bad habit of peering.

It is Paul's mother who has been recommended (by one of her gossips at Mothers' Union) the book about the Method. She is anxious for Paul to Sun, Shift, Palm, Swing and Flash and so correct his short sight, and to please her he is giving it a try. He is open-minded. If you have difficulty in focusing it seems to him reasonable enough to give your eyes special practice, just as you might have remedial classes in Maths if necessary. The Method does include specific focusing exercises – you can jump-change the focus from a near object, such as a watch face, to a more distant one, a calendar on the wall, and back again. An important aspect of the Method is that you should try to do without mechanical focusing aids (spectacles) in the interest of restoring flexibility to the eye. Since they arrived in Normandy he has not worn his glasses at all. Jean-Claude is puzzled by this. Why isn't Paul wearing his lunettes as he did in Paris?

Paul sighs. He has baulked at the linguistic challenge of explaining the Method to Jean-Claude, but when pressed on one occasion (while trying out a complicated Swing-Shift) referred to 'exercises to help the eye' and left it at that.

Jean-Claude shrugged, a contortion which involves most of his face as well as his shoulders. 'The Henglish are crazy.' Actually Jean-Claude, who is an impulsive normal child, suspects that this unfathomable boy he must spend three weeks with, and then three more, may not be a typical English person. And whatever (he wonders) can the co-ordinators of the Scheme have supposed he and Paul might find in common? He cannot see anything at all.

Paul thinks he will end the present unusually long and concentrated eye session with the relaxation technique known as Palming. Not only does the eye benefit from total dark, just as from total light; the mind's eye, with its power to conjure up images, can teach the optical eye something about seeing. If you envisage perspectives, landscapes, converging roads, aerial views of the Panama Canal, you may begin to accustom the eyes to focusing on distant objects. Paul also finds the purple and gold plasma of the dark fascinating to watch as they swirl around and coalesce. He sits as if entranced with his eyes covered by the palms of his hands, and in this attitude is discovered by Jean-Claude.

'Paul? I'm sorry, what is wrong?'

Paul blinks in the light. 'Nothing . . . '

'I thought for a moment . . . ' Jean-Claude does not pursue this but delivers a surprising summons. 'There is an Englishwoman at the house asking for you.'

'An Englishwoman? Who? Who is she?'

'Just an Englishwoman.' (Shrug.)

Work on the Method suspended, Paul returns to the house with Jean-Claude. Unpredictability seems a major characteristic of a holiday in France; half an hour from now you could be doing anything. 'We are going to Normandy in ten minutes – please pack your valise.' 'We are going to Honfleur in five minutes.' 'We are going—' Well, you could be going anywhere. In the orderly suburban life of East

Ewell there is always forewarning, plans and preparations are made the evening before; whether there is a difference or Paul just doesn't understand the language, misses arrangements, he isn't sure. And now a strange Englishwoman. He can think only of one of his more restless honorary aunts – perhaps Aunt Vega has dropped by to say hello? It must be. At the thought of The Vegan he brightens and ahead of Jean-Claude pushes open the peeling ramshackle door of the house.

The dining-room: echoic, austere, unpapered. The face that turns to greet him from the group conversing by the window is unfamiliar, a chignon of blonde hair topping faintly lined features, and his smile for Aunt Vega freezes on his face.

' . . . And may I present M. le duc de Berry.' M. Marret, mock-deferential with his gravelly voice, is having his usual little joke on Paul's surname. In Paris there was even at his insistence a photograph of Paul standing in front of the Opéra (*Voilà, M. le duc devant l'Opéra*), where a fanatic had assassinated the actual Duke de Berry in 1820, after a performance of *Don Giovanni*. M. Marret himself, a squat, swarthy man, will spontaneously assume a Napoleonic pose for photographs, one arm tucked inside his jacket. He is said to have visited Elba.

'And Monsieur and Madame . . . ' Paul does not quite catch the name – Popelin? Poquelin. It seems they are old friends of the Marrets. Monsieur is a seriously tweedy type with dark hair and a ginger moustache. Madame explains in English, a little defensively, 'When you've lived in France for 30 years, Paul, you'll speak French as badly as I do.' Paul is unsure what might constitute a polite reply to this so makes none. And now, *à table*.

At table he is able to note that while Mme Poquelin speaks a confident fluent French her accent is not, indeed, all it might be. She takes her French easily – does not, for instance, trouble to roll the 'r' or to do anything un-English with it. So presumably if you have to speak the language constantly the strain is excessive unless, of course, you are willing to change your personality and become French. Rapid conversation being under way, much of it impenetrable, Paul attends to the first of the usual random succession of courses, some easily ingestible, others less so. The artichokes that appear seem unavoidable by virtue of their odd primacy, so he deals with his as cursorily as he dare, defoliating it with gusto and concealing beneath its debris the final, disgustingly soapy heart. With the shrimps he is faring better than last time, observing which parts the others discard (the sensation of swallowing an entire prickly-legged crustacean is not one to experience twice), when Mme Poquelin looks up from across the table to ask him in English how he has been spending his time at Le Cyprès?

Paul considers carefully. 'Well. We've been to Château-Gaillard, which was built by Richard the Lionheart. And to Honfleur. On the way back M. Marret bought a .22 and we did some shooting in the garden. M. Marret missed a rook . . . I missed the target.'

'Paul shoots like a blind man,' says Jean-Claude. It is true that without his spectacles Paul has had to concentrate hard to get his shots anywhere near the target.

'In French, please,' calls out M. Marret.

'No, Jacques, she addressed him in English!' says Mme Marret.

But Paul continues in his hesitant French. One has played at the ping-pong. Washed the cars. And been for promenades. In the evenings one regards a quiz on television, *l'Homme du Vingtième Siècle*. And one has eaten many *gâteaux à flan*. One can't buy them in England.

'That's true?' says M. Marret, appalled. 'No *flans*?'

'True, I'm afraid,' says Mme Poquelin sadly. 'The English custard tart is a poor thing . . . it's all pastry and pretension.'

Why Paul had to consider carefully: because there are things he cannot tell Mme Poquelin about. The smouldering competitiveness between him and Jean-Claude which started with too many boastful references to Nelson, Napoleon and the Battle of Waterloo and has continued with the odd trial of strength. A pity Jean-Claude is learning judo (the humiliation of being deposited on the floor so effortlessly and repeatedly, and the more terrible one of being seen in tears of frustration and panic – Jean-Claude's parents chancing to return at this awkward moment. 'Why were you enervated?' Jean-Claude was puzzled and genuinely concerned). The increasing wildness of things, the lengthening walks through the woods. The ongoing acrimonious debate about cricket – specifically, is it a game or a sport? A game, says Paul. A sport, says Jean-Claude. 'The Henglish are crazy.'

'The French are crazier.'

'You have not the Henglish humour.'

'The French have no humour to have.'

They bought catapults (as if to settle the matter) in the village store – heavy steel devices which Paul suspects would not be legal in his local toyshop. *Le Cache-cache* is a variant of hide-and-seek played with catapults. There was a scream from the battered woodshed with a hole in the door big enough to admit a cunningly aimed pebble; Jean-Claude got a nasty bump just above his right eye, Paul a nasty glimpse of might-have-been. Someone who ought to be wearing glasses can do harm with a catapult. Someone who has bad ideas can do harm.

Nor can he tell Mme Poquelin about another bad idea, *Les Faisans Ecrasés* (Crushed Pheasants). This game of Jean-Claude's devising is ideal for two players – childish, Paul knows, dangerous too, but what choice has he but to play it? Above the village a quietish unhedged lane leads through fields and past a deciduous wood, the lane being straight for the most part but with a gentle curve hereabouts. Halfway along the eighty-metre stretch between two bends the contestants lie down side by side in the road, their feet in the direction of the vehicle that is to be heard approaching but not yet visible. You are Crushed Pheasants and a smallholder puttering along in his utility Tortoise 2CV or some other local worthy in a more substantial Grande Traction estate is rounding the bend and has just seen you. The winner is the last person to leap to his feet and make himself scarce among the trees as a very angry French driver applies brakes (how can you predict their effectiveness?) and screeches to a halt. Oaths and gestures attend your escape. Crushed Pheasants is a test of nerve and Jean-Claude has never failed to win it. Paul is always more afraid of the driver than the car.

They are eating beefsteaks now, tough and bloody; Paul makes what he can of his while enjoying the chips, which the French seem quite good at. Presently a disturbance occurs, one of those sudden face-slapping flare-ups that characterize life *chez les Marret*. It is, of course, Jean-Claude whose face is slapped ('*Cochon!*') and who is sent from the table ('*Sors!*'). The slap itself was the forthright kind Paul has noted on previous occasions from this particular slapper. What outrage provoked it? What did Jean-Claude say? Paul caught only a certain word, *dégueulasse*, as used by Jean-Claude and his Parisian friends when they are feeling dismissively cynical or contemptuous. Requested by Paul to translate this word he has denied using it – has denied its very existence. It is evidently in some special sense disgusting and unsuited to your parents' polite lunch-party.

Yes, the slapper, Mme Marret, is high on Paul's list of unpredictables. She is kind to him; she charmingly brought him breakfast in bed on his first morning; she speaks English when he doesn't understand. But he feels wary of her feline fury, her hidden claws. Probably it is only a matter of time before he too is slapped and dismissed. Sometimes Mme Marret calls her husband *Cochon* too, or *Salaud*, and though she does not slap his face Paul has the impression she is considering doing so. Instead they just exchange insults for a while. Driving here along the Autoroute de l'Ouest, for example, or rather floating in the big Grenouille DS 19 which is a semi-amphibious vehicle, one of these peculiar rows erupted. *Salaud! Cochon!* The invective flew between the occupants of the two front seats. Clearly they hated each other. A row at 120 kph? Was this wise?

Paul has observed that the French are impulsive – that they do not always consider the consequences of their actions. He remembers *Le Petit*, Alex, with whom he and Jean-Claude spent a day in Paris – *Le Petit*, Mme Buffet's son, with his excited chatter and strangely truncated head – and he wonders whether Alex's accident was caused by quarrelling motorists. ('His brains were in the road,' Jean-Claude explained afterwards.) Or had he perhaps been persuaded to play Crushed Pheasants? However Jean-Claude, in the back of the Grenouille with Paul, seemed unalarmed by his parents' behaviour. Soon they stopped for lunch and everyone was smiling – the wine, probably. Well, it is curious and all very different from East Ewell.

Over a segment of brie (he has declined a helping of the vinegary lettuce), Paul is once more drawn into table-talk.

'M. le duc,' M. Marret begins, leaning forward, 'tell me, does your father hunt? Does he *ride to hounds*?'

'Er – no.'

'He fishes, then?' enquires M. Poquelin from Paul's side of the table.

'No, he doesn't fish.'

M. Marret and M. Poquelin exchange surprised glances. 'Surely,' says M. Marret, 'surely, in that case, he goes shooting? . . . Sometimes?'

'No.'

'Occasionally? A little bird?'

'Never.'

M. Marret and M. Poquelin makes gestures of utter disbelief. 'An Englishman who doesn't hunt, fish or shoot? It's incredible.'

'I can't believe it.'

'Everyone knows . . . *les Anglais* . . . '

'So what does he do to amuse himself?' asks M. Poquelin at last.

Paul knows that whatever he says will not impress, so he merely offers an extravagant parody of Jean-Claude's disdainful Gallic shrug. He gives them shoulders, hands, eyebrows, mouth, the lot. The effect is perhaps more spectacularly insolent than he intends. The ladies laugh and the gentlemen bristle. M. Poquelin's ginger moustache *bristles*.

'Jacques . . . ' intervenes Mme Marret.

'They're joking,' Mme Poquelin tells Paul, in English. 'Just because they're crazy on killing anything that swims or flies . . . '

But Paul knows they weren't joking. He is conscious of having disappointed badly, in some way let the side down; besides, when your Englishness has been appropriated by sporting Frenchmen what have you got left?

It is late afternoon on the same day. The Poquelins took abrupt leave after coffee; they were en route for someone's country estate and a weekend of random slaughter. M. Marret has returned to Paris in the Grenouille, for unknown purposes. Paul and Jean-Claude soon tired of playing table-tennis (Paul lost) and are in the garden browsing through Jean-Claude's collection of Tintin cartoon books. Paul has also been discreetly trying out some of the less obtrusive techniques of the Method. A little quiet Sunning and Palming. Some Swinging: you roll your head and note the mobility of the world's images as they fly by. And Flashing, a rapid-blink technique to test your brain's interpretation of fragments of visual detail. So is it working? – the question his sardonic friend Chris Huggett has asked him more than once.

First, reading: at the moment Paul is reading without spectacles at a distance only marginally less than the (British) average of fourteen inches. Second, distance definition: here the bright sunshine offers perfect illumination and makes him feel positive and optimistic so that at times he thinks, I can see as well as anyone needs to see! I don't need glasses! In more realistic moments he has to admit that at the top edge of the fence he still sees two edges, at the ridge of the house he sees two roofs, and the upper extremities of the cypress are a hopeless blur. He knows this is to be expected, that if you try too hard for early success the Method will disappoint you because it is above all a method of Dynamic Relaxation, not of tension and end-seeking; and yet . . . How about those flashes of pellucid clarity (lengthening if you are lucky into extended periods of 20/20 vision) of which Dynamic Relaxation is said to offer the possibility? Paul has not had one of those yet and he expects one any day. He feels entitled.

Jean-Claude must have abandoned Tintin for he is now hurrying back from the house, under the cypress and through the rest of what Paul, having heard of 'wild gardens', assumes to be one such. This time Jean-Claude's panting excited message is more startling than the other surprise arrangements he has notified to Paul in the past fortnight. Paul queries it.

'Yes, on the road,' Jean-Claude is insisting, 'yes, a driving lesson. Hurry, my mother is waiting!'

Paul hurries. 'It's your first driving lessson?'

'My third . . . The first for you?'

Outside the house the sight and sound of Mme Marret already impatient behind the wheel of the little Bébé 500 ('*Dépêchez-vous mes enfants!*') confirms at least the driving element of the plan. Thrilling though Paul finds this unforeseen promotion to adulthood he hesitates, grasping its seriousness. With the sun's disappearance behind a large black cloud a temporary greyness has settled on the afternoon; as Mme Marret revs up the Baby's engine, an action as usual generative of smoke, he feels the visual confidence of half an hour since evaporate. With her plump beige bonnet and chubby posterior the car is distinct, but distinctly blurred. Going to get my lunettes, says Paul, making for the house.

Five minutes later he takes his seat in the back of the car, marvelling afresh at the effortless brilliance of a world transformed by lenses. But surely the Baby should be carrying 'L' plates?

'So now you can see,' says Jean-Claude.

'Yes, I can see very well.'

'*Formidable*,' says Mme Marret.

Jean-Claude sits in front with his mother, and we go along too, slightly reluctantly, as they drive through the village and up the lane to the open fields. For this initiative all thirteen year olds would surely consider Mme Marret the very image of a modern sporting mum; generous she certainly is, if to a fault. She stops at the first straight stretch

269

and the Baby's handbrake is hardly on before Jean-Claude is out of the passenger seat and round to the driver's side. His mother slides over. Neither Tortoise, elderly cyclist nor startled pedestrian is in sight. Jean-Claude seems to know what to do. The Baby co-operates noisily as they move off. First gear, second gear. Now third. Paul giggles as a row of poplars sails by. '*Doucement*,' warns Mme Marret. '*Doucement!*'

Fourth gear. But the Baby is not going fast enough for fourth – her engine has insufficient revs – she rattles and shudders. 'Go back to third,' says Mme Marret. 'Now! *Débraye!*'

Jean-Claude protests. '*Oh, maman* . . .'

The road is still clear ahead and he stops the Baby labouring in fourth by giving her more accelerator. That's better. The Baby is happier now. They are bowling along and the speedometer reads 52 kph but Mme Marret is not happier. 'That's too fast,' she tells Jean-Claude. 'Slow down. Go down to third! Brake! *Débraye!*'

'*Oh, maman* . . .' Jean-Claude declutches without braking and his mother grasps the gear-lever and throws it into third. Jean-Claude raises the clutch and the Baby decelerates with a wail of pain as her engine does the job of the brakes. 'Stop,' commands Mme Marret, 'stop *immédiatement.*' Jean-Claude brings the car to a halt in the middle of the road. Mme Marret heaves on the handbrake and leans over and switches off the engine. The Baby convulses and dies. Jean-Claude's mother is furious with him. *Cochon! Salaud!* Another front seat drama, sighs Paul.

'Listen, if you want to learn to drive you do as I tell you, you understand? You were going too fast! If you kill someone it's me that'll get the blame!'

'That wasn't fast . . .'

'You annoy me. You *infuriate* me. Get out, you can walk home! Little wretch! Go on, out! Start walking!'

Protesting and shrugging ('*Oh, maman . . .*'), Jean-Claude allows himself to be pushed from the car. His mother slams the door and starts the engine and as she drives on Paul looks out through the rear window and waves, a gesture more gloating than he means it to be, at the receding disconsolate figure. They round a bend, a short stretch by a wood and another bend, these being features of the road Paul recognizes from a previous excursion. Mme Marret is no longer angry. She parks the Baby just beyond the second bend where the road straightens again. 'Now, your turn.' Paul transfers to the driving seat.

He feels unprepared for the wonder of this, his first moment of control over the driving machine – for the rapture of running his fingers over the shiny white plastic of the steering-wheel, so precisely moulded, so businesslike, knowing that this is no day-dream. Through a delighted haze he hears Mme Marret instructing him in her careful English on the art of pedal co-ordination. He understands all this already – hasn't he practised gear-changing and declutching on his father's car, without the engine running? The moment arrives, and 'Now,' says Mme Marret, 'now we drive,' and soon the Baby is *moving*, edging willingly along in first gear and then gathering speed quite alarmingly in second. He stifles another giggle. '*Formidable,*' says Mme Marret in a little while, 'you can drive, you see? Now stop and I'll turn the car round.'

So after a three-point turn Paul is driving again as the Baby heads back in the direction they have come from. This time he feels confident enough to ease the stick into third gear, '*Doucement,*' warns Mme Marret, but he is not going very quickly, just coasting along, '*Doucement!*' and as they round the first gentle bend with the trees on the left Paul sees Jean-Claude lying in the road in the Crushed Pheasants attitude, his feet towards them. Mme Marret breathes, '*Mon Dieu!* What is that, *arrête*,' but Paul recognizes Jean-Claude's challenge and thinks, I'll stop but not *quite* yet – this impulse of his, for it is a thought compressed into an impulse, occupying about a second of time and therefore, if he is travelling at 40 kph, some eleven metres of road. Jean-Claude doesn't show signs of coming alive until the Baby is somewhat closer to him and Mme Marret screams 'Stop!' and pulls on the handbrake and pushes the steering-wheel, 'Stop!' but not soon enough because Paul has just mistaken the accelerator for the brake. The car goes right over Jean-Claude with a bump and Mme Marret screams again and she bangs her head on the windscreen because Paul has now found the brake. She jumps out and so does Paul and they run back to Jean-Claude who is not only not a Crushed Pheasant but still a very conscious one. He looks a mess with blood on his head and pouring down his face and lies laughing and crying in the road holding his head and his arm and then half gets up only to fall over again. Not saying anything but whitefaced and older than before, the bruise darkling on her forehead, Mme Marret runs back to the car and reverses it to where Jean-Claude is swaying around on all fours. Together they help him crawl into the passenger seat of the Baby. Trembling, speechless, Mme Marret gets in the car, slams the door and drives her son away, presumably to the nearest hospital. For a few moments Paul remains standing quite still in the road as the Baby's engine fades. Beginning the walk back to Le Cyprès he soon rounds the second bend and in the road ahead sees, with a flash of unpleasant clarity, consequences – the telephone calls, his return to Paris, Hearts and others trying to be sympathetic, the gathering clouds of disgrace.

CLERICAL ERROR

Gentian Walls

Gentian Walls gave up marketing to take up writing full-time four years ago. Since attending a Creative Writing class at Surrey University, Gentian has written stories and poems but this is the first story she has had published. She is a keen golfer.

CLERICAL ERROR

When I tried to analyse my feeling of antipathy towards the new parson, I could find no single, precise reason for my dislike.

Of course, I knew even before he spoke to me that I was repelled by his moist, full lips with their absurd cupid's bow. Then there was the time he came out from behind the Robsons' family vault, adjusting his cassock. It was only later I realized he must have been there to relieve himself – our church has a certain lack of modern facilities, but that is no excuse. I still blush now at the thought – not that he appeared in any way embarrassed by my presence – he was quite devoid of any finer feelings.

And he wore *scent*. A pervading, musky, powdery smell that made my nostrils wrinkle. *Gentlemen* don't wear scent.

I am probably a little old-fashioned in some ways, although not in my dress, I hasten to add. Mother used to say, good tweeds never date.

My attitude was nothing to do with my age, I am sure. Some silly women seem to go through a strange phase when they reach their fifties; their imaginations play tricks on them and they turn to poison-pen letters, kleptomania and other inexplicable behaviour. But how can a simple physical condition be responsible for such mental weakness? Fortunately, I have always considered myself extremely well-balanced. That view might not perhaps be shared by Elspeth Peabody – however, no sane person would pay any attention to *her*.

But, nevertheless, I do have to admit I spent an unhealthy amount of time observing him. I can see that now.

He was tall, with a broadness indicative more of soft living than of power, for he had none of the hard angles of the athlete. Even from behind there was something disturbing about him: one could not help noticing the plump, almost female, buttocks, snugly rounding beneath the clerical black. Each stride of his heavy legs emphasized the voluptuous curves in a most unseemly way.

How I could think of him in such intimate detail both horrified and disgusted me, for I had never before thought of priests as men – at least, not men in that sense.

I saw him outlined against the sky in the doorway of the church, after that first Sunday service. His mass of blond-white hair seemed slightly raised on each side, and in silhouette gave a strange impression of budding horns. Quite ludicrous, but then I have always been an imaginative person.

Miss Peabody was with him. She had apparently appointed herself as his mentor since he first came from Kansas on the three-month exchange with our own dear vicar. They were examining the plaque commemorating Father's generosity to the parish, and I expect Miss Peabody was boasting of the intimacy she imagines we enjoy, for she looked somewhat flustered when she saw me.

'*Theodosia!*' (She is so insensitive – I have always ignored all her invitations to call her 'Elspeth'!) 'Come and be introduced to the Reverend Brekinridge,' the silly woman smirked. In striking contrast to the fleshy giant at her side, she appeared shrivelled, her walnut-skin furrowed with a network of dry lines.

I suddenly realized his face was like those illustrations of the wind in children's books, all puffed cheeks and pursing mouth. I saw with a disgusted fascination how frequently his pink, pointed tongue slid along the exaggerated curve of his lips leaving a wet trail, both unpleasant and . . . provocative. Provocative, because there was something strange about the way his eyes were fixed on a point some way below my own eye level. It made me uncomfortable, that bold gaze. Uneasy, in a way I can't define.

She must have told him Father had been knighted.

'It's great, ma'am, to meet a real English lady!' That was the first thing he said to me.

I can recall the shock of the American drawl, more pronounced at close quarters than it had been from the pulpit.

And I was unused to such brashness. We British are so much more subtle than Americans when it comes to class and social considerations.

I muttered something while seeking a means of escape, to avoid those eyes probing like sweaty fingers. I was uncomfortably aware of the plump hands engulfing my own, and the scent he flaunted.

My gaze determinedly lowered I saw, with a further sense of shock, his grimy fingernails.

'Cleanliness is next to godliness', Mother had always said. Somehow it was an omen, this clear indication of the ungodliness of the man.

I extricated myself from his grip and hurried home to my cottage, my haven, and washed my hands several times until I was satisfied I had removed all traces of the odour I could detect on my skin, the musky smell, so overpowering in its intensity.

From that moment, just as a cat is attracted to those who find it abhorrent, the Reverend Breckinridge seemed to seek me out. I could not walk through the village without him accosting me, his tone always unctuous, over-polite.

'Hi there, Miss Bow-champ,' (his pronunciation of my name was infuriating). 'Good morning to you. Now let me help you with those bags. They're far too heavy for a little lady like you.' Then, his huge hand with those grey-tinged nails encircling my upper arm, beaming at me as he ignored my feeble protests, he would seize my shopping and guide me firmly to my car. I can remember the faintness which threatened to overcome me as his thigh brushed against my body when he took the key from my stiff fingers to unlock the door. And, as he bent double to arrange my parcels within the small boot, how disturbingly aware I was of the roundness of his rear quarters so near my face. I tried hard to avert my gaze but could not prevent noticing how the great muscles strained the cloth of his trouser seat.

'Thank you, Vicar.' I knew I sounded flustered, not as dignified as I would have liked.

Partly due to our social position, Father preferred Mother and me to keep a certain distance between us and the village people and even, to a lesser extent, the vicar. The other problem was Aunt Alice, Father's only sister. Not that there is such a stigma attached to these things nowadays. Many people have a little nervous trouble, and she was comfortable, well looked after . . .

But Father didn't like to talk about it, it was easier to prevent gossip by not allowing anyone too close. We didn't mix a great deal although, let me hasten to add, we were always kind – just a little aloof. We knew what was expected of us.

The Reverend Breckinridge seemed unaware that he was overstepping the bounds of acceptable behaviour by his excessive familiarity. And I found myself quite out of my depth; yet, for some reason, I could not stop thinking about him. How I wished Father was still alive, I'm sure he would have known how to deal with him.

On one occasion the man called at my home. It was a Thursday afternoon, a time I always set aside for my sewing. It was with a sense of panic that I saw the towering figure approach my gate. I slipped behind the curtain, hoping he would think I was out. But he must have noticed me through the drawing-room window as he passed along the hedge, for he was very persistent. He rang the bell several times before knocking thunderously upon my door. Miss Peabody was passing, she knew I was always at home on Thursdays. She is such a gossip. To avoid speculation, I opened the door to the intruder.

'Evening, ma'am. Sorry I hammered on your door. I think that li'l ole bell of yours isn't working.' He beamed, white-fanged shark's teeth gleaming in the fading light.

Wordlessly I stood aside, hating his invasion of my home, the violation of my refuge. Men had entered the house before, safe men, by invitation. But not such a creature, ingratiating, overwhelming, *unclean*.

He entered the drawing-room, stooping to pass through the door, incongruous among the delicate, carved chairs, the fine china ornaments and bric-a-brac passed down from generations of my family.

'My, this is a charming room, Miss Bow-champ!' He looked around with an interest I found ill-bred.

I motioned him towards a Hepplewhite armchair and winced as his flesh overwhelmed the fragile structure.

'How can I help you, Vicar?' My tone was neutral, polite, if not warm.

'Well, now, Ma'am, I was jes' thinking, maybe I can help you!'

'Help me?' There was honest surprise in my voice. He had caught me off-guard, for it was unthinkable that such a creature could help *me*, surely even *he* could see that.

'Well, Miss Bow-champ . . .'

279

'*Bee*-cham.' I could stand the pronunciation no longer.

'Is that a fact!' The vagaries of our language caused another flash of the too-white teeth. 'You see, Miss *Bee*-cham, I was thinking, you seemed a little peaky. It's my job to look after the folk round here, leastways, that's how it seems to me. So I thought to myself, I'll just drop in on the little lady and see if there's anyways I can help.'

His face seemed childlike, ingenuous. But I knew better.

'You are mistaken – I am perfectly well.' I couldn't keep the stiffness out of my voice.

'Well, that's all right, then. I just thought I'd ask, seeing as how shy you are, if you'll forgive the liberty, ma'am!'

Shy, indeed! I seethed inside, but kept my features under stern control. And I remembered my manners, if only to set an example.

'Will you take some refreshment, Vicar?'

'That's kind of you, Ma'am. Bourbon's my usual, but I'm beginning to get acclimatized to Scotch!'

'I am afraid I do not keep strong drink.' I knew my voice was frigid. 'I do have some sherry. However, I was actually thinking of tea.'

If he was disappointed, he hid it well. He didn't seem to take offence, for the wide grin never faltered. 'Then I'll be pleased to join you, ma'am, and thank you kindly.'

I don't know how I survived the next hour. I watched him try to sip from the dainty cup, his hand with those disgusting nails engulfing the fragile porcelain, while the petticoat-tail shortbread disappeared whole into the cavern of his mouth. He was so . . . so *physical*, so inappropriate in that room, my room. And he affected me in a strange way. I find it difficult to put into words: it was a revulsion tinged with something else I couldn't understand. Something that made my throat dry and my chest tight, just like the pleurisy I had as a child. I don't like to think too much about it. Suffice it to say it was with relief that I watched him walk down the garden path and disappear behind the hedge.

Unfortunately, Miss Peabody was passing the gate once more – sometimes I think she spies on me – and I could hear her ingratiating tone as she twittered on about some triviality followed by a patient reply from the Reverend Breckinridge. I have to keep saying the name to remind myself he is a clergyman and not a workman of some sort.

After his visit, I became apprehensive of the almost certain encounters with him in the village. Often I would cut his polite enquiries short, sometimes, I fear, almost rudely. I knew that he would stand, puzzled, not sure in which way he had offended. I even began to dread leaving the safety of my home. and yet, paradoxically, when I did not see him for a day or two, I would suffer a strange anxiety, almost a need to reassure myself he was still there.

That was when the dreams began. Terrifying nightmares when he would come to me, huge and clumsy and – bizarre. Inexorably, he would cross the carpet to my single bed as I pressed back further into the pillows in a fruitless effort to escape from him. Then he would reach out with damp hands to do unspeakable things . . . And his shiny damp lips would leave a moist trail across my skin . . . And in these dreams, even while I cringed away from him, my revulsion seemed to be tinged with a strange exultation . . .

I awakened each morning, flushed and panting, as though with a fever, my mind invaded with such wicked thoughts, I could think of little else. And when I saw him in the village, a smile seemed to play around the sensual mouth as though he knew too, and understood something that I did not. This worried me, for I was afraid people might guess what was between us.

I used to walk up and down my garden for hours,

distraught, trying to cope with these alien thoughts, totally abstracted. I can see now that I was obsessed. Once, I was shocked to see Miss Peabody standing quite close to me, apparently observing me, although I had not been aware of her until she spoke.

'Miss Beauchamp! I thought you had company. You were having such a conversation!'

Of course, I told her she was mistaken.

She had a very strange expression on her face. I might have thought it one of concern, had the circumstances been different. She is such a foolish woman – her hearing is undoubtably defective. I mean, why would I talk to myself?

I could not bear to hear the other ladies of the parish discussing him.

'Such a good man, so kind, so gentle . . . '

'He's so thoughtful, he visits anyone who's ill. And he has so much patience with the old people . . . '

'Yes, nothing's too much trouble! How lucky we are . . . '

I began to do my shopping in Rodchester, a town a few miles away from my home, to avoid the daily reminders of his intrusive presence. And it was there I saw them.

First I caught sight of the familiar figure with its clerical collar, head and shoulders above the throng of people. Then I saw his companion, a slim, dark girl, half my age. His face was animated, joyful even, as he half-turned towards her, one arm encircling her shoulders, his free hand holding hers to those wet lips. He seemed about to devour her, as though he couldn't stop touching her.

I was shocked beyond belief at this evidence of his perfidy, at this disgusting public display of animal desire. I followed them at a distance, sickened when, at one point, he drew her close and nuzzled her neck, trailing kisses across the skin of her face to her mouth, just as he had done to me.

This betrayal made me very angry. How dare he — spurning me for another. He was nothing more than a womanizer!

I lost sight of them then, and finally returned home to consider what to do. A man of the cloth behaving in such a way. Why, it was a disgrace. It was her fault, of course. A respectable woman would not have allowed such intimacies, in public, too!

I could never understand why her wantonness was not as apparent to others as it was to me. For he brought her to the village, this 'fiancée' of his. Oh, she lodged at the local inn, supposedly taking a holiday from some teaching job in the United States of America. But there was more to it than that, for there was a light in his bold eyes now which had not been there before and, anyway, had I not seen them together that day in Rodchester, when they thought they were safe? The carnality of his nature was exposed for all to see, yet people said that I was mistaken. That I had misunderstood, misinterpreted. In the face of their disbelief I decided that, in future, I would keep my own counsel.

'Mary-Lou' insinuated herself into the society of our village, approved of by everyone except myself. She simpered her way into their homes, insisting all and sundry call her by that ridiculous name — really, Americans are very strange. I tried not to call her anything to her face — and no one ever calls *me* Theodosia. No one — except Miss Peabody, who is totally insensitive to my displeasure.

People seemed to find Mary-Lou pretty — they said she was 'elfin'. She reminded me more of a vole with her narrow jaw and bright black eyes. Yes, definitely more shrewish than elfin.

After she came to the village there was an unpleasant development, terifying in its way. For the Reverend Breckinridge ceased his nightly visits; instead, I had visions, no less vivid, of *her*. But I was no longer sinned against; it was I who committed acts of unimaginable horror. I was transformed into a virago, violent and vicious. The nightmares always had the same starting point, the church, and I would come upon her in some cool corner, pressed against the smooth stone wall. Her skin would look so pale; her face framed by the long dark hair, bright eyes filmed with tears, pleading, terrified. I can feel even now the sense of power flooding through me, knowing I had her at my mercy. To increase my pleasure in her fear, I would bare my teeth in a grimace which I know was not intended to be mistaken for a smile. Then, as she shrank away from me, whimpering, I would produce a knife from my jacket pocket and slowly raise it above my head, before plunging it into that white shoulder ... The blood was so red, spurting shockingly over my hands. And the stench of it stirred me to a frenzy, so that I hacked away at her body until I was exhausted, slashing wildly at every part of her until there was blood and flesh everywhere ...

What horrified me most was that I awakened from these excesses with the same sense of exhilaration I had experienced when I myself was ravished in my dreams.

How could I have such nightly fantasies? There is no brutality in my disposition, I am the very opposite, quiet, inhibited by something deep within my nature. My father was not really violent, either. Of course, he liked to be obeyed, but then I learned when I was very young that it was not prudent to go against his wishes. Mother's expression would be enough to warn me if the threshold of his patience was about to be crossed. Sometimes I wondered if she was a little afraid of him, but perhaps that idea was just a figment of my childish imagination.

Aunt Alice was different, but then, she wasn't entirely well ... One has to make allowances.

Mary-Lou attended church a great deal, sitting in the front pew, staring up at her *inamorato* with what, I am sure, was a totally assumed solemnity. Upon one occasion I am certain I saw the vestige of, dare I say it, a *wink*, an unseemly flicker of his heavy eyelid as he returned her devoted gaze. I was very shocked and glanced quickly at those nearest me but, kneeling with eyes closed, they seemed oblivious to this further proof of his profanity. Not that it was entirely his fault, she was Temptation sent to try him and he lacked the moral fibre necessary to resist.

You might have thought he would be too busy now to continue with his harassment of me. But no, she urged him on to further excesses.

'Now, honey, help Miss Beauchamp with that door!' Smiling sweetly at me, she watched him lumber over to do her bidding.

'It's always a pleasure, Miss *Bee*-cham!' And with exaggerated courtesy, embarrassing in the extreme, he held the door wide. I endeavoured to remain dignified, but could not help but be aware of the sly way she smiled as she watched his parody of the British gentleman.

Another time, we, Miss Peabody and I, were descending from the tower where we had been examining a stone carving which I intended to photograph for the History Society records. As President, I am responsible for collating the information – I do not allow Miss Peabody to influence me, even if she *is* Secretary.

'Angel, take Miss Beauchamp's arm, those steps are mighty steep!' They had appeared in the small doorway, part way up the stairs, which led to a small store-room. What they were doing there is a mystery to me. I had never seen that door open before, and couldn't help noticing how dusty their clothes were in the rays of light entering from a small window in the side of the tower. As he seized my left arm obediently, I tried to shrug him off but, as ever, he was oblivious. Miss Peabody wasn't, though, and I knew she was enjoying my discomfiture. I must have looked foolish, one arm held aloft by that great paw, stumbling down the uneven steps which I could have managed perfectly well unaided.

I looked at that girl with such dislike, she must have felt the malevolence I directed at her. The pale face contrasting against the warm yellow stone was just like the reincarnation of the dream I had had the night before. Why, I even groped for the knife that wasn't there, to wreak havoc on that smooth skin! I was trembling and could feel a fine film of moisture beading my upper lip and brow.

'Are you OK, Miss Beauchamp? You look kinda strange!' She whispered the words in a taunting way; she knew she was safe with the others there, I realize that.

I suppose it was then I decided that the time had come for something to be done. I made no reply, just pulled my arm away with a quick upward thrust, knocking my hat slightly askew with the effort, and left the three of them without looking back. I heard Miss Peabody's breath, sucked in with a decisive click of her dentures, and knew she'd be talking about me as soon as I was out of sight. I was heedless of the impression I made as I staggered off, one hand clutching the hat which threatened to topple, my hair straying from beneath my loosened hairpins. I could feel the three pairs of eyes staring after me in astonishment, but I just had to get away.

I almost ran the three hundred yards to my cottage, not pausing until I was leaning against the cool wood and stained glass of the door which shut out the threatening world. My breath came in hiccuping gasps and my appearance in the hall-stand mirror frightened me. My face was mottled with red patches on my cheeks fading to a greyish-white; my eyes, staring and wild, looked madly back at me. I did not care for my appearance at all. I tried to repair the damage to my hair, but my hand shook so much I had to give up the attempt. I sank down into the nearest chair, and it must have been twenty minutes before I was sufficiently composed to pour myself a large sherry. This was a thing I had never done before, for I never drank alone, always having considered it depraved and unworthy of a gentle-woman. Yet, even as the heady sweetness soothed my parched throat, I began to feel more relaxed, so much so that I helped myself to another. It seemed to concentrate my mind in some strange way, for, suddenly, I saw clearly what I had to do.

I knew then, God was behind me, working through me. I had been chosen to be an instrument of His Will. I have to admit I took a little more sherry in the days that followed, it gave such clarity to my thoughts. It made everything seem so easy. I always took great care to remove the glass from my bedside table in the mornings, for it would never have done for my daily to learn of this change in my habits. She works for Miss Peabody in the afternoons. I often think she must be the source of the never-ending supply of gossip with which that woman seems supplied. It was a pity she found the cache of empty bottles in the larder, it is the first time I have ever seen her lost for words. Instantly, I said I had been making trifles for meals-on-wheels, but I don't think she believed me. From then on I made sure I disposed of them after dark in the litter bin near the village hall.

Once I had made the decision to kill Mary-Lou, my nightmares ceased and I slept soundly for the first time in weeks. I took this as another sign from above.

To begin with, I was not quite sure how I intended to

bring about her demise. That is, until the small kitchen knife appeared in my jacket pocket. I can only think I must have put it there in a fit of absentmindedness. It was true, I found myself doing some very odd things, but I had been under a great strain since the contretemps in the church. However, since I was now sure the Lord was guiding me, I decided it was only right and fitting that His Will be done in His House.

I had the excuse, should anyone ask, that I needed to take some photographs for the History Society. However, I must admit I tried to remain unobserved, for I did not want to put her on her guard.

The weather was warm and it seemed sensible to observe her movements from the tower. Ours is such a small village that it is easy to command a view over most of the houses, as well as the inn where she lodged. It was unfortunate I could not see the vicarage, but this lay behind the church, obscured by a copse of ancient yew trees.

I had been in position for only a short while when I saw her emerge from the side door of the inn and cross the road to the churchyard. She was wearing a disgracefully short skirt, quite unsuitable for the fiancée of a clergyman. I stood back from the parapet and waited for her. I must say, it was an inordinately long time before I heard the heavy door swing open. I was dismayed to hear two voices, and realized she must have met up with *him*. A feeling of panic rose within me and I wished I had remembered to bring my flask, just to calm my nerves. At this point, I decided to postpone my attempt until a more suitable occasion, for, clearly, it would be impossible to carry out my mission unless she was alone.

However, I couldn't leave immediately because I could hear their footsteps approaching the tower, effectively cutting off my only exit. I prayed they would not ascend the staircase, the prayers being answered when I heard the squeak of a key turning in a lock. I realized they were entering the disused storeroom and was thankful because this meant I could leave as soon as the door closed behind them. Sure enough, a few seconds later when all was quiet once more, I gathered enough courage to tiptoe down the roughly hewn steps. As I reached the threshold, I could not resist trying to hear what was going on inside the small room. Thus it was that Miss Peabody found me, bent in a most unseemly posture with my ear to the keyhole.

'Miss Beauchamp! Whatever are you doing?' the wretched woman shrieked at me. She must think I'm deaf, her voice really has the most unmelodious cadence. How she got into the choir, I shall never know.

I felt my face go scarlet as the door was flung wide to show the astonished faces of the Reverend Breckinridge and Mary-Lou framed in the opening. I had the strangest feeling as I looked at the three faces. It was as though I viewed them through a huge magnifying glass which distorted their features into exaggerated shapes, as though they wore rubber masks. The parson's lips were huge and pink as they mouthed words I could not hear, Mary-Lou's eyes seemed to fill her face, while Miss Peabody was all nostrils and ears, like a mad goat. I began to laugh, I really could not help myself, I positively shook with mirth. until Mary-Lou tried to take my arm, that is. My mood changed immediately, and I turned upon her, all the pent-up resentment I had felt towards her coming to the fore.

She must have seen something different in my face for the huge fringed eyes looked frightened as she backed away from me, up the staircase. I know how an animal must feel as it stalks its prey, for the fear of my quarry was palpable. Then she turned with a choked cry and began to run up the steps, while I followed, brandishing my knife and still laughing.

What happened next seems very confused in my mind. I am told that the Reverend Breckinridge caught up with me before I reached the top and struggled with me in an attempt to remove the knife. I remember fighting with him, finding a reserve of strength I did not know I possessed. In the tussle that ensued, somehow he lost his footing. I am sure I did not push him and Miss Peabody could have been in no position to see clearly. I do remember him falling. It was like a dream in slow motion as the heavy body, arms flailing at first, then still, flopped from step to step. A trail of red splattered the yellow stone steps in its wake, until it came to rest, like a sacrifice, beneath a statue of Jesus which was set into the wall. I was aware of the piercing screams emanating from both Mary-Lou above and Miss Peabody below. I had to cover my ears to try to shut out the noise.

I think they must have given me some medication, for I cannot remember much about the days that followed. I can vaguely remember seeing a very old woman they said was Aunt Alice, but that can't have been right, for she didn't recognize me, and I certainly had never seen her before in my life. They've given me the room next to hers, but we have nothing in common. I'm sure she is not well. She sits in a chair all day rocking to and fro or sleeping. Definitely not normal behaviour . . .

It is very kind of you to want to hear my story, seldom have I had so good a listener. Although why I should lie down whilst you sit in that hard chair escapes me. But if you feel more comfortable like that . . . I see you are making notes. I have often thought I might write my autobiography had I the time. Now might be a good opportunity . . .

There is only one thing which annoys me. Miss Peabody has taken it into her head to visit me every day. I never did like her. She never stops chattering, usually about other people. I think she is evil. I have even started to have dreams about her. I hope they won't blame me if anything happens . . .